C000064432

# THE DEATH PRAYER

# THE DEATH PRAYER

*David Bowker*

VICTOR GOLLANCZ
LONDON

First published in Great Britain 1995
by Victor Gollancz
An imprint of the Cassell Group
Wellington House, 125 Strand, London WC2R 0BB

© David Bowker 1995

*All rights reserved. No part of this publication may be
reproduced or transmitted in any form or by any means,
electronic or mechanical including photocopying,
recording or any information storage or retrieval system,
without prior permission in writing from the publishers.*

The right of David Bowker to be identified as author of
this work has been asserted by him in accordance with
the Copyright, Designs and Patents Act, 1988.

A catalogue record for this book is
available from the British Library.

ISBN 0 575 05950 8

Typeset by CentraCet Limited, Cambridge
Printed by St Edmundsbury Press Ltd, Bury St Edmunds, Suffolk

*For Joan Bromley, with love*

# ONE

All day long, the murdered girl walked beside him.

He had sensed her presence most strongly in her parents' home and now, as he made his way through the crowded, narrow streets on this grim December afternoon, he seemed to feel her hand pressing on his heart.

He was a big man and the animated, jostling shoppers parted ranks as he approached, possibly mistaking his brooding melancholy for aggression. People stared at him but Laverne saw no one. He was alone with a dead girl in a monstrous world.

As he turned into High Petergate, the Minster reared before him. Its illuminated towers were framed against an improbably dark sky. Striding purposefully across the road, he passed through the church's western gate.

Its icy vastness consumed him. Out of habit rather than respect, he removed his trilby and smoothed back his thinning hair. As usual, due to his complete lack of religious beliefs, he felt like a trespasser in the House of God. The cathedral was almost deserted and his footsteps echoed dramatically as he crossed the nave. A robed verger nodded impassively as Laverne walked by. Laverne nodded back.

Most of the staff knew him by sight and usually left him in peace, believing him to be a great detective who regularly visited the cathedral in search of divine inspiration. In fact, Laverne didn't believe in inspiration, divine or otherwise. The Minster was one of his favourite buildings, and in the winter months, when the dark nights came early and tourists were thin on the ground, he liked to come here to think.

Sometimes, if an inquiry was going particularly badly, he simply came here to sulk.

Under the Five Sisters window, an affable bearded man in an ill-fitting anorak was bullying two old ladies with his knowledge.

'As a city guide, I would agree with you,' he was saying, 'but as a Minster guide I say rubbish! Rubbish!'

'And what would you say as a girl guide?' thought Laverne, shooting the bearded man a scornful glance that he probably didn't deserve. But the speaker showed no awareness of Laverne's presence and continued to assault his two victims with a deadly cocktail of history and halitosis.

Laverne stopped at the Chapel of Saint Stephen. There was no one in sight. Someone had lit three candles as a votive offering and the altar was ablaze with light. He seated himself in the front left-hand pew and closed his eyes. Still he could see the candle flames dancing; now orange, now green.

Her name was Anjali Dutt. She had been a student, living in a rooming-house in Fishergate. Two nights ago, her fellow tenants had heard a series of violent crashing sounds emanating from Anjali's bed-sit. With the intention of complaining to the landlord, the man in the flat below had actually tape-recorded the disturbance. The police were called and the investigating officers found Anjali at home. Her room was in a state of utter disarray. Nothing had been taken, apart from her life.

Earlier today, he had driven over to Bradford to interview the parents of the deceased. Mrs Dutt had greeted him at the door of her small terraced house and clasped his hand warmly.

'We are Anjali's mummy and daddy,' she had explained.

This information was somewhat superfluous, as Laverne had met the couple on the previous day during their trip to York to identify their daughter's body. Then, they had simply been dazed. But this morning, after thirty-six hours of hell, Mr and Mrs Dutt had begun to understand what had happened to their Anjali.

Together, inseparable in their grief, they made Laverne a pot of tea. Then he subjected them to his 'twenty questions' routine. Had Anjali had a social life? Boyfriends? Was she in any kind of trouble? Had she ever taken drugs?

'Our girl was murdered,' Mr Dutt had suddenly announced with a bluntness that caused Laverne to spill scalding tea on his trousers.

'Yes, sir. I think you're right. I'm sorry,' he replied, gazing steadily into Mr Dutt's troubled eyes in an attempt to distract attention from the steaming brown stain on his lap.

In fact, his first sight of the Dutt girl had prompted Detective Superintendent Vernon Laverne to launch a full-scale murder investigation. The similarities between her injuries and those of the unidentified male discovered in the museum gardens three weeks before were too striking to be ignored.

'Your work must be very upsetting, Superintendent,' Mrs Dutt had remarked.

'When I joined the CID I used to think that I could never be shocked,' Laverne said. 'But after thirty-two years I have to say that yes, I'm still affected by the terrible things that people do to each other.'

This was true. But for Laverne, the worst aspect of the recent murders was their absolute implausibility. He had never seen anything like those bodies, and God knows he had seen enough.

And after his fruitless twenty-nine-month search for the Animal, a man who performed autopsies on fully conscious human beings, Laverne had no stomach for another insoluble mystery. The thought of cramming one more filing cabinet with unhelpful statements and despondent, insubstantial reports filled him with genuine dread.

From far behind him came the sepulchral boom of a great door closing. This was followed by the kind of distant sibilant whispering that those who frequent great churches grow

9

accustomed to and hear without hearing. To Laverne, the sound was vaguely unsettling and he opened his eyes.

He glanced at his watch, dimly aware that he was cheating the taxpayer. Stop moping, Superintendent. You have work to do. But he was not quite ready to return to his office. For a moment, he remained locked within himself, staring at the candles on the altar until everything turned black, apart from that triad of wavering flames.

In Laverne's office on the top floor of Fulford Road police station, Inspector Lyn Savage was scrutinizing a grainy black and white photograph. It depicted a gaunt young man with sleepy eyes and a vacant expression. She glanced up at the rather battered-looking constable standing by her desk.

'That's good, Johnny. But we need more of these. Two are no use. We need a whole batch. Get on to the lab.'

Detective Constable John Andrew Mills shifted his not inconsiderable weight from one leg to the other.

'Will do, boss. I'll give 'em a call as soon as I've checked that registration.'

'No,' said Savage, allowing a glimmer of ice to invade her piercing blue eyes. 'You'll do it now.'

Automatically, Mills launched a protest. 'I've got a pi—'

'*Now*,' repeated Savage with quiet finality.

Mills, who may have been sexist but was far from stupid, gave the Inspector a placatory smile and turned to leave the room. As he did so, he almost tripped over a rotund telephone engineer who was crawling across the carpet on all fours. The engineer was ostensibly present to install direct lines for the present inquiry. Savage had no idea why he was on his knees or what he was searching for, and didn't ask.

She gazed into the window by her head and saw her own face floating coldly there. A gust of wind sprang from the darkness to spray the glass with rain. Something told her that it was not going to be a White Christmas.

Mills had left his copy of one of the grubbier tabloids on

10

her desk. It was folded open on a page that proclaimed BLACK MAGIC LINK IN YORK SLAYINGS. She picked up the newspaper and began to read. With mingled amusement and indignation, she realized that the 'exclusive' story before her purported to reveal the 'previously undisclosed facts' behind the very homicides she and Laverne were currently investigating.

A former witch has revealed that the shocking murders which have baffled police bear three well-known hallmarks of BLACK MAGIC ritual sacrifice.

*IMPALED ALIVE. Both victims were impaled. Impaling is a common method used by witches to dispose of their enemies.

*SIGN OF THE CROSS. The inverted cross, a recognised symbol of the devil, was painted on the bodies of the deceased with their own blood.

*NAKED. Both victims were discovered naked.

The report contained so many breathtaking inaccuracies that Savage laughed out loud, causing the phone engineer under Laverne's desk to jump up and bang his head. There were only two half-truths in the piece: Anjali Dutt was discovered naked and the boy was undoubtedly impaled. The rest was pure fiction.

Not so amusing, perhaps, was the caption that 'our own crime reporter' had printed beneath a blurred photograph of Anjali Dutt. It read: HUMAN SACRIFICE.

Savage immediately thought of the girl's grieving family, and wondered how this garbage would affect them. Then she heard Laverne's voice drifting through the partition wall between her office and the murder room. His hatred of the press was prodigious. So was his temper. She hastily deposited the offending journal in a drawer, and pretended to make notes in a large out-of-date desk diary.

As Laverne entered, she nodded to him absent-mindedly. Then, registering his graveyard pallor, she executed a double-take.

'Yes, Lyn,' he said. 'I look bloody awful. But you could at least have the courtesy to disguise your revulsion.'

He stood still for a moment, peering curiously at the large overalled backside poking out from under his desk. But he was tired and couldn't be bothered to ask how the backside came to be there. Instead, he hung his hat, coat and scarf on the old-fashioned walnut hat-stand he'd brought in from home after his favourite overcoat had been stolen from the staff cloakroom. Then, he slowly walked over to a still-steaming kettle in the corner of the room, spooned instant coffee powder into a cracked Manchester United supporters' mug and slopped in scalding water. Nothing but the best in the North Yorkshire Police.

He sat opposite Savage and she watched him drink. She was rather attracted to Laverne. He could be a surly bastard but there was a dignity to him that commanded respect and an aura of quiet sorrow that elicited her sympathy. The dignity had been earned by his dazzling career with the CID. The sorrow was not so easily accounted for. She knew that he'd lost a son, but that had been back in the early seventies. Could a man stay in mourning for twenty years?

'Anjali Dutt had a boyfriend,' she suddenly announced.

'So I've been told.'

She passed him one of the black and white prints.

He frowned. 'He's cross-eyed.'

'He's some kind of student, apparently, name of Derek Tyreman. And he's been missing from his flat since the night of her death.'

He said: 'Her parents swore blind that she didn't have a boyfriend.'

12

'What do parents know? Besides, she was Asian. He's white. Maybe she didn't want to worry them.'

The phone engineer, still on all fours, crawled out of the room. Savage closed the door behind him.

'We're actually already prosecuting him for shoplifting,' she announced. 'Two previous convictions for the same offence.'

'All right, Lyn,' he snorted. 'I don't need convincing. He's a dangerous master criminal.'

She was accustomed to this kind of response from Laverne, having long since formed the opinion that he was not, strictly speaking, a policeman at all. Visually, it was true that he resembled detectives in photographs from the vintage days of Scotland Yard's murder squad; men with voluminous raincoats, well-trimmed moustaches and a rakish habit of half-smiling, half-snarling at the camera while biting on their pipe stems.

But Laverne showed no regard for day-to-day police work; the repetitive routine of asking questions and studying the answers filled him with boredom and disdain.

'The DCC rang when you were out,' she said.

'Why? Couldn't he get through to Dial-a-Bimbo?'

'He's coming up to see you tomorrow morning. Bright and early.'

He buried his face in his hands.

She regarded him sympathetically. 'Are you all right, Vernon?'

'No.'

'Another headache?'

'No. I've just remembered that it's Christmas Eve tomorrow. I still haven't got Dawn a present.'

'I'll be nipping into Marks and Spencer's in the morning. What size is she?'

He lowered his hands and smiled at her. 'Do you mean it?'

'Yes. It's no trouble. Did you have anything in mind?'

13

He screwed up his face. 'She needs a new dressing gown. A good one.'

'What size is she?'

'Ohh, about your size, but not as big.'

'Not as big?'

Shyly, he cupped his hands in front of his chest. 'You know . . .'

She laughed. 'I'll see what I can do.'

Carelessly, he unrolled five twenty-pound notes from his wallet and passed them across the table. She smiled at him and stashed the money away in her large, sensible handbag. He had the gift of making others grateful for the opportunity of doing him favours. That, she reflected, was power indeed.

Three years before, when the Greater Manchester Police had seven murdered children on their hands and an eighth child missing, they had asked for Laverne's assistance. Savage recalled how overjoyed she had been when Laverne adopted her as a bag carrier, thereby offering her the career opportunity of a lifetime; the chance to observe a brilliant detective at close quarters and to learn his working methods.

After one week with Laverne, she formed the opinion that he was nothing but a fraud; an outrageously lazy man who showed no interest in the efforts of his subordinates to apprehend a man who throttled schoolchildren with his bare hands. While a dedicated team of uniformed and CID officers were working round the clock to prevent further carnage, Laverne spent his time sulking and staring into space. And when a former sex-offender was caught kerb-crawling outside a Bolton junior school and brought in for questioning, the great detective excelled himself. He refused to interview the suspect.

'Talk to him yourself,' he had memorably remarked. 'I'm off to the pub.'

Savage had been so hurt and confused by this act of wilful negligence that she'd immediately drafted a formal letter of complaint to Neville Wood, the Chief Constable for North

14

Yorkshire. She had reason to thank God that the letter was never posted.

Thirty-six hours later, an off-duty Lyn Savage had accompanied Laverne to a churchyard at midnight to find the missing girl safe, well and in the arms of Albert Bomford, a middle-aged cabinet maker from Little Lever near Bolton.

Never again was Lyn Savage to interpret her Superintendent's bouts of moody inactivity as apathy. Indeed, she had grown to think of Laverne as an intuitive genius, and indulged him shamelessly. He, in turn, never patronized or expected her to fetch his coffee. Consequently, their working relationship was happier than most marriages.

'These photos are the wrong size,' complained Laverne. 'They should be snapshot size so that they can be easily carried around. And we need a few dozen. Get on to the lab.'

'I already have.'

Laverne grimaced. Her relentless efficiency never failed to humilate him.

'Something funny cropped up about that tape,' continued Savage. 'The tape that Anjali Dutt's neighbour made of the bangs and crashes coming from her flat.'

'You mean exhibit A.'

'I mean our only exhibit.'

'What about it?'

'The lab ran a sound check on the recording. They're not real noises.'

Laverne, who was slotting slides into a viewer and peering at them dolefully, looked up sharply.

'What are you on about, Inspector?'

'Well, a normal note moves in a curve, apparently. The sound builds up, reaches a peak, and then decays.'

'I know that,' he said irritably. 'I used to play the trumpet.'

'Well, the noises on this tape start and stop abruptly, as if they're synthetically produced.'

'So what are you telling me, Lyn?'

'I'm telling you that I'm tired. That I spend more time with corpses then I spend with my children. And that this inquiry makes no sense whatsoever.'

Laverne shrugged. 'As long as you're happy,' he said.

At six p.m. Laverne and Savage joined their team in the murder room for their second meeting of the day. On one wall there was a large white washable board on which the known facts of the case were recorded. Apart from the dates of the murders, the board was empty.

Laverne was fond of slide shows and had arranged for a projector and screen to be set up for the duration of the inquiry. News of the Tyreman boy's disappearance had raised morale considerably and as Laverne inserted slides into the carousel, his fellow officers took their seats, chatting amiably.

Laverne liked to run a small, tight operation and besides himself, Lyn and two WPCs who were in charge of storing on index cards all the information pertinent to the case, there were only six detectives.

The exhibits were being handled by Tony Lawless. He was thirty-two but looked forty. Loyal and honest, he had a real taste for police work. He was also one of the few policemen Laverne knew who never slagged off colleagues behind their backs. Instead, he slagged them off to their faces, which was why he was unlikely ever to rise above his present rank of Detective Sergeant.

WPC Helen Robinson was a reserved, conscientious woman who looked too shy to be a detective. She was actually an authorized firearms officer and while acting in this capacity had taken part in the bloody attack on the Racecourse Rapist's luxury holiday home.

Detective Constable Peter Farrell, a scene-of-crime officer, had supervised the initial examination of both murder sites. He was a university graduate whom Laverne liked and trusted. But his large vocabulary did not always endear him to the other members of the division. Johnny Mills was a rather crude but good-hearted young man who boxed for the force and had a walnut-shaped nose to prove it. He also possessed an ancient scar on his right forearm, earned by protecting Laverne from a knife-wielding pimp.

The least experienced members of the team, Detective Constables Simon Beale and John Etherington, had cut their teeth on Laverne's previous investigation: the open-and-shut case of a Skipton man who murdered his wife in order to take his girlfriend for a weekend break in Blackpool.

When Etherington had turned off the lights, Laverne flashed the first slide on to the screen with a hand-held remote control unit. Lyn perched herself on a desk beside him.

The monstrous image on the canvas effectively silenced everyone in the room. It was a photograph of a man with a grotesquely broken body. He appeared to be reclining casually on a set of iron railings. The slide, taken from the vantage point of a step ladder, failed to indicate that the corpse owed its elevated state to the three railings embedded in its back.

The man's inverted face occupied the foreground of the scene. His bulging eyes seemed to stare, imploringly, into the room. His left leg was hidden. His right leg, impossibly, had been so hideously broken at the knee that its foot hung level with his right shoulder. The foot was shoeless, half-covered by a dismal grey sock. The overall effect was that of a ventriloquist's dummy, carelessly abandoned.

'Murder number one,' said Laverne. 'A young white male. Found outside the museum gardens on November twenty-eighth. He was evidently homeless. We don't know his name. Bone analysis tells us he was no older than nineteen.

'He was malnourished for his height – six foot four. None the less, he weighed eleven stone and I believe it would have taken at least three exceptionally strong men to impale a body of that size on blunt spikes. The wounds in his back are deep and clean. He was impaled in one go. Think about the force that made that possible. Unbelievable.

'To make matters worse, the railings are over six feet high. So these strongmen would have had to have been on stilts, or at least ten feet tall themselves. No. I can't figure any of this out. I see by your faces that you can't either.

'We find no evidence, on the youth's body or on the ground surrounding it, that anyone has been near him. It's as if he's flown there. And, looking at his multiple fractures – one hundred and forty-two in all – he could have been dropped from a great height. But apart from the wounds caused by the railings, his skin and muscle tissue is unharmed. There is virtually no bruising.'

A voice from the darkness said: 'We know all this, sir.'

'You know it all, do you, Tony?' snapped Lyn. 'Share your knowledge, then. Come on. Whodunnit, Sergeant?'

There was muffled laughter, followed by silence.

'The damage to the skeleton,' continued Laverne, 'includes grotesque dislocation of all the major joints. The term "grotesque dislocation" was supplied by Dr Swallow, the pathologist. A very serious man, our Dr Swallow. Not given to fanciful expressions.

'But the fact that the dead man's left shoulder is suddenly three inches broader than his right causes Dr Swallow grave concern. When an arm is that far out of its socket, the word grotesque strikes him as more exact than fanciful.'

Laverne raced through a series of x-rays, showing the boy's shattered and fantastically displaced bones.

'The bloody stupidest thing is that all this damage – just look at it – takes place after the man is dead. The cause of death, as with the Dutt girl, was asphyxiation due to heart failure.'

The police photographer's murder scene studies of Anjali Dutt began to appear on the screen. She was naked, huddled in a corner, her broken legs crossed in a grisly parody of relaxation. Her face was masked by the blood and brains that had tumbled from her flattened cranium.

One of the team exhaled in distaste.

'Yes,' said Laverne. 'I quite agree.'

Wordlessly, he sped through the post-mortem shots. The

18

penultimate slide returned them to the scene of the crime; the girl's mouth frozen in a catacomb howl, her arms flung above her head in an attitude that suggested panic or extravagant exultation. Laverne, who had made a study of the sad sign language of the dead, was convinced that, despite appearances, the girl's gesture was accidental and meaningless.

'She died of heart failure. But after her death, as with the boy, she appears to have been hurled around. Or should I say fired? The damage to her head resulted from a single collision with the wall above her bed. The forensics team estimate that to crush her skull in a room that size she would have had to hit the wall at a speed of not less than one hundred miles an hour. She wasn't shot from a cannon, so how did it happen? We don't know.

'As with the boy, Anjali's bones were dislocated at the knee, elbow, shoulder and thigh—'

There was a flash of light as the door to the murder room opened and closed.

'What was that?'

'Etherington, sir,' said Mills. 'I think he was feeling a bit claustrophobic.'

Laverne nodded philosophically.

'Should I go after him?' suggested Lyn.

'No,' said Laverne. 'Let him sort himself out. Now where were we? Yes ... these dislocations. They interest me. In both cases, they look deliberate. They remind me of nasty little kids who pull the legs off spiders. Know what I mean? Systematic, inventive cruelty.

'Except torture wasn't the motive. We're pretty sure that both these people died before their injuries were inflicted. That's good news for them, of course, but it doesn't help us much.'

The final photograph was a close-up of the bite mark under Anjali Dutt's left armpit.

'But we do have this. A set of teeth marks made around the time of her death. The imprint was deep. A bite like that

19

seems to point to some sexual motive, but neither of our subjects were interfered with – not in that way, at any rate. Professor Stockton, the man who took the plaster cast of the boy's mouth, is going to build a model of the attacker's teeth for us. Johnny – see to the lights.'

Laverne winked at Savage, who took this as a sign that the boss was tired of talking. She faced the team, slipping easily into her impression of a brisk, no-nonsense policewoman. She hated role-playing but had long since learned that if she was her quiet, unassuming self, no one paid any attention to her.

'You all know about the spot of difficulty we've had with our tape-recording?' she said.

'Not proper sounds?' offered Beale helpfully.

'Yes. That's what we've been told. But those noises almost certainly accompanied Anjali Dutt's murder. How could they have been produced? Any ideas?'

'Maybe the tape-recorder wasn't working right,' Mills suggested.

Someone sniggered.

'What's funny about that?' Mills demanded, indignantly looking around for his secret taunter.

'This is only a theory,' ventured Farrell, adjusting his glasses nervously. 'But perhaps the sounds on the tape originate from some kind of electronic sampler and were made in a recording studio.'

Now it was Mills's turn to snigger. 'What'd be the point of that, then?' he demanded.

'A calculated act of deception? I don't know. Maybe the recorded sounds were played on the dead girl's stereo with the deliberate intention of misleading us all.'

Laverne nodded. 'That's an interesting idea, constable.'

There was silence while everyone wondered why the idea was interesting.

'Now on to the main business of the day,' announced Savage. 'The photo Tony is about to pass round – when you're *quite* ready, Sergeant – is the only picture we have of Derek Tyreman.

'He's twenty-two years old. A third-year psychology student. He left his lodgings on the night that Anjali died – and he left in a hurry, leaving his books, record player, most of his clothes. He was expected home in Haywards Heath a week ago. Sussex police are interviewing his parents for us – they'll be sending any info they get as soon as possible, along with a better likeness, hopefully. The snap you're seeing now is taken from his Student Union card. It's three years out of date.

'Obviously, we feel that Mr Tyreman's sudden disappearance is not a coincidence. Finding him is our top priority. We are very interested in talking to him. He knows something.'

Laverne added: 'He must be the only one who does.'

That night Laverne slept badly. Although the details of his dreams were indistinct and ever-changing, he was vaguely conscious of living in a new and unfamiliar house which was huge, dilapidated and haunted. When he awoke it was 5.18 on the morning of Christmas Eve and his chest was bathed in hot sweat.

As he opened his eyes to the heavy darkness, a litany of names passed through his head. Graham Allen. Mark Hendry. Lindsay Pike. Heather Knowles. Annette Ketley. Susan Hamer. Paul Richardson. All the children murdered by the Bolton Strangler. He hadn't thought about them for years.

At his side, Dawn Laverne murmured in her sleep. He turned towards her for comfort and she instinctively laid an arm across his ribs.

Of course, those children were not his responsibility. They had all died before he'd joined the murder hunt. It wasn't guilt that assailed him, but the sheer brutishness of the world in which he was living. Heather Knowles, nine years old. Killed behind her grandmother's grave while, fifty yards away, two sextons were enjoying a skive and a quiet smoke. Where was her grandmother at the time? If God exists, what was he playing at?

He placed a protective hand on Dawn's dreaming head and, breathing in her warmth, tried to think happy thoughts.

But he couldn't think of any.

'It doesn't feel like Christmas,' said Laverne.

Six hours had passed since his early-morning gloom-attack and he was walking beside the Ouse with Geraint John, the Deputy Chief Constable. As always, the sight, sound and smell of the grey surging river infused him with a shock of wonder and melancholy.

The DCC was one of his oldest friends. They had first met three decades ago as uniformed constables on the streets of Manchester's Moss Side. Although John hailed from Salford and Laverne was born and bred in York, they had chosen not to re-enact the Wars of the Roses. Instead, they had boozed, brawled, competed for the attentions of barmaids and done all the unsavoury things that male police officers have always done. But that was a long time ago.

Like Laverne, John was a big man, but his face had retained a boyish openness. His smile was generous, almost defenceless in its warmth. He seemed to find some kind of release in his old friend; a licence to forget his rank and be as loud, ribald and immature as he pleased.

'What about the *Sun*?' he grumbled, '"Ritual murders" . . . Where'd they get that from?'

'Journalists don't need to get anything from anywhere,' said Laverne. 'They tell lies.'

'Unlike us police lads who are always so scrupulously honest,' added John, punching Laverne lightly in the kidneys. 'Still, you'll crack it in a week, Vernon. You always do. You'll be driving along, minding your own business, and you'll suddenly see a gang of ritual murderers coming out of Tesco.'

'I didn't catch the Animal,' observed Laverne sourly.

John waved a dismissive hand.

'He's dead. All the experts say he was the type. He's copped it. Suicidal manic depressive with psychotic tendencies. Prone to advanced paranoia with fucking knobs on.'

Laverne laughed. John cackled warmly, pleased with himself.

'Oh aye. Catch these buggers and you've got that OBE in the bag, matey. The Chief gets his knighthood, I get his job, the wife gets a new coat and everyone's happy. Eh? Anything you need, just let me know. And you want more merry men on the team, Vernon. Everyone's watching this one. You need a proper sized team. What's the matter with you? You're not playing five-a-fucking-side, you know.'

'I've got the right people,' asserted Laverne. 'I don't need you sending me all the wrong people. Just bugger off.'

'Bugger off? That's no way to talk to your commanding officer. It's "Bugger off, sir," when you speak to me.'

A cold, dispiriting wind was beginning to blow from the river. They ascended to street level at Lendal Bridge and ambled down Museum Street. Above, legions of grey cumuli were gathering to murder the day. The distant Minster was little more than a Gothic blur.

'Actually, Vernon,' said John, abruptly pausing to stare directly into Laverne's eyes, 'I'd like to ask a favour.'

Here it comes, thought Laverne. Another guest appearance at yet another charity ball ('Ladies and gentlemen: the detectives amongst you will already have identified the suspicious character on my right . . .').

'No,' said Laverne, 'I'm not giving any more speeches, Geraint. I don't care how many minibuses the handicapped kiddies need.'

John grimaced. 'It's worse than that. We want you to give a statement to the telly bastards.'

'You're joking, aren't you?'

'It's part of the job, old flower.'

'My job is catching criminals,' said Laverne with a swagger that he instantly regretted. 'I don't keep a score sheet but I

23

reckon I've nailed more killers in the past ten years than all
the other poor sods on the force put together. That ought to
be enough.'

His friend looked pained. 'Look, I know what you think of
the press. I'm not so keen on 'em myself. But me and the boss
reckon that if you don't use the media, they use you.'

Laverne's heart sank. He knew that 'me and the boss' really
meant 'the boss' and that a refusal to co-operate would reflect
badly on Geraint. It was no secret that Chief Constable
Neville Wood only ever wanted to hear two words from his
staff. The first was 'yes' and the second was 'sir'. Many of his
subordinates, including John, would have dearly loved to utter
two other words to Mr Wood. But, alas, they had families to
support and mortgages to repay.

They passed the entrance to the museum gardens. The area
where the unknown man had been impaled was still boarded
off. A patrol car was illegally parked in front of the gates.
Laverne would happily have ignored the vehicle but John
rapped on the windscreen to awaken its occupants. Their
initial reaction to this disturbance was hostile disbelief, followed by alarm as they recognized the DCC.

John walked on, chuckling with sadistic glee. 'That shitted
*them* up.'

'So what do you want from me?' Laverne asked. 'I'm not
giving a press conference.'

'No, no, of course not. Just say something about the missing
bloke. What's his name again?'

'Tyreman. Derek Tyreman.'

'Aye. Just say something like: "Derek Tyreman is obviously
a fucking murdering swine and we'd like him to help us with
our inquiries. And give him a good kicking."'

Laverne sighed. 'It's a bit much, Geraint.'

'Well, miss out the bit about the kicking.'

'Yes. Very droll. You know damn well what I mean.'

'You know what you are, chuck?' said John, clasping

24

Laverne's right shoulder. 'A moaner. A bloody moaner. Come on, I'll buy you a drink.'

While John and Laverne were strolling towards the Angler's Arms, where they were each to consume four pints of best bitter, Detective Inspector Savage was working through her lunch hour. Most of the team were out searching for Anjali Dutt's missing boyfriend. In the company of Lawless, Savage was interviewing a homeless man who answered to the name of Minstrel.

He was a tall malnourished individual in his mid-forties, swaddled in layer upon layer of unsightly rags. But Minstrel's most striking feature was his face, which was grimy to such an extent that he resembled a cartoon character who has mistaken a stick of dynamite for a cigar.

Two uniformed constables had found him flapping his arms frantically outside the York museum. He was reputed to be a regular trespasser in the museum gardens after dark and Savage hoped that he had known the murdered boy.

In return for ridiculously sweet coffee and a turkey sandwich, Minstrel allowed his prints to be taken. Savage's offer of a shower and a change of clothing had unfortunately met with a brusque refusal. The tramp had not bathed for some considerable time and he filled the tiny interview room with the smell of damp and a sickly sweet stench that Savage recognized but preferred not to think about.

It occurred to her (and she was not proud of the thought) that the greatest single factor that prevents us from helping the less fortunate is not a lack of compassion, but the possession of a sense of smell.

'More,' he demanded pettishly as Lawless heaped sugar into Minstrel's umpteenth cup of coffee. 'I need me vitamins.'

'Have you remembered what your real name might be?' asked Savage.

The man thought for a moment. Then he suddenly stood to attention and saluted. 'Peter,' he announced.

'Your name's Peter, is it?' pressed Lawless. 'That's your name, then?'

'Minstrel,' answered the interviewee, seating himself.

'Which is it?' asked Savage, in her best 'the police are your friends' voice. 'Peter or Minstrel?'

'Peter Minstrel.'

Lawless sighed. 'That's not your name. Nobody's called that.'

'Well, forget about that for now,' said Savage, wondering why conversations like this always made her feel so foolish. 'I'm going to show you a photograph. I'm going to ask if you've ever seen this man before.'

She carefully laid the best police mug-shot of the murdered boy on the table before Minstrel. To Savage, the photograph was merely a portrait of a dead person. All corpses looked the same to her. But there was just a chance that the man before her would see beyond the open-mouthed, despairing death mask to recognize a real person who had lived and breathed.

Both police officers studied Minstrel fixedly as he picked up the photograph. He subjected it to a baleful scrutiny. He then replaced it face downwards on the table as if he had been dealt a particularly unlucky card.

'That's him,' he said gruffly.

There was an untimely knock on the door. A laughing constable rushed in, saw that there was an interview in progress and backed out, uttering muted apologies.

'That's who?' asked Savage sharply. 'Who is that man?'

Minstrel hung his head. 'Teddy,' he mumbled.

'Teddy? Did you say Teddy?' said Lawless.

'Terry!' snapped Minstrel. 'Deaf bastard.'

Lawless began to blurt out a warning. Savage silenced him with a glance.

'Peter, was this man a friend of yours?'

There was a long silence.

'I'm fed up with this,' said Minstrel eventually, screwing up his face. 'I want to speak to a proper police sergeant, not her.'

26

Savage took a deep breath. 'I'm an inspector. That's higher than a sergeant. Won't I do?'

'No! You're a woman. I need a proper man inspector.'

'You need a bloody good kick up the arse,' opined Lawless.

There was a pause while Minstrel evaluated this suggestion. He then coughed nervously and said, 'I'm not sayin' another word till you get me some biscuits. Chocolate.'

While Lawless went to the canteen on this major errand, Savage took the opportunity to observe the ragged man carefully. Like many people who have been destitute for long periods, he appeared to slip in and out of sanity. He also possessed a remarkable gift for avoiding eye contact. Every now and then he winced, as if the world revolted him.

When Lawless returned and Minstrel was munching on a chocolate wafer, Savage reactivated the tape-machine.

'So the man in the photograph was called Terry?' said Savage.

The vagrant man nodded cautiously.

'Do you know where he came from? I mean, what part of the country?'

'He were English,' said Minstrel with belligerent pride, as if imparting a fact of enormous consequence.

'And you were his friend?'

'Terry were ill,' Minstrel volunteered. 'He couldn't walk. I were looking after him.'

'Why would you do that?'

'He couldn't walk,' he repeated, mystified by the question.

'Did you know his full name? Did he have a surname? A second name?'

Minstrel nodded and began to dip his second chocolate biscuit into the lukewarm coffee. There was a long pause, during which the electric clock on the wall emitted a faint metallic click.

'Well?'

'Well what?'

'What was Terry's full name?'

'Terry Thomas.'

Lawless snorted.

'Terry Thomas,' echoed Savage sceptically. 'Like the actor?'

The tramp looked confused. Savage reached for her fountain pen and, without enthusiasm, recorded the name on a blank sheet of foolscap. She then offered it to Minstrel.

'Is that how it's spelt?'

'Aye.'

'How do you know?' said Lawless. 'You're not even looking.'

Realizing that Minstrel was possibly illiterate, Savage decided to drop the matter.

'You say Terry couldn't walk,' she continued. 'Why was that?'

'Gone lame.'

'Why had he gone lame?'

He shook his head. Then, on a whim, he chose to lie extravagantly. 'The police attacked him. They stamped on his legs.' He pointed to Lawless. 'He was one of 'em.'

'Now that isn't true, is it? What really happened? Won't you tell us, Peter?'

Pacified by her tone, Minstrel said, 'He were ill. Then he got better. He flew off.'

Savage sighed wearily. 'I think you're playing games with us. I don't believe you know this man at all.'

Peter Minstrel stared threateningly at her left ear. This was the closest he would ever come to looking into her eyes.

'I-know-Terry,' he chanted.

'All right. When did you last see him?'

'Last night. He came flying over with all his friends. Like this, they were . . .'

Minstrel stood up and gave a passable impression of a glider. Savage and Lawless exchanged amused glances.

'Peter,' asked Lyn. 'What day of the week is it?'

'Sunday.'

'Try again.'

'Tuesday.'

'It's Friday, Peter. And do you know what's special about tomorrow?'

He thought for a moment. Then, triumphantly, he cried: 'It's Saturday!'

'Peter. Do you know the name of this city?'

With absolute conviction, Minstrel said, 'Leeds.'

'No. This isn't Leeds,' said Lyn, placing her pen in the inside pocket of her jacket and calmly gathering up her notes. 'You're in York, Peter.'

His brow furrowed in genuine perplexity.

'Didn't it used to be Leeds?'

Laverne stepped out of a confectioner's in Low Petergate, bearing a dainty gold carrier bag. He felt intoxicated and rather ashamed of himself. After their seasonal drinking session, John had offered Laverne a lift back to Fulford Road in his chauffeur-driven Daimler. Laverne had refused on the pretext that he needed to walk in order to collect his thoughts. In truth, he was Christmas shopping on the firm's time.

Nothing he bought for his family ever satisfied his desire to give, and it was his custom to keep buying until the shops were boarded up, in the hope that his loved ones might doubt his thrift, his taste, but never his devotion.

The carrier bag contained a pound of assorted chocolates for his wife and eight ounces for Inspector Savage. Each selection occupied a silvery casket, bound with blue ribbon. These gifts effectively exhausted his ideas for stocking fillers and he turned left into Stonegate in the hope that its bright window displays might inspire him.

The street was crowded and to avoid bumping into people, he was compelled to shuffle rather than walk. Christmas muzak of the most odious kind floated out of a gift shop.

A drifter with an oil-blackened face was standing in the shop doorway like an unlovely sentry, daring the public to enter. As Laverne passed, the man lowered his eyes and mumbled something. It sounded like: 'No God. No God.'

The path ahead was blocked by a troupe of carol singers bearing candle lanterns. They looked like an advertisement for designer 'Winterwear' from an exclusive mail order catalogue. A beaming well-fed boy shook a collecting tin under his nose.

'What are you collecting for?'

'This choir,' answered the boy cheerfully.

'That's not a very good cause, is it?' said Laverne.

The boy's smile disappeared and Laverne felt obliged to restore it by dropping a coin into the tin.

Moving forward, he noticed a teenage boy with his arm round a girl's throat. She was about two years his junior, and was screaming as she struggled. Laverne was about to break it up and give the boy a stiff caution when the girl exploded into fits of giggles and breaking free from her assailant's grip turned and fell into his arms. They immediately began to kiss, with excessive zeal. The mock-strangulation had all been part of some banal adolescent courtship ritual.

Then he saw the young woman. She was tall, dark and emaciated, clad in torn dungarees and a tattered flying jacket that was several sizes too large for her. At first glance, Laverne took her to be a religious zealot in search of converts.

Wearing a serene smile, she was addressing the passers-by as if she knew each of them personally. They, in turn, were ignoring her completely.

With his mind clouded by drink, it took Laverne a few moments to appreciate the girl's predicament. When he realized that she was begging, he pushed his way towards her.

'Any change? Can you spare any change, please?'

She watched Laverne approach. He read apprehension in her eyes. Did he look *so* like a policeman? Glancing down, he was appalled to note that despite the cold, she wore no shoes or socks. Her feet were black, bruised and bloody.

'What's with the bare feet?' he asked bluntly.

30

She paused, unsure whether to reply to this dour stranger. Eventually she said: 'I like to feel free.'

'Free to catch pneumonia?'

He stood there for a moment, simply appraising her, and he felt her discomfort as she stared down the street, then back at him. It was a quick, nervy action that Laverne associated with prostitutes. But this girl was no prostitute. Her eyes were too soft for that; there was no hardness in her face at all.

She smelled strongly of patchouli oil. In his ignorance, Laverne mistook the pungent scent for marijuana, a drug of which he strongly disapproved. This did not prevent him from reaching into his overcoat, extracting a bank note and pressing it into her hand. She examined the gift as if it were a mirage.

'Twenty pounds?' she marvelled. 'Are you sure?'

When he smiled encouragement, she giggled with mildly hysterical delight. She was beautiful and Laverne suddenly felt old and foolish. Buy her a drink. Offer her a decent meal. No. It hurts to look at her. He patted her arm and turned to go, but she seized his hand.

'This is great of you. Really. Most people just ignore me.'

He would have liked to follow this observation with a witty riposte but was too drunk and embarrassed to think of one. Instead he said, 'Never mind,' and walked on.

*Never mind?* What was *that* supposed to mean? He blushed hotly at the thought of his own verbal ineptitude, aware that the girl was staring after him in genuine amazement.

Perhaps he had been rash. The money he had parted with had been intended for his annual indulgence: a bottle of good malt whisky. His Christmas was now destined to be a more sober affair than he would have liked. But she had moved him. Not because of her gentle manner or her bare feet. Then why? As the answer came to him, he stopped in his tracks, realizing that the last time he had seen that face, it had been staring up at him from a mortuary slab. The girl was the image of Anjali Dutt.

31

# TWO

'Merry Christmas, sir. We thought your arteries needed hardening up and this is the stuff to do it.'

Everyone hammered their fists on the table appreciatively as Mills handed Laverne a bottle swaddled in the cheapest Christmas wrapping paper that money could buy. Afraid that the present might be a hoax, a gift-wrapped bottle of water or a flagon of methylated spirit, he tore off the paper contemptuously, only to reveal a bottle of Glenmorangie. He had got his malt whisky after all.

Slightly humbled, he smiled shyly round the table at his murder team, and they beamed back at him, raising paper cups full of the worst wine any lavatory attendant had ever recycled and dared to sell. Asked to obtain two litres of decent Liebfraumilch, Mills had returned with half a dozen bottles of dry white bile. It was difficult stuff to swallow, even for police officers. Mills seemed to like it, however.

'Thanks very much,' said Laverne, holding his gift aloft like a trophy. 'I haven't got you anything, you know.'

'Puddin'!' shouted Lawless, who had drunk too much.

Helen Robinson, who didn't drink and was therefore better suited to the task than most, carried a number of miniature Christmas puddings over on a tray. Also on the tray were two large plastic jugs of bright yellow custard.

With cheery absorption, and one or two cackles of manly delight, the small assembly devoured their dessert. They were seated at a long table in a corner of the otherwise empty canteen. The rest of the division had already held their various celebrations and there was a melancholy 'end-of-term' feeling in the air. Everyone, apart from Lawless, was in a hurry to pull their crackers and go home. Lawless was waiting for an opportune moment to ask WPC Helen Robinson out for a drink. But Robinson was eager to get home to her boyfriend, and Lawless, whether he liked it or not, was destined to spend another Christmas Eve with his wife.

After the pudding, Ivy and Florence, the canteen staff, walked by. They were buttoning their coats and carrying shopping bags. In previous years, their services would have been required well into the night, but the division had been tightening its belt and their overtime had been cut. They exchanged the usual pleasantries on their way out, advising the police officers not to do anything *they* wouldn't do. The murder squad chuckled obligingly at this pleasantry. No one expected canteen ladies to be original.

Laverne was the next to stir. 'Well, time to go home and kick the cat.'

'Don't forget Dawn's present,' Lyn reminded him.

He hadn't forgotten. The dressing gown that Lyn had bought for his wife on his behalf lay, ready-wrapped, under the desk in his office. This was where he went now, but he was in no hurry to go home.

Long after his colleagues had left the building, Laverne sat alone, spinning in his swivel chair, humming cheerfully to himself, but in his mind seeing a woman with no shoes, begging in the winter streets of York.

Shortly after six, Lyn Savage edged her car, a silver Peugeot, into the narrow drive of her home. The voice of Phil Collins, the hippest recording artist she ever listened to, died and hovered in the air as she turned off the stereo. She stepped out of the car and winced as the icy cold enwrapped her.

Sleet, not snow, was wafting down from a filthy orange heaven. Locking the car, she glimpsed a cluster of iridescent lights through the living-room window and realized that Ian had finally got his act together and dressed the tree.

Despite the knowledge that, for the first time ever, Christmas Day would not be spent with her family, she experienced a warm rush of pleasure. Tomorrow she would work, but tonight she would bathe, change and devote herself to Ian and the girls.

At the sound of the keys rattling, Lucy, their Great Dane, charged at the front door and emitted a sonorous 'Woof!' Lyn eased her way into the hall, while the dog breathed Pedigree Chum into her face and strained to get past her, eager to escape. Ian arrived in time to yank the dog back by its collar.

'Lynny,' he said affectionately, aiming a kiss at her cheek, but because of the dog's exertions missing and kissing the air. 'We've got a visitor,' he announced, taking her coat and absent-mindedly dropping it on the floor.

There was a hint of annoyance in his voice that told her the visitor was unwelcome. She guessed that Mrs Dart had called round on one of her impromptu visits. Mrs Dart was a talkative neighbour who only ever appeared at mealtimes.

Jane and Michaela rushed out to embrace her legs. She crouched down to envelop her daughters as Ian closed the door behind her.

'Who's here?' she whispered.

'Someone to see you,' he said, irritatingly, ignoring her question.

'Mummy, you smell of beer,' observed Michaela, who was no more diplomatic than a five-year-old could reasonably be expected to be.

'It's wine, darling.' And to Ian, she said: 'Who is it?'

Ian merely grinned oafishly and nodded towards the tall figure emerging from the study. As soon as Lyn saw the worn, polished black brogues on her visitor's feet, she knew she was in the presence of a fellow police officer. As he approached, the children drew away from him instinctively. For all his charm, Geraint John was an intimidating man.

'Happy Christmas, Inspector,' he said simply.

34

She felt her face burning, and he must have noticed her discomfiture, for like a conjuror deceiving his audience, he showed her his empty hands and said, 'Nothing wrong. I come in peace.'

Then, seeing that she was unconvinced, he laughed and said, 'I was just passing and I thought I'd drop by to say hello . . .'

There was a silence, while all three adults savoured the sheer preposterousness of this statement. Geraint John and his highest ranking female detective had only ever exchanged a dozen words, half of them barely civil. In fact, the last time Savage had passed Geraint in a corridor, he had not even deigned to acknowledge her presence. This was clearly not a social call.

Remembering his manners, Ian said, 'Why don't you go back into the study and I'll bring in a little something?'

Lyn was quick to realize the implication of this proposal. She sighed apologetically at the Deputy Chief Constable.

'Hasn't he even made you a cup of tea?'

Geraint shrugged. 'It doesn't matter,' he began, slyly aware that this was the perfect way of saying, 'No. Inconsiderate bastard, isn't he, your husband?'

Lyn glared at Ian. 'You are useless sometimes, you know.'

'I'll make some tea, shall I?' said Ian hurriedly.

'And for us,' cried Jane. 'Dad. And for us.'

'For you too, my leetle one,' said Ian affecting an unfunny Gallic accent. Then, all fake-eagerness, 'Mr John? Tea or coffee? Or maybe something stronger?'

'Whisky and soda?' suggested Geraint, obligingly.

'Just tea for me,' snapped Lyn, cutting short her husband's next question.

Ian retired to the kitchen with the children in tow. Lyn followed her enormous guest into the study, where his overcoat was already draped over the armchair by the fire. *Her* armchair.

'Honestly,' she reiterated. 'I can't believe Ian didn't get you a drink. How long have you been waiting?'

Seating himself with care, Geraint said, 'Oh, only about twenty minutes.' (There it was again; that genial smile that meant, 'Yes. That arsehole kept me waiting for all that time without offering me so much as a custard cream.')

She sat in a hard-backed chair and surveyed her visitor, taking in his powerful neck, the weight of his shoulders, the full head of greying hair cut short at the neck and parted at the side. Who was he, this scoundrel of a barber who gave every policeman in the world the same spectacularly bland haircut? He deserved to be taken into immediate custody and charged with intent to ridicule officers of the law.

Geraint, relaxed enough to make her feel like a guest in her own home, adjusted his cufflinks. As he did so, she caught a wiff of his cologne. Coming from a privileged background, it was a scent she recognized; Blenheim Bouquet by Penhaligon of Covent Garden. It was the smell of money and swaggering male vanity.

Anticipating her first question, he launched straight into the offensive. 'I'm sorry about this, Lyn. It's a stupid time to pick. I know that. But I needed to talk to you.'

'I thought you said there was nothing wrong,' she countered, mildly indignant.

'There isn't. Not yet, anyway,' he answered cryptically, still smiling.

'So why are you here? If you don't mind my asking.'

'It's Vernon,' he said. 'To tell the truth, I'm a bit worried about him.'

She nodded again, seeing nothing resembling worry in the big man's face. His expression was mild, a study in calm cordiality. He looked like a mature male model on the cover of a knitting pattern.

'Have we got a few minutes?' he enquired.

'Of course.' What did he expect her to say? No, I'm off duty, so kindly piss off out of my house. Sir.

36

He said: 'I needn't remind you that anything I say to you now is said in confidence.' A glint of controlled malice flashed in his eyes, and was instantly replaced by prefabricated warmth.

'Why needn't you? Remind me, I mean,' she challenged, noticing that the gas fire was on full. Had he turned it on himself? Would even the DCC be so presumptuous? She saw the casual way he was picking his fingernails and dropping the results on the carpet and decided the answer was yes.

Without replying to her question, he said, 'Why don't you take off your scarf?' She declined. In fact, she had been about to remove the scarf but didn't want him to think she needed his permission.

'Yes. Vernon,' continued Geraint. 'He's an old friend of mine, you know. We were young bobbies together. We know each other socially. I like the lad.'

'So do I.'

'I know. That's why I'm here. But Vernon isn't everyone's cup of tea, you know. He has a tendency to rub people up the wrong way.'

'I had noticed.'

'Yes. This job you're on now ... There are people who didn't want him to handle it, you know.'

This shocked her. Her face felt as if it had caught fire. 'What are you talking about?' she said.

Geraint looked away, studied the carpet and sighed, like a bad actor in a television soap attempting to convey regret. 'I'm talking about your friend and mine.' He coughed loudly. 'I'm telling you this in confidence, Lyn, but I had to fight to get Vernon on this inquiry.'

'Does he know?'

'Does he hell as like.'

'But why? What's he supposed to have done?'

He saw outrage in her face and raised a placatory hand. 'Listen, this is your house and I'm here on your time. You can ask me anything you like. I can't guarantee you answers to all your questions, but I'll try. That's the best I can do.'

'What about the question I've just asked you?' Too late, she heard the cold composure in her own voice. Both her tone and her precise, clipped enunciation were a clear and not entirely wholesome statement of the self-confidence and supremacy of her class. It was the voice of a lady, addressing a particularly stupid tradesperson. Geraint, however, didn't seem to notice.

'It isn't so much what he's done, Lyn ... More what he *hasn't* done.'

'Meaning what?'

'Well, let me put it another way ... How long have you known your boss?'

'A long time.'

'Right. And if I asked you to write a book about his working methods, how long would it be?'

She smiled at the absurdity of the question. 'Oh, about two hundred and forty-four pages ...'

He snorted. 'Two bloody paragraphs. That's how long that book'd be. If you were lucky. You haven't got a clue how his mind works and neither have I. I mean, I know he's no good at cards, because I've beat him at pontoon on several occasions. But I don't know how he thinks in his job. Police work is team work. You know that. As a policeman, Vernon's meant to communicate with other policemen. I mean, officers. But he doesn't, does he? Vernon talks to no bugger.'

'He gets results,' she said quietly. This was self-evident, but pitted against the full weight of Geraint's scornful pragmatism, it seemed a poor defence.

'Yeah. But how? He doesn't tell anyone. Did you read his last report?'

'I typed it.'

'Come off it, you *wrote* it.'

She grinned. 'What makes you say that?'

'Oh, just a little phrase that caught my attention ... "The

38

subject was manifestly guilty." Since when did Vernon know a word like "manifestly"?'

She blushed. He laughed and pointed at her like a schoolboy. 'Who's "manifestly guilty" now, then? No, I'm a detective meself, remember.'

She smiled at this. Geraint hadn't been a detective since the early seventies, but he still liked to pose as one of the lads. A man who, in spite of the endless bureaucracy of his expense-account, chauffeur-driven existence, claimed to have looked Death in the face, and on occasion shaken hands with him.

'Vernon's reports don't make sense. If a detective gets it right, we want to know how. Every time Vernon gets a break, it has bugger all to do with the investigation he's leading. Someone's murdered at the races in York and, as luck would have it, Vernon has a feeling the killer is a pools winner who lives in Newmarket. It's rubbish. I'm sorry, but it is. There's a lot of "feelings" in Vernon's reports. But no logical deduction. None at all. You're a policewoman.'

'Officer.'

'That's what I said. You're a police officer. A good one, from what I've heard. You didn't get where you are today because of feelings. Well, did you?'

She felt herself growing angry. 'But that's what he's *like*. He isn't an intellectual, he relies on his instincts. The police are only people, for God's sake. People are all different. We're gifted in different ways. Vernon's gift is his intuition.'

'Intuition . . .' echoed Geraint, as if the word was a euphemism for excrement.

'What's wrong with that?' she demanded. 'I cannot believe I'm having this conversation. I mean, this man has saved lives. There's a little girl in Manchester who recently celebrated her twelfth birthday because of that intuition you're sneering at. Every year we get a card from her parents, just to let us know that they'll never forget. I'm sorry, but as far as I'm concerned, that's a more eloquent testimonial to Vernon's worth than a piddling report.'

As she spoke, Geraint made frequent attempts to interrupt, but she shouted him down. When she'd finished, he said, 'Hey. Now, just hold on a minute, there. I'm on Vernon's side. And I'm glad to see that you are too.'

But Lyn would not be appeased. 'If you're on his side, why are you sneaking about behind his back? I'm sorry, sir, but I'm disappointed in you.'

To her astonishment, Geraint roared with spontaneous laughter. 'Dear me,' he said eventually, 'couldn't you just crawl to me like every other bugger?'

Ian chose this inopportune moment to enter, carrying a tea tray. Geraint eyed him calmly and with some amusement, although Savage had no idea what was amusing about a man carrying a tea tray.

'Tea and whisky for the needy. Mince pies for the greedy,' Ian announced brightly, seemingly unaware of the stupidity of this remark and the tension in the room. As he departed, he added, rather tactlessly, 'If you don't hurry up, we're going to watch that video without you, Mum.'

'You were saying?' grinned Geraint, cupping his hands around a Johnny Walker whisky glass.

His nonchalance disarmed her. If he was angry with her or wished Laverne ill, he was a superb actor. 'Well . . . just that Vernon does his job. He catches murderers.'

She poured hot, black Earl Grey into a cup and stirred it slowly. The peace was broken by the thunder of the children bounding upstairs. Geraint laughed again, raised his eyebrows in the direction of the sound. 'Air raid,' he joked.

After a short silence, he continued. 'You say he catches murderers. But how? I mean, what do you say to young CID officers when they ask you how you came to arrest the Bolton Strangler?'

She shrugged. 'No one's ever asked me.'

He bit into a mince pie. 'Good pastry,' he spluttered. 'You make these?'

'No. My husband did.'

He leered. 'A "new man", eh?'

'No. A man who can turn an oven on.'

He hastily changed the subject. 'You didn't take to Vernon at first, did you?'

'No. He gave me a rough ride, actually. My first job as Detective Sergeant and he gave me zero support.'

'That's right. Danny Phipps recommended you. Manchester police couldn't stop the Strangler and you'd done so well on that child abuse case. We thought your expertise would come in handy. But the old fella buggered you about, didn't he? Said, "I'm not doing that" and "I'm not talking to him."'

She was amazed. 'How did you know that? I thought only I knew that.'

He winked, a little smugly. 'Not much escapes me, you know. Oh, no. Seven kiddies dead, we lend Manchester our best detective, and he just sits on his arse gathering piles.'

Savage smiled at the memory. 'He reduced me to tears on one occasion. I couldn't believe it. I thought he was a complete fraud.'

'You weren't the only one. Manchester rang up and said, "What've you sent us? We've had another child abducted and this clown has gone visiting churches."'

She laughed. 'I never knew that.'

'Oh, aye,' said Geraint. He laughed also, but his eyes hardened before the laughter had died away. He sipped his whisky, rolling it around his cheeks like mouthwash. Then he stared at her for a long time. Silent scrutiny was a textbook interrogation technique, designed to unnerve the suspect into talking. There was no way it was going to work on Savage, but she didn't blame Geraint for trying. Eventually, he got bored and broke the silence himself.

'And how has he been behaving lately? Vernon. Noticed any strange behaviour?'

'No. Nothing.'

'Stranger than usual, I should say. Because I know by your

41

face that you agree with me. You know damn well that nine out of ten murders are solved within days, because they're committed by idiots who know the deceased. You also know that the other ten per cent are usually never caught, because the police are crap. If the public knew *how* crap, they'd be terrified to go to bed at night.'

'That is *so* cynical,' she said. 'And completely unfair. We simply don't have the money or resources to mount lengthy investigations. That's what happened with the Animal. The trail went cold, and in the end it felt as if we were pouring money down the drain. As an organization, we're not given the chance to be efficient, because we're undervalued and inadequately funded.'

'I couldn't agree with you more,' said Geraint slyly. 'In fact, I didn't mean a word I said. I just felt like testing your professionalism. You've passed the audition with flying colours. I'm impressed, Inspector. You're a very good advert for the force. Or service, as you probably call it.

'Now, I want you to do something for me. I want you to keep an eye on Vernon. Report back to me on all his movements. This'll just be our little secret.'

Gracefully, she placed her cup and saucer on the desk beside her. 'I see. You're asking me to spy on my own boss.'

'Oh, don't be daft,' he scoffed. 'I just want you, as a highly trained observer, to keep a record of all his movements.'

'Why should I?'

'Like I said, questions are being asked about him. The knives are out. It's up to you and me to watch his back. I'm not asking you to write anything down. I just want you to phone me, once a week, or once a day if things are really moving. There have been two very nasty murders. I just want to know what Vernon is doing about them. That's all.'

'I can't help you, I'm afraid,' she said, hearing the tremor in her own voice.

'Just our secret. I give you my word,' he pressed. 'And if

you fancy trying for Chief Inspector in the New Year, you could do worse than ask me to be your sponsor.'

'Oh? What makes you think I want promotion?' she snapped. 'I'm happy where I am, thank you very much. I have no desire to go back into uniform.'

'Who said anything about going back into uniform, Lyn? Exceptions can always be made for exceptional officers . . .'

She rose to her feet. 'I'm sorry, sir. I'm going to have to ask you to leave.'

He ascended, not to leave but to seize her by the wrist with surprising urgency. 'Listen, I'm sorry. I didn't mean to insult your intelligence. Or your integrity. You don't meet many genuine people in this job. That was silly of me and I really am sorry. Now, why don't you sit down and hear me out?'

Without a word, she acquiesced. 'Like I said,' he continued, 'tongues are wagging. And not without reason. All right, he's had some amazing successes. But why didn't he catch the Animal? That Standring woman was cut to pieces in her caravan while you and Vernon were five hundred yards down the road. Where was that famous "intuition" of his then?'

She shrugged irritably.

'It doesn't add up, does it?' he stated. 'It just doesn't . . .' He searched her face for some sign of accord, but found only cold resentment. 'So you won't help?'

'He's my colleague. And my friend. And I honestly thought he was yours.'

Geraint seemed a little stung by this.

'He is. Make no mistake about that. I love the man to bits.'

She sighed. 'So what are you trying to do to him?'

He looked away, struggling to think of a concise and honest answer. 'I'm trying to save him from himself, Lyn. I swear to God, I am.'

These words chilled and depressed her, because she had met enough liars to know that the DCC was telling the truth. He drained his glass and dithered for a second, uncertain whether to place it on the table or the tray. He chose the tray. Then he stood, and eased himself into his overcoat. Keys jangled in his pocket.

'Do you ever see Vernon outside working hours?' he asked.

'No. Only at functions. What about you?'

'Now and then. I shouldn't think either of us get out as much as we used to. Getting old.'

In the hall, he straightened his scarf in front of the mirror. She unbolted the front door. He reached out, as if to shake her hand, then pressed an embossed calling card into her palm.

'That's my home number. Call me anytime if you change your mind.' He looked at her earnestly. 'Don't say anything to him, will you?'

'No.'

'I need a promise on that score.'

She took a deep breath. 'You've got one.'

'All the best, now.'

With this benediction, he stepped through the open door and reached the gate in six massive strides. Without glancing back, he raised a hand and a black Daimler ghosted into sight. Lyn suddenly noticed an unfamiliar pair of leather gloves resting on the table in the hall. Instantly, she snatched them up and rushed down the path. A door slammed and the car began to move away. She glimpsed Geraint in profile, settling into the back seat. Reaching the kerb, she called out and waved the gloves in the air, but the vehicle merely gathered speed. At the end of the road, the Daimler's tail-lights blinked and the car swept out of sight.

She bathed, changed and attempted to slip into her mother-as-best-friend persona, but the cute, slick Disney cartoon she watched with the children bored her and she found the songs that accompanied it sickening. The DCC's visit had planted a nagging anxious pain in her gut, and she could think of nothing else. In short, her Christmas Eve at home felt like any other night of the year, only not as Christmassy.

When the girls were in bed, Ian brought in two glasses and a bottle of Cognac. He turned off the television, poured equal measures of the golden liquid into the glasses and passed one to her.

He kissed her once, softly, on the cheek and said, 'Would it be very stupid of me to wish you a happy Christmas?'

'Stupid? Why stupid?'

'Well, you're obviously feeling deeply pissed off about something. So what with you working tomorrow and you being fed up anyway, me wishing you the compliments of the season might sound a bit, you know, inappropriate. Or just plain stupid.'

Knowing how sensitive he was, and afraid that he might spend Christmas worrying that she was having an affair – which was what he always suspected when, as now, she was too tired or anxious to shower him with constant praise and affection – Lyn decided to unburden herself. She told him exactly what Geraint had asked of her.

She rarely discussed her work with Ian and he listened in rapt silence, afraid to interrupt in case she thought better of her indiscretion. When she'd finished, he said, 'So what are you going to do?'

'I've told you. Nothing. Vernon's a friend as well as a colleague. I refuse to tell tales about him to anyone.'

'But you must admit, it does seem a bit far-fetched, when you think about it.'

'What does?'

'The amount of luck your boss has. He's had more coincidences in his career than a character in a Thomas Hardy novel. I mean, what about Banford?'

'Who?'

'You know, the Bolton Strangler.'

'You mean Bomford. What about him?'

'Well ... weren't you just driving by a school or something?'

'Close,' she said. 'It was a church.'

She refilled their glasses, and with the alcohol warming and relaxing her, she told him, for the first time, how they'd caught the Strangler.

It had been the night of the great storm, and driving down from Buxton after interviewing a particularly useless 'witness' they had passed overturned lorries and cars, eerie and abandoned in the glow of their headlights. Every so often, Laverne's Rover would lift and glide across the road, carried by the wind. Lyn urged Laverne to stop and sit it out. They had a flask of hot coffee, there was enough fuel to keep the car heated. She wasn't wild about the company, but the thought of being blown into the path of an oncoming vehicle appealed to her even less.

'I think we'd better stop, sir.'

Ignoring her, he gently accelerated. A whole branch, wrenched from its trunk by a gust of biblical force, hurtled across their path, bouncing once on the bonnet before spinning off into the dark.

Count to ten, Lyn.

'Sir: at least slow down.'

He flicked open the dashboard with one surly hand. 'There should be some toffees in there,' he directed. 'Help yourself, and, while you're at it, unwrap one for me, would you?'

Then he wrenched on the car stereo and, without looking, violently slammed in a cassette. Immediately, a forties-style band blared up and a female voice that Lyn didn't recognize began to sing about the secrets of love. This secret love? The secret of? The lyrics were inaudible, as was most of the accompaniment. The gale-force wind made sure of that.

Resentfully, she unwrapped a sweet and passed it to him. He accepted it without thanks and began to suck on it noisily. The sound aggravated her, but she comforted herself with the thought that tomorrow the five-page letter of complaint that she had drafted about Laverne would be on its way to their Chief Constable, Neville Wood. He was almost certain to take Laverne off the inquiry and she would be noted as an officer of initiative and daring. Perhaps.

They passed a house with a missing roof, its splintered rafters poised to swallow the sky. Almost involuntarily, Lyn said, 'Oh, how terrible.'

'Yes,' said Laverne. 'They'll be a bit sick when they wake up.' Then he laughed drily to himself, confirming her opinion of him as a callous lout.

Apart from the calamitous howling wind, broken by the odd indistinct phrase of jazz, the journey continued in silence. It was 12.06 a.m. before Laverne, reaching the end of the Buxton Road, halted the car outside the gate of Norbury Church.

'It's a little late to stop now, isn't it?' she enquired.

Then she saw that Laverne was shaking and his face had turned a ghastly shade of bluish-white, the colour of her father's face in hospital after his final heart attack. The resemblance frightened her. If he was dying, what would she do?

Thinking quickly, she remembered passing a large police station half a mile back. If his condition worsened, she would drive him there. The local police would speed him to the nearest hospital, magically absolving her of all responsibility.

'Are you all right?' she asked, in the time-honoured manner of well-meaning idiots. He was patently not all right. But he heard the question and turned to fix her with a strange, unfocused stare.

'He's in there,' he slowly intoned.

'I don't understand. Who's in where?' she asked.

Laverne seized her arm. His hand was shaking so acutely that her entire body, in turn, began to tremor.

'The Strangler,' he said. 'This is where I saw him.'

She felt a large droplet of sweat leave her left armpit and

descend to her ribs. 'What do you mean? When did you see him?'

'He's in there,' he said, recovering his composure slightly, releasing her arm, nodding in the direction of the churchyard. 'The man we're looking for. You have to trust me, Sergeant. I know I'm right.'

'You're over-tired,' she reasoned. 'Neither of us know where he is or who he is. Do we? You know we don't.'

'It's a lovely night for criminals,' mused Laverne, almost wistfully. 'They love the wind, and this is a storm. In a storm, every noise is unfamiliar. Burglars and murderers can make as much noise as they like on a night like this. You hear a door banging and turn over in your bed, blaming the wind. The next thing you know, there's a knife at your throat.'

Light flickered in his eyes; a quick, manic light that she distrusted and feared. But as he raised the collar of his overcoat and left the car, duty compelled her to follow him. She snatched a hefty police torch from the dashboard and stepped out into the maelstrom. Should anything happen to him, should he fall and suffer a seizure while his mind was disturbed, she would be held to account. 'I let him wander off and stayed in the car because it was windy,' would not be a strong defence.

By the time she reached the gate, Laverne was already moving down a straight path that led to the church. The path was flanked on either side by neat beds of graves. The wind bellowed in their ears and made them stagger. Savage had to fight to catch up with him, and every so often, twigs and scraps of newspaper leapt out of the darkness at them like predators.

'Back!' she shouted. 'Let's go back!'

'What?' he asked, cupping his ear like a deaf old man in a farce.

'I'm taking you back,' she yelled, tugging ineffectually on his arm. Ignoring her, he walked forward, and even with the wind against him he was still strong enough to drag her along.

48

There was a dull, low rumble and Savage turned to see a black mass rise from behind a grave and hurtle through the air towards them.

With all her strength, she dived into Laverne's back and toppled him, just as the flying object spun over them, crashing into the church wall and removing a crescent of masonry. It was an iron wheelbarrow, and but for her swift action might have smashed their skulls.

Realizing their luck, they laughed with relief as they dusted themselves off. Again, Savage urged Laverne to give up this madness. In answer, he clasped her shoulder, silently asking for her support.

The north side of the cemetery was vast, overgrown, and sheltered from the street lamps by the bulk of the church. The looming spire above them seemed to rise directly out of the darkness, fashioned not from stone but the very fabric of night. At their feet, glimmering crosses and headstones, sagging and broken, pierced the earth in miserable profusion. And in their ears, the gale roared.

There was a bad feeling here; of past evil and evil impending. Years later, attending a conference in nearby Macclesfield, Savage had returned to this scene alone, in daylight, on a pleasant spring morning, only to find the same promise of sudden desolation hanging over the peaceful, sunlit graves. It was a garden for murderers to walk in.

Tonight, terrified and freezing, Savage was the first to see movement. She grabbed Laverne's arm and pointed towards the far church wall, where a lone gravestone appeared to be stealthily creeping along the ground. Savage raised the torch but Laverne snatched it from her and turned it off.

So they stumbled on without light, frequently halted or hurled back by the gale, until they were within yards of the moving object. Then, rudely, Laverne snatched the torch from his companion's grasp and shone its beam at the pale shape by the wall. It was a portly middle-aged man wearing a beige anorak, carrying an ungainly blanketed bundle in his arms. Suddenly illuminated, he froze, staring incuriously back at Savage and Laverne, his spectacles pools of silver light.

'Police!' shouted Laverne.

The man remained perfectly still, but the wind whipped back the blanket, revealing a human leg. Instantly, forgetting all her training, Savage rushed forward and relieved the curiously passive figure of his burden. In seconds, Laverne was at her side. Although the man in spectacles merely watched calmly as Lyn unfolded the blanket, Laverne roughly pushed him aside, knocking him over.

Then he shone the torch on Lyn's hands as they uncovered a child, a girl in school uniform. She was about nine years old. This was Lesley Wright, the Bolton Strangler's last intended victim. As Lyn searched for a pulse, the child moaned.

'She's alive!' bellowed Savage in triumph. She was always to consider this moment to be the highlight of her career.

The elated sergeant gathered the child up into her arms, while Laverne roughly dragged the abductor to his feet. After being knocked down, the man in spectacles had continued to lie on his back in a docile manner, as if awaiting further instructions. Laverne cuffed his wrists behind his back and the four figures made their slow, faltering way to the road. As they passed through the church gate, a yew tree, torn up by its roots, fell heavily across the path where they had walked moments before. Under the circumstances, this narrow escape hardly seemed worthy of comment.

Laverne sat in the back of the car, eyes on his prisoner. Lyn took the wheel, with the now reviving child beside her in the passenger seat. She executed a rapid three-point turn and they headed back to the police station on Buxton Road.

Albert Bomford, the Bolton Strangler, spoke only once. As the car pulled away from the kerb he said, 'I'll do whatever you want. But promise you won't tell my sister.'

As it turned out, his sister already knew.

\*

Ian shook his head and exhaled. 'But that is so unlikely, don't you think? In fact, it's more than unlikely. It's ridiculous.'

'I know. But it happened. I was there, as they say.'

'And what was Bomford doing so far from Bolton?'

'His mother was buried at Norbury Church. He was looking for her grave. He was a religious crank who thought the children of today were being raised in a Godless world. By strangling them, he believed he was preparing them for the arms of Jesus.

'Most of his victims were killed near places Bomford associated with dead members of his family. The idea being that the spirits of his relatives would keep the children safe until Judgment Day. As he went on, he took more and more risks. He seemed to think Jesus was helping him stay out of the law's clutches.

'He obviously had every intention of strangling Lesley Wright and leaving her on his mother's grave, which would, of course, have given us a vital clue to his identity. But we caught him, and saved her life.'

'And did you ever ask him how he did it?'

'I've told you . . . strangulation.'

'No. I mean Vernon. Did you ever ask him how he knew Bomford was in the graveyard?'

'I tried. Once or twice. I honestly don't think he knows.'

'But in the car he said, "This is where I saw him." What did he mean by that?'

'I don't know,' she replied curtly. 'What difference does it make?'

'Differensh?' he echoed, mocking her drunken slur.

'Shut up. I'm making a serious point, here. No one knows where Shakespeare's talent came from. I'm sure Shakespeare didn't know, either. If someone has a gift, we should treasure it, give it space and let it grow, so we can share its benefits. But to treat a man with suspicion because he's too good at his job . . . To me, that is unintelligent, cheap and morally indefensible.'

'Yes,' he pressed. 'But if I was the Chief Constable—'

'But you're not.'

'No, but if I was, *I'd* be suspicious. You say he doesn't know how he solves these murders. Well, I don't believe that. I just don't. I think he *does* know, but won't say. And – don't jump down my throat – but if Laverne's out of favour, where does that leave you? How do you think they're going to treat the woman who remained loyal to yesterday's man? You know what the police are like, Lyn. They'll freeze you out.'

Her eyes blazed. 'Look, let's drop it. You probably mean well, but you're just making me angry . . .'

He took the hint. The clock in the hall gently chimed midnight. 'Cue the ghost of Christmas past,' he said.

He hurried to the Christmas tree, a small, perfectly formed live pine that on twelfth night would be lovingly planted in the garden and left to die. The tinsel-strewn branches shook as he foraged through the pile of parcels beneath them. He produced a solid-looking box, ostentatiously wrapped in purple and gold paper, and proudly handed it to her.

'Happy Christmas.'

'But we can't give our presents now,' she said.

'Why not? It's Christmas.'

'Yes, but I wanted to give the presents tomorrow night when I've finished work and we're all together.'

His face dropped. 'Oh. All right, then.'

He was obviously disappointed. What the hell did it matter? 'No. Actually, you're right. Let's open them now.'

'Not if you don't want to.'

Why did they always have to play this game?

'No. I want to. You're right. I'll be too tired tomorrow.'

She unearthed his present, small and expertly wrapped. He opened it recklessly, whereas she uncovered hers with great care and deliberation in order to re-use the expensive paper. His present was a watch he'd been coveting but had not dared to buy. Hers was the latest miniature Japanese colour television, with a screen the size of a tea bag. It was just what she'd never wanted; a ludicrous gift, especially when there were so many things she actually needed. But at least the children would like it.

'You clever thing,' she lied. 'It's lovely. How did you know I wanted one of these?'

'Because I know you,' he said, with tragic irony. Immediately, she took him in her arms and squeezed him as if he were about to take a long sea voyage. For a full minute, they indulged in inane, nauseating love talk and then went to bed.

Later, while he slept, she lay awake at his side. Whenever she closed her eyes, she found herself walking the interminable corridors of the police station. This vision was not conducive to rest. Her right temple throbbed with tension, and she decided to go down to the kitchen for some painkillers.

She left her bed and slipped into her dressing gown. Ian mumbled and turned over in his sleep. She passed the girls' room, where Father Christmas, who both daughters were afraid of, had thoughtfully leaned two loaded pillowcases against the door frame. The stillness was almost palpable. She guessed it was about one-thirty.

At the top of the stairs, she paused for a fraction of a second to brush the hair out of her eyes. Immediately, she knew that something was wrong. From the landing, she could see most of the hall below. Facing each other, on opposite sides of the hall, were the doors to the living room and the study. Before retiring she had, as always, closed both doors, shutting the dog in the living room. But both doors were ajar, and a triangle of yellow light shone out of the living room into the hall.

Her heart began to pound. She listened intently. Not a sound. Slowly, with great care, she began to descend. The third stair creaked and she grimaced, pausing, alert to the slightest noise from below.

It was then that she saw Laverne, in profile, leave the study,

53

cross the hall from left to right and enter the living room. He moved rapidly, in perfect silence, and although he passed the foot of the stairs, he neither looked up nor showed the least awareness of her presence. Still dressed in the brown tweed suit he'd been wearing the previous day, he had looked and moved like a bold, experienced house-breaker.

Where was Lucy? She had always been an efficient guard dog. Why wasn't she barking? Incautiously, Lyn rushed downstairs and charged into the living room. There was no one there. The dog, drowsily, looked up from its enormous basket. Alert to its owner's unease, the animal rose to its full height, drawing level with Lyn's ribs, its shining black eyes alive with curiosity. Her Christmas present rested on the sofa, emanating the metallic perfume of new electronic toys. She guessed that Laverne had passed through the living room into the kitchen and, clutching the dog by its collar, went to investigate. But the kitchen was empty.

Aloud, she said, 'All right. Where are you? Come on out.' She sounded ridiculous to herself; her voice seemed to have raised its pitch by a full octave. But as she waited, and listened, it occurred to her that she was quite alone. Yet she felt sure she had not imagined it. An hallucination could walk across a hall, but could it open doors and turn on lights?

She wrenched at the kitchen door, finding, to her alarm, that it was unlocked. Drunk or not, this was one duty that Ian had never been known to shirk. She opened the door and the dog rushed out into the dark garden. Moments later, it returned, panting and mystified, searching for some clue to her strange behaviour. Nervously, she stepped out into the dark. The garden was quite deserted.

'Come on, Vernon,' she said, addressing the cold, damp air.

Nothing. Then, somewhere in the distance, the rattle of a goods train.

Guiding Lucy by her collar, she circled the house until she came to the front door, then walked to the end of the drive and scanned the road from right to left. Christmas lights shone in dark hedges and porches. Empty cars gathered frost outside their owners' homes. But there was no trace of Vernon Laverne.

# THREE

Jennifer, Laverne's daughter, was arranging a bunch of crimson roses in an old cracked jug. It was five past ten on Christmas morning, and she was crouching over the grave of her kid brother while Laverne, hands thrust deep into the pockets of his sheepskin overcoat, stood guard and shivered.

The child was buried in the shadow of All Saints Church, Huntington, and every Christmas Day, to please Dawn more than anything, Laverne and his daughter made this pilgrimage to the graveside to wrench away the weeds and leave fresh flowers.

The stone was plain and white. The simple inscription read:

TOM LAVERNE

Oct 8, 1970 – Jan 5, 1974

WE WILL ALWAYS LOVE YOU

'I'm not keen on this,' said Laverne, pointing with his toe to the foliage climbing the headstone.

'Oh,' said Jennifer, 'I think it looks rather nice.'

'You would.'

'It looks sort of Pre-Raphaelite.'

'Yeah. But I hate the Pre-Raphaelites, remember.'

Jennifer had been to art school and Laverne had developed a keen interest in her subject, perusing the illustrated books she'd brought home and taking great pleasure in deciding what was art and what was rubbish.

'The Pre-Raphaelites,' he liked to say. 'Now they're art, all right. But they're still rubbish.'

Jennifer had left college with a First, but to his lingering disappointment had done nothing with her qualification or her talent. After art school, she had struggled on for two years, painting intermittently and talking vaguely about the possibility of taking an MA.

Then, a year ago, at the age of twenty-four, she had met an actor called Michael Berensford. Her artistic aspirations were immediately shelved. She and Michael had hastily married and in October Jennifer had given birth to Harriet, Laverne's first grandchild. What irked him about this course of events was that Jennifer had always found painting difficult, despite her immense talent, and marriage and motherhood had now provided a convenient excuse for her to opt out of art altogether.

Of course, her new roles as wife and mother brought heavy responsibility, but notwithstanding this, he was disappointed. When Jennifer had originally decided to study art he'd lectured her about the perilous career route she was taking, but later, seeing her evident happiness and her ability flourishing, he'd become a convert to the idea of having an arty daughter who wasn't like other people's children. And now that she'd traded in her studio for wet nappies and a life of little wifedom, he felt, obscurely, that she'd betrayed him.

Yet his disappointment might have been surmountable if he'd liked Jennifer's choice of husband. As it happened, Michael, or Michael Berensford as Laverne loved to call him, was not Laverne's idea of a man. For a start, his real name was Michael Caine, but because there was already another member of Equity with that name, Laverne's son-in-law had rechristened himself. In Laverne's opinion, the fact that he'd chosen Berensford, or could imagine, in a million years, that Berensford was an impressive sounding title, summed the man up.

As he and Jennifer walked back to Laverne's Rover, where Michael Berensford was waiting, he tried to repress these thoughts. Christmas was bad enough, without bearing grudges.

But the indescribably smug way that Berensford grinned as they entered the car instantly reminded Laverne why he was bearing a grudge in the first place.

Michael had recently had his blond hair permed. Bored with being cast as upper-class *Brideshead Revisited* types, he had auditioned for a role in a new drama series about footballers, called *On the Game*. Before the audition, he'd had his hair done in an authentic footballer's style, and had impressed the southern casting director – who had probably never met a northerner in her pampered life – with a crude caricature of a Yorkshire accent. Laverne, who had a very real Yorkshire accent but had never been offered an acting role because of it, found this all highly offensive.

Michael Berensford was currently high on his latest success, and kept making excitable jokes about scoring and playing the game, to remind everyone that he would shortly be a household name.

In Laverne's eyes, Michael had already committed his first crime of the day by failing to accompany Jennifer to her brother's grave. Michael had pretended to stay in the car out of tact, saying that their visit to Tom's grave was 'a personal experience that he had no right to share'. To Laverne, the whole point of joining a family was to share its personal experiences.

But he hadn't said anything, and hoped to God that his self-control would last the day. Silently, he drove back to the house, feeling like a chauffeur with Jennifer and her husband holding hands in the back.

Laverne lived in an old stone-floored farmhouse, dating back to the last century. In the late sixties, when it was bought, it had mud floors and no running water. Twenty-five years and several bank loans later, it had become what estate agents call a 'charming, spacious period property in a sought-after area'.

The cottage was shaped like an elongated cross, bisected by a central porch. The roof was thatched. Bryony and green ivy scaled the walls. The rear windows faced west, overlooking rolling farmland and the distant church, and in the summer prolonged sunsets bled into the fields and made Laverne and Dawn feel they were living in a rustic dream.

Now, as the car eased up the gravel drive, the Christmas lights in the living-room window glittered like jewels and Dawn appeared at the door, rocking Harriet in her arms and smiling, the ludicrously proud grandmother.

The smell of roast turkey filled the hall. The sound of Harriet's wailing filled the living room. Auntie Anna, a guest in the Laverne household every Christmas, said bluntly, 'She started crying as soon as you went out of the door. She hasn't stopped since.'

Anna was in her eighties, a diminutive black woman who lived in the poorest part of Leeds and in her youth had performed in cabaret with Dawn's mother in a musical duo called *The Two Shades*. Their finest hour had been supporting Danny Kaye in Bradford. Anna now saw herself as an authority on all aspects of show business life, and naturally took a keen interest in Michael Berensford's career. She also, apparently, saw herself as an authority on babies, despite never having given birth to any.

'You know why she's crying, don't you? She wants her granddad. That's what it is.'

Willing to try anything, Dawn passed the red-faced wailing infant to Laverne. At once, miraculously, the child stopped crying. General laughter greeted this event, but Laverne was not unduly surprised. 'She knows she's safe in the long arms of the law,' he commented.

'It's time for her feed,' said Jennifer.

Reluctantly, Laverne surrendered the child to its mother, who, a little forwardly to Laverne's way of thinking, offered it a swollen breast to suck. Anna watched this spectacle with interest, and every so often gave Jennifer helpful snippets of advice on how to improve her technique.

Laverne went into the kitchen to help Dawn dish out the food. 'How's the man I love?' she said, winding an arm about his waist.

'I don't know,' said Laverne. 'I haven't seen him.'

Although in her forties, she was still an exceptionally handsome woman, and like her daughter had large dark eyes under gloriously thick eyebrows. She was also Laverne's best friend and sleeping with one's best friend is always an agreeable arrangement.

'Isn't Harriet gorgeous?' she said.

'A monkey,' joked Laverne. 'A small, ugly monkey.'

Dawn hit him. 'She's got her grandfather's hair.'

'She's hardly got any hair,' said Laverne, walking straight into the trap.

Dawn laughed, pulled him close and gazed lovingly up at him. This process usually gave her a stiff neck, for he was a full eight inches taller than her. 'Was everything all right?' she asked quietly.

He knew she was referring to their son's grave, and quickly said, 'Oh, yes. Fine.'

'And I hope you weren't rude to our new son-in-law while you were out?'

He chuckled with sly delight. 'What, me . . . ?'

'Vernon!' she said, almost laughing herself, but holding a warning finger under his nose. Twice he tried to speak, and twice she silenced him.

In Wilmslow, Cheshire, Professor Fred Stockton, Consultant Odontologist, was climbing the stairs of his huge, wood-stained, creaking home. His large belly was heavy with turkey, pudding and brandy. He was a severe-looking man with sparse grey hair shorn close to his skull, steel-rimmed spectacles glinting on a square, sour face. Those who knew him loved him, but getting to know him was not easy.

Because this was a day of leisure, he wore a checked waistcoat and a white shirt with a yellow bow-tie. The dandiacal effect of this ensemble was completed by a pair of heavy corduroy jodhpurs and shiny brown brogues. Most of his clothes were bought by mail order from a shop in Regent Street that catered for rich outdoor types with no taste.

Stockton saw himself as a country gentleman, and, to be fair, possessed the qualities of the breed. He liked shooting and, given the chance, loved nothing better than the kick of a gun against his shoulder and the answering crash of a deer falling to earth. It wasn't that he disliked wildlife. He was grateful to it, for giving him something to shoot at. He would have liked to have been in Scotland now, but his wife had condemned him to Christmas at home, with her mother and her mother's entourage.

This entourage was invisible and entirely confined to his mother-in-law's imagination. Senility had resurrected the old woman's dead husband and a host of other deceased friends and relatives, and for the past hour she had held a heated debate with these uninvited guests while Stockton and his wife had tried to watch the James Bond film on television. It had been, in Stockton's view, a typically miserable Christmas and it was a relief to close his study door behind him and turn his mind to more serious matters.

He had spent the previous morning in York, examining and photographing the bite wound on the body of Anjali Dutt. What he saw was unsettling enough to prompt his speedy return to the lab at Manchester's University Dental Hospital, where he developed the photographs immediately, with only a pissed security guard for company. By the time his suspicions were confirmed, it was six p.m. He telephoned Laverne at Fulford Road, but received no answer.

Deciding that it could wait until Boxing Day, he collected together his findings and went home. But the matter had continued to plague him, and now, Christmas or not, he could not resist the compulsion to pick up the phone and dial.

The phone rang six times, and was answered by a neutral-voiced switchboard operator. Stockton asked for Laverne and was unceremoniously connected. On the second ring, Lyn Savage picked up the receiver.

'DS Laverne's office. DI Savage speaking.'

'Inspector. Happy Christmas.'

A silence. 'Who is this?'

'Freddy Stockton.'

'Oh, hello, Mr Stockton. I thought you'd be listening to the Queen's speech.'

'No,' he said. 'Ridiculous woman.'

'Who? Me or the Queen?'

Stockton made a noise that might have been a snort of mirth. Then again, he may just have been sniffing. 'Is the Superintendent around?'

'No. Will I do?'

'Certainly. By all means.' Stockton liked Savage. He had only met her once, briefly, but the memory of her pellucid blue eyes and large breasts had stayed with him.

'Inspector, there's no easy way to say this, but we have a problem.'

'Mmm?'

'As you know, I've made a cast from Mr Unknown's teeth. And yesterday, I took some first-rate photographs of the bite mark on the dead woman's body.'

He paused, allowing this to sink in. 'I developed the photographs immediately and I have to say that they don't match up to Tyreman's dental records. In fact, no similarity whatsoever.'

'Oh.' He heard disappointment in her voice. 'Well, thanks anyway. It was good of you to let us know . . .'

'Hang on,' he said hastily. 'That isn't the problem I was referring to.'

His eyes strayed to the top shelf of the heavy bookcase on the wall, which was lined with copies of his best-selling odontology manual *The Criminal Mouth*. The book had become a classic in its field, and would keep its author in ammunition and loud waistcoats for many years to come, despite its rather controversial claim that potential wrong-doers could be identified by the Neanderthal positioning of their molars.

'No,' he stressed. 'The problem is as follows. You can rule out our Mr Tyreman. But the bite does match up extremely well to the teeth of the first murder victim.'

'I'm sorry,' said Savage, 'I'm not with you.'

'No,' he said. 'I can't say I blame you. I'm not with me, either. But there's no doubt about it. In my opinion, the bite on the second murder victim was inflicted by victim number one.'

A long silence. 'But that's impossible.'

'Yes. Isn't it just? But it's obviously the same set of gnashers, m'dear. Even a layman could tell that.'

He was seated on his desk, juggling with a plaster cast in a polythene bag. 'I'm looking at the dead lad's teeth now, so to speak. Fairly distinctive. I won't blind you with science, but teeth are highly idiosyncratic. There can be no mistake.'

In sympathy, he added, 'All I can think is that the, er ... When did they die? Do you have the dates handy?'

'Uh ... somewhere.' The sound of shuffling papers. 'The boy on November the twenty-eighth. The girl on ... December the twentieth.'

'Hmm. I don't suppose the girl could have died before the boy, or on the same day? And the pathologist has simply made a terrible cock-up? Hmm?'

'No,' said Savage firmly. 'Dr Swallow is like you, Professor. He's clever, dedicated, a complete professional.' (I think I'm falling in love, thought Stockton.) 'Pathologists do get the times of death wrong, but both these bodies were warm when they were found. Or at least, not cold. The girl definitely died *after* the boy.'

Sighing, Stockton said, 'How very inconvenient.'

'Yes,' said Savage, dazed by this new revelation.

'Horrible murders, these,' said Stockton conversationally. 'They don't make sense, do they? Terribly difficult job you people have on your hands.'

'Yes,' she repeated.

'Maybe I can buy you a spot of lunch next time we meet?'

'What? Just me on my own?'

'Well, yes. I mean, no. You and the Superintendent,' he said, cursing his cowardice.

She laughed in his ear. It sounded faintly mocking. 'Thank you, Professor. Send in your report as soon as you can. And happy Christmas.'

As soon as she had replaced the receiver, Savage mouthed a silent expletive. Farrell, who was the only other member of the murder team on duty, smiled sympathetically. Today they were sharing Laverne's office. 'Was that as bad as I think it was?'

Bluntly, without fuss, she related Stockton's findings. Farrell, who had been copying names from Anjali Dutt's address book on to a computer, emitted a low whistle.

'This case reminds me of *The Exorcist*,' he said.

'I haven't seen it,' Lyn replied. 'What do you mean?'

Unwilling to elaborate, he dismissed the thought as insignificant.

'You went to university, Pete. Can you tell me what's going on here?'

Farrell could never resist an opportunity to air his ideas, whether he had any or not. 'Well, suppose Anjali and the murdered boy were friends. Lovers, even. The bite mark might have been a deep wound, made before his death . . .'

They both scowled simultaneously, knowing this to be a feeble explanation. Undeterred, Farrell said, 'All right. Forget that. I don't know how the bite got there. But I have been thinking about the dislocated limbs. I wonder if there might be any poisons that can cause those kind of convulsions? Some toxins, like strychnine and brucine, are primarily convulsants. In massive doses—'

'No,' she interjected, cutting him dead. 'Someone else suggested that. But no poisons were found in the bloodstream of either victim. The boy took amphetamines on a regular basis, but not on the day of his death. And once again, you're pinning your hopes on the notion that our forensics people are idiots, that they don't know how old a wound is or wouldn't recognize a liver full of arsenic if it hit them in the eye.

'You've seen more pathologists at work than me. I don't know, maybe you have good reason to distrust them. But if the path lab makes mistakes, then so do we all, and hoping that they've been incompetent because we can't come up with any ideas ourselves smacks to me of sheer laziness.'

Farrell smiled patronizingly and adjusted his glasses. 'But isn't it also lazy to place unquestioning faith in experts? Pathology is still in its infancy, and much of it is mere guesswork. Swallow strikes me as a competent man, but there's a poison called Ricin that he couldn't spot in a thousand years, because it's practically impossible to trace. It's derived from castor oil beans, and one-hundredth of a milligram would be enough to kill us both.'

Interested, she said, 'And does it cause violent convulsions?'

He blushed. 'No.'

She smiled wryly. 'Well, if you find any untraceable toxins that do, let us know.'

They went back to work, he peering unhealthily into the computer screen, she sorting through a cardboard box that had once held bananas but was now full of Anjali Dutt's possessions. She removed small stuffed animals, cheap trinkets, tiny bottles of scent, laying them out on the desk before her. There was no particular method to this process; she was simply looking and thinking. Extracting a small pack of cards, bound together with an elastic band, she paused. Like playing-cards, their backs all displayed a uniform design: a horned moon above three wavy lines and the letters SD, all in silver on a black background. The card faces were white, and boasted one hundred – Savage counted them – separate statements or tokens of advice, such as 'As of now, my life is wonderful' or 'All the flowers in my garden will bloom'.

'Pete?' said Savage, passing the cards over the desk. 'Any idea what these are?'

He stopped typing and flicked through the pack, frowning in his studious way. 'Yes,' he announced, after a few moments. 'They're affirmations.'

'Pardon?'

'Affirmations. Cards to meditate on. The idea being that if you repeat what's written on the card, over and over to yourself, your life will be wonderful. Or, indeed, all your blooms will flower.'

'I've never heard of that. What did you say they were called?'

'Affirmations,' he repeated, glad to be of use.

She wrote down the word on a cheap notepad.

'And what do you do with them again?'

Patiently, he repeated himself, and she jotted down a few key phrases. 'And who uses these cards, would you say?'

'Ah . . .' He puffed out his cheeks as he pondered. 'Well, anyone really. They're just another new age prop as far as I know. Like crystals and aromatherapy oil. All these ideas come from those Californian cults that teach that we have to undo the harm done to us as infants and learn to love ourselves, and that spiritual people can still be rich. Like rebirthing, primal therapy. You know the kind of thing.'

But her expression was blank. This was unfamiliar territory. 'So you think Anjali could have been mixed up with one of these cults?'

'Well . . . not necessarily. She may have been given the cards as a present. I mean, my sister gave me a crystal because she thought it'd help me to sleep. And it works, if I hit myself over the head with it. I, personally, am not the mystical type. Anyone seeing the crystal in my flat, however, might easily jump to a different conclusion.'

66

The phone rang. Lyn answered it. She heard the prattle of party noise at the end of the line. Then the voice of Johnny Mills. He sounded extremely drunk. 'Yes. Yes. The same to you, John. Yes, I'll tell him.' She replaced the phone, laughing and shaking her head. 'That was Mills. He rang to say he's thinking of us, and for some reason particularly wanted you to know he's already drunk twelve pints.'

Farrell smirked. 'So much for the changing face of the force.'

'Back to these cards. What does SD stand for?'

'I don't know,' he said. 'But the printer's name is on the bottom, look. "A. W. Watt, Halifax." They'll be able to tell us.'

'Shit,' said Savage. 'There'll be no one at work till next week.'

'Maybe there's an A. W. Watt in the phone book?'

'Well, I certainly don't feel like looking now. Do you?' Savage got to her feet and stretched. 'I'm sick of the sight of this office,' she complained. 'Let's go out.'

Wondering whether his leg was being pulled, Farrell smiled uncertainly. 'Where to? The pictures?'

'No, I'm serious. I don't feel we're getting anywhere. Do you mind if we take another look at Anjali's flat?'

'Well, er, fine. Yes. If you think it'd help. But how do we get in?'

She reached into her drawer and held up a set of keys. 'These might help.'

'I thought we'd given them back to the landlord.'

'We gave him one set,' said Lyn. 'But Anjali had a spare set that he didn't know about.'

Leaving the office lights on, they donned their coats and hurried out. They avoided the lift and took the stairs, where there was an institutional smell of chalk and disinfectant. In the late afternoon, the darkening windows reflected their descent. Their feet clattered noisily on the polished steps. Even now, before they'd left the building, they were each secretly regretting their decision to embark upon this macabre return journey. In the basement, a radio played loudly. The song that drifted up the stairwell to greet them was 'I Wish It Could Be Christmas Every Day'.

They travelled to Fishergate in Lyn's car. The roads were quiet. Throughout the city, people in party hats were gathered around tables or televisions, suspecting that everyone in the world was having a better Christmas than them. Savage suspected this also, and she happened to be right.

The building in which Anjali Dutt had lived was in an advanced state of dilapidation. It was a three-storey Victorian terraced house and, like most properties rented to students and the unemployed, was merely a means for its owner to make money without doing anything in return. The entrance hall stank of urine, and subsidence had buckled the tiled floor.

There was no light bulb on the stairs, and even though it was a freezing winter's day, gnats seemed to be rising from the stair carpet and flitting around their heads during their ascent. On the first landing, dance music throbbed behind an unpainted door. The smell of rotten eggs drifted out from a squalid shared lavatory.

'This place should be condemned,' said Farrell.

'So should the landlord.'

On the top floor, Savage inserted a Yale key in the door of Anjali's flat. Grim-faced, they entered. Savage flicked the light switch and a naked light bulb illuminated the scene. The odour of death, although faint, was still perceptible; a sharp, sweet smell of the butcher's slab, disagreeably augmented by cigarettes and incense.

Their feet resounded hollowly on the bare boards. The only floor covering was a hand-woven rug beside the single bed. The rug was black with dried blood.

Lyn's gaze was drawn to the hunched outline in yellow chalk drawn under the window where the floor met the wall. Within and without this image were dark, caked patches of gore. Similar stains were splattered and smeared on the walls and ceiling. It was as if the girl had been bounced around the room like a plaything.

The police had not helped, emptying drawers and cupboards and leaving their contents strewn across the floor. 'Who searched this room?' asked Savage angrily.

'Mills and Etherington,' answered Farrell.

'Look at the mess they made,' she said, in disbelief.

'You just can't get the staff these days,' concurred Farrell.

Then she turned to face the wall above the bed, inspecting the deep crater that had been made by Anjali's skull when someone, or something, had bashed out her brains. A trail of what looked like iodine and congealed mince stretched from this hollow to the bedspread.

'Dear God, what happened, Pete?' sighed Savage. 'What went on here?'

Treating the question as rhetoric, Farrell produced a gleaming new brandy flask. 'Do you like it?' he queried. 'A Christmas present from my fiancée.'

'Well, good for her,' said Lyn, accepting the proffered flask and taking a swig. She hadn't eaten since breakfast and the alcohol rapidly flooded her with warmth and well-being. She passed the flask back to Farrell.

'That's enough. I'm driving, remember.'

'Yes, of course,' said Farrell respectfully, who wasn't driving, so swallowed half the contents of the flask.

Savage walked to the window and looked out on to grey cheerless Fishergate. In the street below, a small child was wobbling by on a tricycle under its father's doting supervision.

'I think we need to use a bit of lateral thinking,' said Farrell slowly. 'Because what seems to have happened here can't possibly have happened. I mean, it may *look* as if she was thrown around the room by invisible strongmen . . .'

'Strong persons,' corrected Savage.

'Strong persons,' repeated Farrell cheerfully, savouring the phrase. 'But we know that can't possibly be so. Don't we? Yes, we do. Just as we know that the first victim wasn't dropped from a passing aeroplane.

'All we can be sure of is that these deaths are not what they appear to be. A while ago, I remember clearing the scene at a suspected murder. A man was found on the city wall, a huge gunshot wound in his head. It was one of Ron Vestey's inquiries. After half a day, he worked out that the guy hadn't been murdered at all. The victim shot himself, but only succeeded in blowing out half his brain. He'd dropped the gun and staggered on for half a mile before he died.'

'A charming story.'

'Isn't it? Well, I think the same principle applies here. We should ignore the obvious.'

'The only flaw in your argument being that absolutely nothing about this case is obvious.'

Savage turned her gaze to Anjali's bookshelf. 'Why were these books left here, for God's sake? Honestly, I sometimes think I'm working with complete and utter morons.'

'Well,' reflected Farrell. 'Yes ... but let's be fair. There wouldn't have been much point in bringing these books in. They're just student textbooks.'

'What? Even this one?' asked Savage, picking a dusty brown volume off the shelf. She read the title aloud. '*The Secret Science Behind Miracles* by Max Freedom Long? Funny title for a textbook.'

'Not really,' said Farrell. 'She was reading psychology, remember.'

She opened the book at random, and tried to read. Irritatingly, Farrell peered over her shoulder.

'See?' said Farrell dismissively. 'A textbook. Multiple personality. Freud. Jung. Per-so-na. That's not going to help us, is it?'

She flicked through the book abstractedly, ignoring him.

Farrell said, 'Lyn?'

She looked up, realizing that he was standing extremely close to her.

70

'Yes?'

His face was thoughtful and composed as he said, 'I think you and I should have an affair.'

She laughed derisively, and then saw that his expression hadn't changed.

'No, really. I think we should have an affair.'

She felt sick. 'Don't be bloody stupid.'

He coloured slightly. 'Who's stupid? It's you who's been coming on to me, remember.'

With mounting dismay, she said, 'When, for God's sake? I've never even thought about you in that way.'

He became angry. 'Then why are you always staring at me?'

Disgustedly, she hurled *The Secret Science Behind Miracles* at him and stormed out of the room. Realizing the full extent of his blunder, Farrell rushed after her.

The book that hit him in the face remained on the floor to gather dust, open at a chapter headed 'The Incredible Force Used in Magic, Where it Comes From, and Some of its Uses'.

There was nothing else for it. After dinner, and brandy, and coffee and more brandy, Laverne realized he was going to have to play Trivial Pursuit. It was a game that his family loved and Laverne despised. He tried to wriggle out of it by claiming that he wished to watch a film on television, but Anna helpfully pointed out that as he owned a video recorder, he could tape the film and still play.

Laverne's main objection to the game was that it brought out the worst in his son-in-law. Michael was one of those people who played this general knowledge quiz with excessive zeal, refusing the opposing team a point if they couldn't reproduce the exact wording on the card. He acted as if winning was conclusive proof of his intellectual superiority, apparently unaware that the originators of the game weren't intellectuals, just entrepreneurs who wanted to make money, and that, besides, some of the answers printed on the cards were wrong anyway.

Harriet slept out in the hall as the adults played. Laverne and Anna formed one team, Dawn and Jennifer another. Michael volunteered to play on his own, explaining that he already held an unfair advantage over everyone else: 'I've got this amazing memory, you see. Very useful for learning lines. Plus my general knowledge is exceptional. At RADA, I spent my spare time reading an encyclopaedia.'

Dawn nudged her daughter. 'Bit of a clever-clogs, your husband, isn't he?' she said good-naturedly.

'Bit of a something,' muttered Laverne.

'What was that, Vernon?' said Dawn, fixing him with an admonitory glare.

The game proceeded. After an hour, Michael had won five wedges, mother and daughter two, Laverne and Anna none. Laverne's low score was due to his readiness to listen to Anna, who only wanted to answer entertainment questions and whose extensive show business knowledge was frequently contradicted by the answers on the card.

'S'truth,' she marvelled, when she and Laverne had failed to get their pink wedge for the fifth time. 'These answers are all wrong, aren't they? You want to take this game back. You want to ask for your money back.' Then she shrieked with laughter, showing warm abandon. Laverne saw Michael raise one eyebrow as if he considered the sound undignified.

'Hey, Michael,' he remarked, 'that was very good, the way you moved your eyebrow just then. Very good indeed. Play your cards right and you could be the next Roger Moore.'

Laverne got up to refill their glasses, and to take a peek at his sleeping granddaughter. 'Your granddad loves you,' he said, 'but I'm afraid your dad's a prat.'

As the evening wore on, and the beer cans at his heels increased in number, Michael became loud and belligerent. Catching Dawn and Jennifer trying to cheat, he'd pointed out that they shouldn't play at all if they couldn't play fair. This had reduced them to fits of the giggles, and Michael Berensford had grown even more annoyed.

When Laverne and Anna were on the pink square for the sixth time, the tension came to a head. It was Dawn's turn to ask a question. 'Who was the first presenter of the long-running seventies game show *The Golden Shot*?'

Anna looked into Laverne's eyes. 'Oh s'truth, love, what's his name? I can see his face. Oh, it's driving me mad . . .'

'Benny Hill?' said Laverne for a joke.

'That's him,' shouted Anna exultantly. 'Benny Hill.'

'Is that your final answer?' asked Dawn.

Laverne and Anna engaged in harmonious dialogue. 'Yes,' said Laverne.

'Correct!' lied Dawn.

Dawn and Jennifer cheered. Laverne congratulated Anna, who was unaware that she had been the recipient of an act of charity. Michael, however, was not so easily fooled.

'Just a minute,' he complained. 'Let's see the card.'

But Dawn was already sitting on it. 'I can't find it. I've just shuffled the pack.'

'Show me that card or that last answer is null and void,' he threatened.

This remark met with general derision. 'Michael, darling, it's only a game,' said Jennifer.

'I'll never be welcome in this family,' he sulked.

'Not with a haircut like that, you won't,' mocked Laverne, earning another reproving glance from his wife.

Anna was smiling. She seemed to be quite enjoying the disagreement.

Dawn gave her son-in-law a cuddle and said, 'Michael, love, of course you're welcome. Don't be like this.'

Mollified, he said, 'I'm sorry. It's the actor in me, I suppose. I was the same as a child. I get so caught up in the drama of things . . .'

At that moment, there was a deafening crash from somewhere above. Startled, everyone held their breath.

'What the hell was that?' cried Dawn.

Laverne leapt to his feet and hurried out into the hall. Harriet had awoken and was whining. Sensibly, Laverne picked her up and took her in to her mother, before running upstairs.

He searched all the bedrooms, but there was nothing out of place. Yet from below it had sounded as if the roof had caved in. Knowingly, Laverne turned off all the lights and walked through each room again in the dark. He said aloud, 'You could at least have the guts to show yourselves.'

Brooding, he returned to the living room and the pale, concerned faces of his family.

'What was it?' asked Jennifer.

He shook his head, already staring at the baby.

Dawn was shifting Harriet's clothing, minutely inspecting the wailing child's body. 'Vernon,' she said urgently. 'Have you seen this?'

'What?'

She pointed to a pair of livid purple bruises on either side of the infant's left thigh. 'Look,' she said, appalled. 'It's as if someone has pinched her.' She demonstrated the action with her thumb and forefinger. 'How did that happen? Who'd do that to a baby?'

The question created a long silence, in which anxiety passed from one adult to another like a virus. Michael, for once, was rendered speechless. Anna shook her head repeatedly. 'It's wickedness,' she declared. 'There's no other word for it.'

And so Christmas Day in the Laverne household ended on an uncomfortable note. Jennifer and Michael, understandably, were eager to get away. After their departure, Laverne, Dawn and Anna had a nightcap and tried to relax by watching a Morecambe and Wise video, but their disquiet was not so easily vanquished. They drank up and prepared for bed.

Once in his pyjamas, Laverne wandered through the house, checking the windows and doors. His tour completed, he climbed the stairs. Anna was sleeping in the room next to his and as he reached the landing, the glow under her door winked out. Dawn, too, was drowsing as he climbed into bed beside her. He reached for the bedside lamp and extinguished the light.

He lay awake for a while, imagining all kinds of movement in the near darkness. But gradually the sound of Dawn's deep, even breathing lulled him to sleep.

Then, once again, he had the dream that had plagued him since boyhood. He dreamed that he was in a crypt full of sleeping stone knights. The only way out of the crypt was a black tunnel, peopled by invisible murderous beings that could see in the dark. Laverne, heavily armed, was waiting for an enemy that had vowed to destroy him. Laverne believed that his enemy would emerge from the black tunnel, but while his back was turned a stone knight arose from its tomb and, with its sword, hacked Laverne limb from limb.

He awoke, panting, his pyjama jacket glued to his back with perspiration. He sat upright and with a jolt of surprise realized that Dawn was sitting up in bed beside him. She clutched at his arm. 'Listen,' she hissed. 'Can you hear that?'

'What?' It was so still that he could hear nothing but his own blood buzzing in his ears.

'There,' she urged. 'Listen.'

This time, Laverne detected an unusual noise. Before he'd had chance to evaluate the sound, it was repeated. It could only be described as a low groan and it seemed to be coming from the landing outside the door. 'For God's sake, Vernon,' said Dawn, 'what *is* that?'

Unable to reply, he reached for the bedside lamp. He pressed the switch, but nothing happened. 'Damn,' he said. 'The bulb's gone.'

There was another groan, this time louder and more harrowing. It was impossible to tell whether the sound was human or animal in origin. The groan tapered into a long, throaty rattle. Then the bedroom door handle turned, and the door itself slowly opened.

75

A figure in white appeared in the room. It said, 'Is someone poorly?'

It was Anna. Laverne leapt out of bed and led her to Dawn. 'It's all right, Anna. We're all right.'

'Vernon, turn on the light,' commanded Dawn.

Standing by the door, he said, 'I'm trying to. The power's off.'

There was a shuffling noise at the top of the stairs, then a hoarse 'Ahhh' that sounded uncomfortably like a gasp of recognition.

'Come on!' shouted Laverne, taunting something unseen. 'What are you afraid of?'

Dawn came up behind him, encircling him with her arms. He could feel her body trembling against his, as together they filled the door frame, barring the way to whatever waited beyond the threshold. Laverne could detect no movement in the murk, and was uncomfortably reminded of the dark tunnel in his nightmare.

From the bed, Anna cried in distress, 'Who is it? Make them go away.'

Something breathed into Laverne's face, causing him to flinch. There was a sense of great menace in the air. The temperature had dropped sharply. It was now fiercely cold. Dawn and Laverne held on to each other. Their eyes, rather than growing accustomed to the dark, were gradually discerning less and less. All around them, the darkness was deepening. Afraid of what might follow, Dawn pressed her face into her husband's arm.

A soft footfall sounded on the stairs, and was accompanied by a deafening chorus of groans and pitiful sighs that came from every conceivable direction.

Anna appeared beside Laverne and Dawn, quaking violently. They each embraced her, forming a human triangle.

A warm wind, smelling of damp earth, roared through the house, rattling the doors and windows. Then, at last, peace . . . disturbed only by the sound of Anna, quietly weeping.

# FOUR

'What do you reckon, Neil?' asked James Merton with forced heartiness.

His son didn't answer, but continued to play with the new Sega computer game that Merton had bought him for Christmas. The boy was sitting crosslegged on the floor in front of the TV screen, his face blank and expressionless. He may have been deep in concentration. Then again, he may have been wishing that Merton had bought him the game he'd asked for, rather than this cheaper alternative.

'Is it any good, do you think?'

This time, Neil emitted a faint murmur of assent. Merton was constantly amazed by how much modern children took for granted. And if that made him an old fogy, so be it. The entire house had been decorated in the boy's honour. Brightly coloured balloons sprouted from every available corner. The live Christmas tree in the hall sagged with the weight of thirty-one chocolate angels and an army of musical redcoats that played 'Deck the Halls' at the flick of a switch, but Neil did not appear to be impressed. Did he seriously imagine that his father had gone to such extremes for his own benefit?

Neil had recently celebrated his tenth birthday. He was small for his age. Small and wiry, like his father. His hair was a rather Christopher Robinish nest of golden brown curls, and although he was of staunch Anglo-Saxon lineage, something about his lean, graceful frame reminded Merton of an African child. So much so, that Merton could no longer watch famine appeals on television without reaching for his credit card.

Leaving the boy to his computer-induced coma, Merton climbed the stairs to the bathroom. As he urinated, he inspected his reflection in the mirror on the door of the bathroom cabinet. He looked fit for a man in his forties. He felt that his neatly trimmed beard gave him the aspect of a dashing mountaineer. But his eyes were tired and uncertain.

Merton, who prided himself on his capacity for ruthless introspection, thought he could read desperation there. Perhaps Neil could see it, too. Children are like animals. They can smell over-eagerness, and are repelled by it. They like you best when you can take them or leave them.

Passing Neil's room, he stared through the open doorway, saw the boy's sports bag perched on the neatly made bed. The sight reeled him in. He touched the bag's handle affectionately, then decided to unpack it. After drawing back the zip, he marvelled at the exquisite, almost Japanese dexterity with which the bag had been packed; first shirts and pyjamas, then sweaters and jeans, all meticulously pressed and folded. Then socks at the bottom, neatly gathered into balls, with four pairs of fresh boxer shorts laid flat beside them. His wife's handiwork.

Carefully, Merton lifted each layer of garments and deposited them in their predestined drawers. Lastly, he withdrew a toilet bag, adorned with cartoon jungle animals, and rested it atop the dressing table. He patted the bag, as if in welcome, knowing that it would soon vanish, along with its owner.

He descended to discover that Neil had not altered his position. The game's soundtrack, a cheap and cheerful melody, was infuriatingly repetitive. Merton crouched behind his son, feigning interest in the little man on the screen who was busily leaping in all directions to avoid various hazards.

'How are we doing?' he wondered aloud.

'Best score yet,' was the laconic reply.

Merton wandered into the recovery room to check up on Lottie, an ancient sheepdog from a nearby farm. Her working life was over, but the dog's owner could not bear to part with her. On Christmas Day the animal had been brought in with a particularly virulent cyst above its left ear. Merton had operated, and kept the dog in overnight for observation. Lottie's head was now framed by a rather comical lampshade, designed to deter her from scratching the dressing.

As he opened the door the old dog tottered to her feet expectantly, hoping to see her owner. At the sight of Merton, she immediately sank down again, disappointment clearly written in her primeval amber eyes.

'That's right,' said Merton gently. 'It's only me, girl. You don't want me, do you?'

Reassured by the dog's alert demeanour, he went into the kitchen to prepare lunch. Neil had turned down Merton's offer of a second Christmas dinner, and asked for beefburgers, baked beans and oven chips. As a rule, Merton would not have dreamed of eating such garbage, or foisting it on others. But he wanted his son to feel at home. So he grilled four burgers, microwaved the chips and accidentally boiled the beans.

They ate at the small living-room table. Merton slotted a compilation tape of Christmas hits into the stereo in a pathetic attempt to create a festive atmosphere. After one mouthful, Neil asked him what was wrong with the burgers.

'What do you mean?'

'They're all dry.'

'I put 'em under the grill. It's more healthy that way. Less fat.'

His son pulled a face.

'What's the matter?'

'Nothing. It's just that I always have them fried, at home.'

That phrase again. 'At home.' Merton said 'Why don't you rub it in, Neil? Eh? This is your home too, you know. When you're here, you should feel that *this* is your home.'

Flushing slightly, the boy chased a soggy chip around the plate with his fork, as if goading it. Merton sighed. 'I suppose there's something wrong with the chips now?'

The phone rang. Merton tried to ignore it until Neil suggested, with irritating maturity, that the call might be important. He walked out into the hall and with ill grace snatched the hand-set from its cradle. He was fully prepared to be brusque, but the caller's voice immediately disarmed him. It was a tearful teenage girl. Her cat had been attacked by a dog. Could he please come right away? Without hesitation, Merton assured her that he could. The girl's mother, sounding as distraught as her daughter, came on the line to supply an address in the nearby village of Holt Cross.

Merton and Neil drove there in the Land-Rover. The mother and daughter were waiting outside their home, shivering in the cold, and the cat, a young tabby, was lying on the pavement at their feet, draped in an old cardigan and whining plaintively. Merton moved the garment and examined the cat briefly. Its back was broken.

'I'm sorry,' he said gently, and the two words emptied all hope from the watching faces of the mother and daughter. 'There's nothing I can do for her, I'm afraid, other than put her to sleep.'

The young girl held the cat while Merton administered a lethal dose of anaesthetic. Within seconds, the animal's head began to nod drunkenly, and then its entire body surrendered to death. Merton asked the owners if they wanted him to take the cat away. They demurred, so he carried it inside for them. The man of the house, hovering anxiously in the kitchen as if awaiting a birth, thanked Merton and asked what was owing. Merton waved his arm, dismissing the thought. There could be no question of any fee. But perhaps, if their goldfish was ever ill, they could bring it to him? This made the family laugh. Once again, Merton offered his condolences, and steered Neil out to the waiting van.

During the drive back, Merton said little. He felt his son's gaze on him for most of the journey, but kept his own eyes on the road. 'Yes,' he eventually said aloud, as if explaining something to himself for the first time. 'Animals aren't like people. A person in a wheelchair can still lead a rich and full life, Neil. But a cat that can't run and jump can't really have any kind of life at all.'

On their return to the surgery, Neil, suddenly drawn to his father, asked numerous questions about the job, which Merton was happy to answer. Yes, he did sometimes 'feel funny' about making sheep and cows well again, when they were only destined for slaughter. 'But, you know, son, if you were a cow, and knew your life was going to be short, wouldn't you sooner spend that short life feeling fit and healthy?'

'No,' stated the boy firmly. 'I'd sooner die, before they could get me.'

That night, a harsh wind whipped up from the east, orchestrating the trees around the house and singing hollowly in the drains. Neil came downstairs in his pyjamas, complaining that he couldn't sleep. He claimed that he could hear the dead cat crying under his window. Merton, who had himself been a sensitive child, let his son snuggle beside him on the sofa, watching a cosy Billy Wilder comedy on television. When the film was over, Neil went to bed of his own accord. As he tucked the boy in, Merton was startled by an unexpected question.

'Dad: who was Sweaty Betty?'

Merton tutted in disapproval. 'Where've you got that from?'

'Who was she, Dad?'

Merton stroked his son's hair affectionately. 'You shouldn't use that name, son. It isn't nice.'

'Why not?'

'It's unkind.'

'Yes, but who was she?'

'Her real name was Mrs Standring, and she was a poor woman who never did anyone any harm.'

'Was she really murdered?'

'Now. Come on . . .'

'Was she, though?'

Merton seemed to deflate. 'Yes, Neil, I'm afraid she was.'

'Did the police think you did it, Dad?'

'All right, who've you been talking to?'

'Mum told me.'

'What? That the police thought I did it?'

'No. She said you helped the police. But on the news, when it says "helping the police with their enquiries", it really means that the police think they've got the man who did it. Doesn't it?'

Merton beamed in admiration. 'Clever lad. Yes, that's exactly what it means. But your mother didn't mean it that way. You see, no one round here used to bother with Mrs Standring. They ignored her. The only people who bothered with her were me and Mr Martin at the farm. So when she died, Mr Martin and me had to say what we knew, you see. We weren't under arrest or anything. We really *were* helping the police, because nobody else knew much about her. Does that answer your question?'

'Yeah.'

'Good. Right, then.' Merton's right hand was resting on his son's head. In his memory, he saw that same hand wrapping a dying woman's intestines around her neck. Don't worry, Neil. Your daddy would never hurt you.

He ruffled the boy's hair and left the bed. Before he had time to cross the room, Neil said, 'And why couldn't they catch the man who killed her?'

'Come on, now. Sleep.'

'Yes . . . but they didn't catch him. What if he tries to kill someone else?'

There was a pause. Neil raised his head slightly from the pillow. His father was standing at the door, with the light behind him. Neil couldn't see his face.

'Shush, now,' said Merton softly. 'It's late. No more questions . . .'

# FIVE

Laverne returned to work in a foul mood. The unresponsive glare that greeted Lyn Savage's breezy 'good morning' discouraged her from politely enquiring after his health, or the quality of his Christmas. His ashen face and sullen demeanour told her all she needed to know. She returned to her paperwork, leaving him to sulk and sigh until he felt like speaking.

DI Savage had already decided that nothing was to be gained from asking Laverne for an account of his movements on Christmas Eve. Her original conviction that he had broken into her home had been replaced by an overwhelming compulsion to dismiss the experience as an hallucination brought about by overwork. And when she'd mentioned her nocturnal sighting of the Superintendent to Ian, he had laughed rudely and suggested that Laverne had been secretly living in the cupboard under the stairs. Or perhaps she thought the dog had let him in?

Farrell entered, brandishing a sheet of scrap paper. He approached Savage, his manner cautiously deferential. The Inspector and he had not discussed his recent *faux pas*, mainly because of her fierce outrage at the time. As far as she was concerned, that was the end of the matter. She bore him no grudges and, in truth, was more disappointed in herself than in Farrell. She felt she'd handled the incident badly, and given the chance would have played the scene again with a dash of humour and rather more self-control.

'I've just been in touch with that firm,' he said, avoiding direct eye contact. 'You know . . . A. D. Watt.' She frowned.

'Printer of affirmations? The "S.D." on the back stands for Sheelagh Daye.'

He placed the sheet of paper on the desk in front of her, and pointed to the name, neatly rendered in his very best hand. 'She's a psychotherapist, and she designed the cards herself. Made up all the messages herself, too. You can only obtain the cards directly from her. "One Hundred Affirmations by Sheelagh Daye." And . . . she lives in York.'

'Whereabouts?'

'Ellis Square.'

Savage raised her eyebrows. 'Hmm . . . There must be money in this psychotherapy game. Any previous?'

'Previous what?' he quipped. 'Psychotherapy?' He laughed artificially.

She regarded him coolly, to show that he had not been entirely forgiven.

He blinked, his smile evaporating, and tapped the sheet of paper. 'It's all there, anyway . . .'

When Farrell had left the room, Laverne put down the dictionary he had been pretending to read and said, 'What was all that about?' Savage told him about the cards and, for good measure, just to see the smile on his face, passed on the findings of Dr Stockton. Laverne listened morosely, not reacting. He was leaning on one elbow with his fist pressed into his cheek. When she'd finished, he said, 'Well, then. That explains it.'

'Explains what?'

'The whole inquiry. The girl was killed by the first murder victim. Who, in turn, was killed by some other corpse. Like they say on the telly, "It all fits." Haven't you worked it out yet, Inspector? Our chief suspects are the undead. All we have to do now is round up all the local corpses with a criminal record and this case is in the bag.'

'That's funny,' she said, grimacing to show that it wasn't.

She handed him the affirmations. He shuffled them deftly.

'They're called "affirmations",' she explained, attempting

84

to sound authoritative. 'You draw a card at random, and sort of contemplate it.'

He plucked a card from the deck. It read YOU ALREADY KNOW ALL THAT YOU NEED TO KNOW. He smiled thinly. Then, with composure, he replaced the card, reshuffled the pack and set it squarely on the table in front of him. He sat back, waiting for Savage to elaborate.

'Sheelagh Daye,' she read, straining to decipher Farrell's writing. 'According to the PNC, two convictions for drugs offences. Possession. But nothing since 1978.'

'What is she, then? Some kind of hippy?'

'A psychotherapist.'

He snorted. 'Like I said, some kind of hippy.'

She glanced at the clock. 'Shall we go in now?'

'Go in where?'

'The morning meeting.'

'No,' he said.

'What do you mean?'

'I mean no,' he repeated, reaching for his coat. 'You can have a meeting if you want one. I'm off to pay a visit to our friend Sheelagh. Who knows? If she isn't undead herself, she may know someone who is . . .'

Ten minutes later, Savage rang Sheelagh Daye's doorbell. Laverne and the Inspector were waiting on the steps of a cream and blue Georgian townhouse. An elaborate holly wreath hanging on the door potently evoked the flavour of a Dickensian Christmas, and a wino squatting on the pavement across the square completed the effect. The entryphone fizzed and crackled. Through the static, a cold female voice said, 'Yes?'

'Police,' said Laverne. 'We'd like to speak to a Mizz Sheelagh Daye.'

The entryphone went silent.

'That's "Ms", by the way,' advised Savage, helpfully.

'Why? What did I say?'

'You said "Mizz".'

Laverne grunted dismissively. It seemed like an age before the door finally opened, and they were confronted by a hard-faced blonde woman with a broken nose and pale, mistrustful eyes. 'What is it?' she demanded tersely.

'We're police officers,' said Savage. 'We'd like to ask you a few questions, if we may.'

'What's going on? What sort of questions?'

Laverne held the affirmations aloft. 'You already know all that you need to know,' he intoned satirically.

She admitted them to a bright kitchen that smelled faintly of curry. The cabinets, table and chairs were made of matching pine. Asocially, Daye waved at two empty chairs, then sat down and lit a cigarette. She drew a mouthful of smoke deep into her lungs, then snorted it out through both nostrils with surprising vigour. 'You couldn't have picked a worse time, actually. I'm with a client.'

'It shouldn't take long,' said Laverne, using his trilby to waft the smoke away from his face.

Savage glanced at a child's picture book resting on the table, its cover towards Daye. She squinted to read the title: *The Differently Abled Princess.*

Daye aimed her protuberant pale blue eyes at them, apparently disliking what she saw. Unruffled, Savage and Laverne stared back at her. Laverne began to utter formal introductions, but Daye cut him short.

'Get to the point, will you?'

'All right,' smiled Laverne equably. Then, like a stage magician, he made a fan-shape with the set of affirmations. 'As you probably know, a York woman was murdered last week. Her name was Anjali Dutt, and these cards were found among her belongings.'

'So?'

'You designed these cards,' he said, telling her rather than asking.

Daye shrugged. 'That's right. What about it?'

86

'Are they on sale in the shops?'

'No. They're for private use. I sell them to friends and clients. And in answer to your next question, no, I don't know how your murder victim got hold of them.'

'She's not "our" murder victim,' said Savage sharply. 'She's yours, too. We should all feel a responsibility to the victims of crime. They're not an alien species.'

Laverne showed Sheelagh Daye the photograph of Derek Tyreman. She instantly denied all knowledge of him. Savage asked her to study the likeness more carefully and Daye gave it another cursory glance. She lit a second cigarette, without finishing her first – the police officers could tell that something was bothering her. Without giving her time to think, Laverne shoved a photograph of the impaled boy under her nose.

'I suppose you don't know him either?' he said evenly.

Daye shook her head resolutely.

Savage asked, 'Would you mind telling us what your business entails? I mean, what is it you do, exactly?'

'Well, first of all, it isn't a business—' Sheelagh snapped.

A young man in his early twenties ambled into the room, and beamed ingenuously at Laverne and Savage. He looked pleasant enough, but he was wearing dungarees. For some reason, this made Laverne want to kick him.

'Stewart,' said Daye, leaning back in her chair and injecting an embarrassingly flirtatious tone into her voice. 'These people want to know what I do for a living. What should I tell them?'

Obligingly, Stewart said, 'Life healing. She's the most fantastic life healer.'

'Oh, yes,' said Laverne. 'What's that, then?'

Daye and her young protégé exchanged amused glances. Didn't these people know anything?

'Life healing is only *the* fastest-growing personal growth system in the Western hemisphere,' Daye said.

'That's right,' nodded Stewart. To Laverne's annoyance, he sat down at the table next to Sheelagh and helped himself to one of her cigarettes. His presence seemed to lend Daye confidence, defusing the tension that had been steadily building up in her since their arrival. Laverne would gladly have told Stewart to leave, but this was only an informal interview and Sheelagh Daye was one of those annoying types who know their rights.

'Is it some kind of religion?' asked Savage.

Daye and the young man sniggered.

'What's so funny?' said Laverne.

Daye looked into his eyes defiantly. 'It isn't a religion. It's a method. A method that "helps us to become ourselves". I wish I'd said that, but unfortunately I didn't. It's a quote from a book called *The Universe and Me* by Tyne Culloch.'

'Never heard of him,' said Laverne.

'For your information, "he" is a "she",' sneered Daye. 'And if you're after a simple guide to life healing, you really ought to read that book.'

'I never read fiction,' said Laverne.

'Actually, Sheelagh,' Savage interrupted, 'it'd save us a lot of time if you explained life healing to us.'

Daye made a great show of weary unwillingness.

'Go on, Shee,' urged Stewart. 'You're great at explaining things.'

This appealed to her vanity. 'Oh, God. All right. Well, life healing originated in the early seventies, out in California.' Laverne made a grumbling noise in the back of his throat, to show that this didn't surprise him. 'A group of like-minded people – Tyne Culloch, Hugo Prince and Sandy Weinstraub – met in a meditation class and decided that meditation, in itself, couldn't answer their problems.'

'What problems?' interrupted Laverne.

Daye ignored him. 'So they began to consider other approaches. Hugo Prince went to Honolulu and studied the ancient Huna religion. And he brought enough knowledge back with him to develop life healing as a viable alternative health system.'

'And how does life healing work?' frowned Savage. 'I mean, what does it involve exactly?'

'It's too complicated to explain in a single sitting,' yawned Daye. 'But basically, life healers undo complexes and crippling phobias by using repeated commands. We help people to be healthy, successful and happy by what some would call hypnotic suggestion, but I prefer to call magic.' She turned to Stewart. 'Is that fair, Stu?'

Stu thought it was fair.

The photographs were still on the table. On an impulse, Savage pushed them towards the man in dungarees. 'How about you? Seen any of these faces before?'

'It's hardly likely,' apprised Daye.

'Let him speak for himself. Stewart?'

Stewart, clearly flattered to be included, flicked through the snapshots. 'No . . . no . . . but, hey, I've seen this one. I know this guy.'

He was tapping the likeness of Tyreman. 'Shee: look,' he enthused. 'Don't you recognize him?'

'No,' she retorted, tight-lipped.

'Yes you do. You must.' Her foot was pressing urgently against his, but he failed to decipher its meaning. 'Wasn't he at your birthday party?'

'I don't think so.'

Belatedly, he read the tension in her face. Confused and helpless, he looked back at Savage. She smiled at him.

Laverne spoke first. 'Well, Sheelagh? Is he right?'

'How should I know? There were two hundred people at that party.'

'When was it?' said Savage.

'November the third.'

'She's a Scorpio,' grinned Stewart inanely.

'Do you keep an appointments book?' asked Laverne.

'What if I do?' returned Daye, belligerently grinding her cigarette into an oval ceramic ashtray.

Smoothly, Savage said, 'We need to see that book, I'm

afraid. The man we're seeking, the man Stewart here believes he's seen in this house, may very well be guilty of murder.'

'Er, no way. My client list is absolutely confidential.'

'Well, Sheelagh,' advised Laverne, the hint of a smile at the corners of his mouth, 'it's like this: either you give us that book now, or we come back with a warrant and turn you and your nice little house upside-down. It really is up to you.'

Sheelagh Daye, bullied into silence, stared at Laverne with unadulterated hostility.

'Wow,' commented Stewart. 'Heavy.'

Derek Tyreman, a scarf veiling the lower half of his face, a woollen hat pulled low over his ears, was walking through the market place. It began to rain, starting as a light shower and promptly turning into a vigorous torrent. He bowed his head in obeisance towards the heavens, but made no attempt to seek shelter. He genuinely wanted to get wet. He was drugged from cold and lack of sleep, and felt that pneumonia would be no more than he deserved.

His ears ached, his feet hurt, his throat was sore. His head felt hollow and bloated, like a Hallowe'en pumpkin. He had now exhausted his tiny circle of friends. No one would help him. For three nights, he had slept on the floor of a squat at Heworth Place until one of his hosts had sighted his photograph on the front cover of a newspaper and asked him to leave. It would appear that even the dispossessed had their standards.

The tabloid headline had asked, 'IS THIS THE BEAST OF YORK?' In fact, Tyreman looked more like a suffering saint than a beast. He had deserted his lover, leaving her to die in abject terror, and was now convinced, utterly convinced, of his own worthlessness. But being worthless was a condition he would have to live with. And, despite everything, he did so want to live.

After a week of roughing it, he had lost a stone in weight. He was five feet eleven inches tall, and now weighed one hundred and thirty-eight pounds. He had a little money; a few hundred left in a deposit account, but that would not last long. Soon he would be hungry, as well as sick at heart, weary, permanently anxious.

The rain abated and the sun did its feeble best to shine. So he walked aimlessly, through crowds shopping for bargains in the sales. He had noticed that the dirtier he grew, the more invisible he became. This was what it was like to be without status. No one acknowledged you. It was almost miraculous, this state of eerie non-being.

Perhaps this was why the police had driven past him time and time again over the last few days. Perhaps they simply could not see him. He tittered foolishly to himself, imagining what he would say to them on his arrest. 'If you were any good, if you were not completely useless, you would have found me a week ago,' he said aloud. Two fat men eating chips stared at him as he passed, then shouted abuse at his retreating back.

In his feverish state, he had begun to see significance in every chance event. His path seethed with omens. That morning, a laughing infant in a pushchair outside All Saints Church had tried to touch him. He gratefully interpreted this as a sign that he was free of the taint of evil, for children and animals were highly sensitive to unholy vibrations.

Now, walking up crowded Davygate, he felt comforted by the bodies milling around him. Comforted because, as Sheelagh Daye would say, these people loved him, even if they didn't know it yet. Then another sign from Heaven: he heard a coarse-voiced woman say to her neighbour, 'He left her. But she still sees him.' Tears welled up in his eyes, for he took this to mean that although he had abandoned Anjali, she had not abandoned him. I left her. But she still sees me.

Outside Betty's Tea Room, he almost collided with a uniformed constable. Raw fear flowered in Tyreman's empty stomach. But the officer was young, a fresh-faced boy, and he was obligingly posing for a quartet of laughing American girls who were taking turns to be photographed with him. The policeman, transfixed by the warmth of these women and their glowing, healthy faces, failed to notice the crazy-eyed, unwashed man edging past him with exaggerated stealth.

Tyreman arrived at the museum gardens but no sooner had he passed through the open wrought-iron gates than a voice called out to him.

'I say! Hello, I say!'

Once again, panic surged through him and he was compelled to turn and face the speaker. Tyreman's gaze fell upon a plump, innocuous man in late middle age. He had a full, boyish head of chestnut-brown hair, neatly parted and combed in a late-fifties style. The face was round, brick-red, with small, disappointed eyes. He wore a navy blazer that most men of his generation would have described as 'smart', and a matching blue and white tie, tucked into a V-necked sweater. Had the blazer been unbuttoned, Tyreman might have seen that the sweater bore a small sporting insignia on its breast.

'I say,' repeated the stranger, using the expression to mean 'excuse me'. He spoke with the kind of falsely polite London accent that upper-class British actors who thought they could 'do Cockney' employed in old pre-war films. Pressing his advantage, he offered Tyreman a small, pink hand. 'I say, you wouldn't know where I could get a really good cup of tea round here, would you?'

'You could always try the Salvation Army.'

The stranger laughed, a little too readily. 'No, no, no. You don't understand. I'm offering to buy you a cup of tea, old chap. You look as if you could use some refreshment. I know I could. Let's share a pot of tea. My treat. Do you know a nice café?'

Stunned, Tyreman said, 'There's always Betty's.'

'Where's that?'

Tyreman eyed him sceptically. 'You're in York and you don't know where Betty's is? I don't believe you.'

92

The man looked startled. He raised his hands defensively. 'No. Honestly, old chap. I'm a stranger here.'

Tyreman gawped foolishly. 'Oh. Well, it's a tea room. Betty's Tea Room. I thought everyone had heard of it.'

His companion tapped him on the arm. 'Lead the way.'

Bemused, Tyreman retraced his steps. The red-faced man hurried along at his side, taking short, rapid strides. 'My name's Tony. And yours is?'

Tyreman didn't reply.

'I'm on holiday, actually. Staying at the Viking Hotel. It's top notch. The carpets come up to my ankles.' An uneasy chuckle. 'Mind you, they should do, the prices they charge.'

'We don't have to go to Betty's,' said Tyreman, his fear of capture suddenly overpowering his insidious hunger. Tony, who had once been penniless himself, took this to mean that the scruffy young man was ashamed to be seen in genteel surroundings.

Kindly, he said, 'No, no, no. Only the best for us. I insist. My treat, old chap. By the way, I don't believe I caught your name?'

'Claude,' lied Tyreman, as the famous Tea Room came into sight. He was thinking of Claude Rains, the actor who played the Invisible Man.

'Claude,' repeated Tony dubiously. 'Nice name. You don't often hear it these days.'

They passed the gilt and glass windows and crossed the threshold. The delicious smell of freshly brewed coffee filled their mouths and nostrils. They went downstairs, and waited in front of a rope barrier. Presently, a sweet-faced teenage waitress came forward to seat them. 'Smoking or non-smoking?' she enquired.

'Oh, non-smoking, I should say,' said Tony, looking to Tyreman for confirmation. 'Non-smoking?' Tyreman gave a complacent shrug. 'Non-smoking, I think,' Tony repeated to the girl in a conspiratorial tone.

She led them to a small table in a dark corner and left them to study the menu. 'Have whatever you like,' chirped Tony. 'Anything that takes your fancy. I should say so!'

Wearily, and without any visible sign of gratitude, Tyreman ordered Earl Grey tea and a mixed grill with plenty of toast. Tony settled for coffee and a tea-cake. The food took a long time to arrive.

Abstractedly, Tyreman watched a heavily bejewelled woman who was sitting at a table in the centre of the room, blithely blowing cigarette smoke over her two young grand-children as they rammed cakes into their small round faces. On the table before her rested an unholy mound of chocolate éclairs, in which she showed no interest. The cakes were merely for show, like the glittering Rolex on her plump, tanned wrist.

At his side, Tony was chatting cheerfully. There was no stopping the man. Tyreman noticed that he smelled of Old Spice aftershave and at close quarters saw that his soft eyes were ringed by dark concentric circles and his skin was slack and wrinkled, like old leather. 'I used to be in the rag trade, you know. My mother was an invalid. Now that she's passed on, I've only myself to worry about. If I want to go away, I just pick up sticks and go. On Saturday night, I thought to myself, "I wouldn't mind York." On Sunday morning, I'm boarding a train at King's Cross Station!'

When Tyreman's food came, he remembered to eat slowly and carefully, guarding against nausea. He was still cold and his feet felt numb inside their damp boots. Tony watched his guest eat with proprietorial satisfaction, occasionally punc-tuating his soliloquy with a dainty mouthful of tea-cake. For him, this moment held all the warmth and magic of a great romance. He was not motivated by lust, but by the desire to enjoy, discreetly, the company of a handsome young man. Admittedly, his guest wasn't remotely handsome. He could have been cleaner, too, but to Tony most young people looked grubby nowadays. At least this one wasn't coarse or aggressive.

For Tyreman, the greasy repast had a sobering effect. His mushroom-laden steak exploded with flavour in his ulcerated mouth, and his sensible decision to chew his food restored his strength, and with it his self-awareness. Gradually, he awoke to the absurdity of his situation.

'You can take your hat off, you know,' joked Tony. 'It isn't compulsory to wear a hat in here, unless I'm much mistaken.'

Tyreman gave the sad man at his side a long, critical look.

'A few drinks afterwards?' suggested Tony lamely. 'The hotel bar is very pleasant. Very salubrious.'

But Tyreman knew there could be no drinks, no more foolishness. After his meal, he would get out of York. He had been pushing his luck, and it was time to leave.

'I didn't know they allowed dogs in here,' said Tony disapprovingly.

Tyreman stopped, in mid-mastication, to ask Tony what he was talking about. Tony was not a confident man, and on being challenged, his jowls coloured with embarrassment.

'Weren't they dogs? They were sniffing around under our table, anyway. Blooming great things.'

Tyreman, who had seen nothing, thrust out his right hand involuntarily, casting the contents of his tea cup on to the table cloth. Murmuring words of motherly comfort, Tony began to dab ineffectually at the spreading brown pool with a paper napkin.

Tyreman felt a crawling, prickling sensation in his feet and began to pray aloud. 'God, oh God, don't let this be happening . . .'

Tony was surprised by this outburst. 'Steady on,' he counselled. 'It's only a bit of spilt tea.'

Tyreman motioned to stand but his feet gave way and he crashed heavily to earth, taking the table and its contents with him. The other diners and a nearby waitress froze, mutely studying him as he lay shaking on the floor, covered with coffee and crockery, a half-consumed tea-cake stuck to his chest. Tony addressed the room in an unsteady voice.

'It's quite all right. I think he's having a fit. It's all right. I'm going to get help . . .'

Then, in his heavy, half-tottering fashion, he rushed up the stairs and out into the street. There he wavered, aquiver with indecision. By now, it had occurred to him that if an ambulance was required, the paramedics might question him, and pass his name on to the police. Then the police might consult their records and discover that he had once been cautioned for loitering in a public convenience.

Appalled by this prospect, Tony fled back to the Viking Hotel, where he locked himself in his room for the remainder of the day.

# Six

The Queen Victoria wing at York Infirmary is, as its name suggests, the oldest and ugliest part of this vast, under-funded establishment. Since mid-afternoon its corridors had resounded to a series of harrowing screams. Hearing these cries, patients and visitors alike found it easy to imagine how operations had sounded in the days before anaesthetic. But now, in the early evening, an uneasy calm had descended on the hospital, disturbed only by hushed voices and clinking plates, and here and there, as required, the sound of laughter and quiet restrained weeping.

Laverne and Savage, working overtime, were walking up a long, narrow passage, their way lit by a procession of naked light-bulbs. Their shoes clattered noisily on the worn, polished linoleum. Garish paintings by local schoolchildren had been pinned to the fly-spattered walls in an attempt to lighten the atmosphere, but the colourful stick-men with their blob heads merely served to highlight the pervading mood of gloom and foreboding.

At the end of the corridor, the police officers turned right, following the sign for ward C12. They passed through a set of flimsy double doors that looked like props from one of television's cheaper hospital soaps, and approached reception. Behind the desk, a woman with a home perm that had gone badly wrong was reading a magazine. Sensing their presence, she slowly raised her face, her expression quickly changing from indifference to servility as Laverne flashed his identification. 'Dr Gregg? Oh dear, I'm terribly sorry. You've just missed her. She's gone for her lie-down.'

'No she hasn't,' barked a militaristic voice from behind. They turned to see a tall, lumbering woman, her face hard and unyielding, her frizzy light brown hair tied back in a ferocious bun. They introduced themselves and, without a flicker of warmth, she showed them into a small cramped office. Most of the floor space was taken up by a low camp bed.

The subject of Derek Tyreman seemed to rankle her. 'If you want my opinion,' she said, 'there's nothing wrong with him. He's been yelling his head off for most of the afternoon. He can't walk, and I have to admit that he doesn't appear to have any feeling in his feet and lower legs. But we can't find any physical cause for that.'

Dr Gregg was not paid to make moral judgements and so, like any doctor or nurse, threw them in free of charge. It was her informed belief that the new boy on her ward was a habitual drug-taker, reaping the rewards of a wasteful and decadent lifestyle.

It exasperated her to think that her meagre budget, which she felt ought to be used to help people who were ill through no fault of their own, should be squandered on those who had visited misfortune upon themselves.

And now, to make matters worse, her precious time was being taken up by this tall, surly policeman and his buxom partner. He was gazing around her office with an obvious low regard for its contents. Nor did he appear to have noticed that Gregg was studiously directing everything she said to his female colleague. It was coming to something, she reflected, when a man was too ignorant to notice he was being snubbed.

'His parents should be here by this evening,' the woman was saying. 'In the meantime, Detective Superintendent Laverne and myself would like to talk to your patient alone, if we may.'

Dr Gregg shrugged. Under different circumstances, she would have taken this opportunity to assert herself by saying, like doctors in films: 'No, I cannot allow that. My patient must, on no account, be disturbed.' But she could not, in all conscience, make such a pronouncement because she didn't believe Tyreman was genuinely ill, and therefore didn't care whether they disturbed him or not.

So she said, 'Go ahead. I only hope you get more sense out of him than we did.'

Savage smiled. 'Thanks, Doctor. And I'm afraid we'll have to post an officer outside his door on a twenty-four-hour basis. Sorry.'

Gregg tutted and scowled.

She felt Laverne's eyes on her and, without meaning to, looked up at him. To her horror, he winked at her.

'What's he supposed to have done?' asked Gregg.

Savage didn't reply. Disgustedly, the doctor rose and held open the door to indicate that the meeting was at an end. Laverne and Savage stepped out into the corridor. A middle-aged orderly shuffled by, wheeling a rattling trolley. Then Gregg led the way to Tyreman's room. Her wooden sandals made a clacking sound as she crossed the floor.

Tyreman was lying on his back in bed, his head lolling forlornly. The far side of his room was obscured by a faded screen, displaying a floral pattern. A wastepaper basket beside the bed was piled high with dead, dried-out daffodils and tulips.

'I'll make sure you aren't interrupted,' said Gregg flatly, leaving them to the bleak room and the pale unfortunate on the bed.

Tyreman had been washed shortly after his admission to the infirmary. He was wearing pale blue cotton pyjamas that were not his own. His eyes were open but glazed; fixed, apparently, on the anachronistic brass bedknobs at the foot of his bed.

In contrast to the stifling warmth of the hospital, Tyreman's room was surprisingly chilly. Laverne coughed and saw his breath rushing before him.

'Is he conscious?' queried Savage.

99

'I dunno,' said Laverne.

Slowly, Tyreman shifted his head on the pillow so that his watery, red-rimmed eyes could accommodate his visitors. In a calm, hoarse voice he said, 'He left her.'

Laverne drew up two plastic chairs and they seated themselves.

'Who left who?' asked Savage.

Tyreman grinned unpleasantly, baring discoloured teeth. 'But she still sees him.'

Laverne looked at Savage, and raised his eyebrows as if to say, 'This is going to be a waste of time.' However, convention demanded that he at least try, so he said, 'Derek, where were you on the night of December twenty-first?'

'Ana,' said Tyreman.

Laverne dismissed this utterance as meaningless babble. 'The night your girlfriend died,' he said, purposefully speaking slowly and plainly. 'Where were you?'

Tyreman closed his eyes, as if in pain, 'No, no . . .'

Laverne said, 'Where were you when she died, Derek?'

'Ana, ana,' echoed Tyreman.

'What's he saying?' Laverne asked Savage.

She frowned. 'It sounds like "a 'nana".'

Laverne continued, 'What do you mean, Derek? What's he on about? Is he asking for a banana?'

Tyreman leaned forward, and opening his eyes seized Laverne's arm. 'He's praying me dead.'

'Sorry . . . I'm not with you . . .'

Tyreman promptly began to scream at the top of his voice. The effort darkened his face and made the veins on his neck protrude. Hastily, Laverne freed his arm and sat back, unsure what to do next. The door opened. A rather plump, ungainly nurse thrust her head into the room to snap, 'You! Just shut it!'

Astonished, Tyreman went silent. The door closed. Somehow, the nurse's outburst, being unprofessional, had created a far worse impression than her patient's lapse into hysteria.

100

After his exertion, Tyreman's energy seemed to ebb away. His eyes grew heavy, and his head rolled towards the wall. 'The Death Prayer,' he whispered, slipping into a heavy slumber.

Behind the screen, a floorboard creaked. The window beyond rattled briefly in its frame. Laverne and Savage pushed back their chairs and crept out into the corridor.

'What the hell's a "Death Prayer" when it's at home?' Laverne wondered aloud.

'I doubt it means anything,' said Savage. 'I mean, his mind's clearly disturbed.'

Dr Gregg was standing a few yards away, deep in discussion with a male colleague. She was holding a clipboard and jabbing at it emphatically with a cheap Biro. Sensing their presence, she looked up suddenly and, taking care to address Savage not Laverne, she said, 'Well? Any joy?'

Before the DI had time to respond, Laverne answered, injecting sardonic exuberance into his voice. 'Yes, thanks, Doctor! Thanks for all your time and patience!'

Scowling, Gregg returned her attention to the clipboard.

As they departed from the ward, Savage gave Laverne a jocular smack on the wrist. He smacked her back. Sniggering like naughty schoolchildren, they walked down the corridor to the waiting lift.

The telephone rang, violently rousing Sheelagh Daye from her reverie. She was in her sitting room on the first floor of the house at Ellis Square, so lost in anxious reflection that she had not noticed the day slipping away. She had to fumble in the dark to locate her mobile phone. 'Yes?'

A familiar voice sounded in her ear. A voice she dreaded, yet had been longing to hear. 'Yes . . . yes. They came and went. But they took my appointments diary. It's got everything in it. Everything. I just don't know what you expect me to do.'

A pause, as the caller advised her. With her free hand, Daye groped blindly in the dark, searching in vain for her cigarettes.

'What? Now?' The voice at the end of the line was calmly insistent. 'All right . . . Give me an hour.'

She turned on the light and rushed to the bathroom, to urinate and wash her face and hands. Then she bounded downstairs to the kitchen, snatched up her shoulder bag and leather jacket and left the house, slamming the door behind her.

Moments later she was behind the wheel of her shiny BMW, leaving the city, heading west on the A59. As she drove, her sense of wounded injustice grew stronger. This time he had asked too much of her. She owed everything to the man she was going to see: her wealth, her self-esteem, her glorious career. But today he had compelled her to lie, and this she could neither forgive nor understand. It was true that she had no great love of the police, but she had turned to life healing to cleanse herself of deceit and hypocrisy. When the police discovered that she had lied, how would she defend herself? No, this time he had gone too far.

The car in front, a Citroën 2CV, seemed to be proceeding at an inordinately slow pace. Normally, she respected careful drivers, but in her present mood every minor setback seemed like a personal attack. She prepared to overtake but, as she glanced in the rear-view mirror, experienced a peculiar hallucination. For a split-second she seemed to glimpse thick yellow smoke billowing out of the back seat.

A hasty glance over her shoulder contradicted this impression. She looked in the mirror again, now seeing only dark empty upholstery and the flicker of pursuing lights through the back window.

How odd. She shivered involuntarily. Steady, Sheelagh. You're getting jittery. She passed an illuminated sign. 17 DEATHS ON YORK ROADS LAST YEAR. Slow down, now. Let's not add to this year's statistics. She eased the pressure on the accelerator, and let the innocuous Citroën slip away.

There seemed to be something wrong with the car's heater. Although the twin fans roared, her feet were tingling with the

102

cold. She lit a cigarette and inhaled deeply. But even this familiar comfort failed to relax her. And although she was only travelling at forty miles an hour, she was closing on that bloody Citroën again. Its ridiculous little rear bumper curled upward to form a complacent Gallic sneer.

She covered the brake with her right foot, and eased down gently. Safety first. But when she tried to lift her foot from the pedal, Daye found that she could not feel it. She panicked, and the cigarette dropped from her mouth to her lap, where it began to smoulder. The dead weight of her leg on the brake pedal resulted in rapid deceleration. Despite her seat belt, she lunged forward, nodding her head at the windscreen. As she released the steering wheel, the car skidded ninety degrees on the wet road, neatly presenting its profile to an oncoming Ford Escort. It was as if the BMW was offering itself up in sacrifice.

The three seconds before collision gave Sheelagh Daye time to reflect on her situation. She understood perfectly what had just happened to her, and what was about to happen, and she drew back her lips to scream. But her throat was dry and no sound came. The last thing she saw before she lost consciousness was a face in the mirror. Its features were indistinct, but it appeared to be grinning. Then a piercing white light and she felt herself spinning outwards in all directions, as if a bomb had exploded inside her.

It was to be another seventeen hours before news of Daye's accident reached Laverne's desk. The appointments diary had been thoroughly perused, and although nothing incriminating had been found therein, Savage and Laverne were both of the persuasion that Daye had lied, and should be brought in for questioning. A squad car was sent to Ellis Square, where a garrulous housekeeper informed her uniformed visitors that Ms Daye was in York Royal, recovering from a road accident.

This news was promptly radioed back to the murder team.

'It doesn't surprise me,' observed Savage darkly, as Laverne drove to the hospital. 'Nothing in this inquiry is going according to plan.'

'Now, now. That's not like you, Lyn.' Laverne gave her one of his rare, twenty-six-tooth smiles. 'The moans and groans are more *my* department. You're meant to be . . . what is it? A fresh-faced ambassador for the new, positive police service of today.' A vague gleam of humour appeared in her eyes. Encouraged, he carried on. 'Eh? Washes whiter, launders the evidence more effectively than ever before.'

They arrived at the hospital and Lawless, who was waiting at the main reception, led them to Sheelagh Daye's bed. She was in Intensive Care, connected to an ECG and a confusing network of wires and drips. Her head was encased in a helmet of plaster. Her eyes were ringed by livid circles, and her face had inflated to twice its normal size. Her jaw was wired, and traces of dried blood showed at the corners of the mouth. She was utterly unrecognizable.

Laverne puffed out his breath resignedly.

'Yeah,' said Lawless. 'I know.'

'No one told us she was this bad,' Savage complained.

Laverne was annoyed. 'We've wasted our time. Again. She's not likely to answer any questions in this state, is she?'

Lawless agreed regretfully and then hesitated, remembering something. 'She did come round, though. At lunchtime. Kept moaning and pointing with her one good arm. Me and a nurse had to try and guess what she wanted. We had a hell of a time, but we got there in the end.'

Laverne and Savage turned to face him. He reached into his jacket and produced a worn brown leather wallet. There was a white envelope sandwiched inside it, which he handed to Laverne. 'We reckon this is what she wanted us to see.'

Laverne withdrew a small greeting card from the unsealed envelope. The cover was illustrated with a silver crescent moon over three rippling blue lines. Inside the card, the message read:

QUEST FOR THE HIGH SELF
*You are cordially invited*
*To a weekend*
*That will change your life*


Below this was a phone number with an Ilkley dialling code. Laverne held the card at arm's length and mumbled something disparaging.

'What's the matter?' asked Savage.

'Well, look at it. "Quest for the High Self." We're up against a load of bloody nutters . . .'

After work, Savage and Laverne went for a drink in the Angler's Arms. It was her idea. Usually, she had no time for off-duty socializing and had always looked down on the pub-and-canteen culture that came between most police officers and their families. But she needed to talk to Laverne, alone and in private.

They sat at a table in a corner of the small, cosy bar. Savage sipped a gin and tonic and a foaming pint of bitter rested in front of Laverne. Savage never actually saw him drink, but every so often she glanced at his glass and noticed that it was a little emptier.

'So what's coming?' Laverne asked quietly. 'Are you about to tell me you're applying for a transfer?'

'No. Absolutely not.'

'I'm not even warm?'

'No. In fact, you're practically at the North Pole, old chum.'

'Hey! Less of the "old" . . . I just wondered what this was in aid of.' He nodded at their surroundings. 'Normally, you can't wait to get home.'

Away from the office, divested of his authority, he seemed strangely shy. She felt a sudden flood of warmth for him. 'I thought it might be nice to talk things over, see what we had going.'

He looked alarmed. 'What? You and me, you mean?'

She almost choked on her gin. 'Give me a break.'

He granted her a half-smile of relief. 'Oh. Sorry. I thought my luck was in there, for a minute.'

'No. I just want to know what we're going to do next. I've got a bad feeling about this inquiry. Don't ask me why . . .'

'No need to ask you why. Someone takes a bite out of a corpse. The only realistic suspect is another corpse. In my book, that's enough to give anyone a bad feeling.'

'Do you think the psychotherapy link's a red herring, or should we follow it through?'

'We follow it through. Or at least you do . . .'

'What's that supposed to mean?'

'I would have thought it was obvious. We've tried knocking at the front door, and got nowhere. So let's go round the back. I think someone should go on this faith healing weekend.'

'Life healing.'

'That as well. Someone should pretend to be a civilian, and find out what they can. And I think that someone should be you.'

'Er, only one problem, Vernon. I'm off at New Year. Three days' leave.'

'Cancel it.'

'No way,' she retorted indignantly. 'We're all going to my mother's. It's been arranged for months. No. You'll have to send one of the team.'

He shook his head. 'Can't do that.'

'Why not?'

'They're all daft.'

She tutted in disapproval. 'Rubbish! Farrell's got a degree. Helen Robinson has got five A-levels.'

'Yeah. But I bet she hasn't got an A-level in undercover surveillance.' (She grumbled to herself.) 'Can't you go, Lyn?'

'I've already told you. No.'

He pondered for a moment. 'Ah, well. I suppose it'll have to be me, then.'

She froze, recognizing this as precisely the kind of behaviour that Laverne's enemies were looking out for. 'No, Vernon. You mustn't.'

'But what choice do I have? It's either you or me.'

'For God's sake!' The oath came out louder than she'd intended. A young couple at a neighbouring table turned to stare. Ironically, she raised her glass to them. Half-smirking, they looked away. 'You *cannot* go yourself. You're a senior police officer. The whole point of having rank is learning to delegate responsibility.'

'I know. That's why I tried to delegate the job to you. But you turned me down . . .'

'Vernon, I agree that a covert operation is a good idea. But just this once, let's play by the rules. So far, this is the oddest inquiry I've ever worked on.'

'Same here.'

'Right. Good. So why make it even odder? Hmm? Let's have a bit of order and rational behaviour at our end of the proceedings. So that no matter how strange things get out there, everything we do is rooted in good, old-fashioned logic. Does that make sense?'

He nodded slowly. 'Makes a lot of sense.'

This pleased her. 'Yes. It does, doesn't it? No one can deny that you've had more than your fair share of inspiration in the past. You've bent the rules, and it's paid off. And good for you. But this time round, let's play it by the book. Let's behave like real police officers.'

His eyes narrowed with cynicism. 'What? And fail to catch the murderers?'

She let this go. 'Send one of the team. That's what they're there for.'

He stared pensively into his beer, watching the beads of gas charging to the surface. She realized with a ripple of surprise that the glass was now only half-full. She had heard of secret drinkers, but this was ridiculous. Gradually, he raised his head and levelled his eyes at hers.

'You know that isn't true, Lyn. The team are just for show. Because people expect them to be there. But all the real work – the work that makes a difference – is done by us. You and me, Lyn. We're the *real* team.'

She blushed, simultaneously flattered and dismayed. For an instant, she was tempted to tell Laverne about the adverse attention his unconventional behaviour had been attracting. But she had given Geraint John her word, and was not the sort of person to break a confidence.

Calmly, she said, 'Yes. That's really the way you see things, isn't it? We've got a team of first-rate detectives at our disposal and you insist on behaving like Clint Eastwood.'

Laverne was amused by the comparison. 'It's a fault, I admit that,' he conceded. 'But I work better on my own.'

'And what's my role in your scheme of things? I'll tell you, shall I? When people ring up to find out where you are, I'm the poor idiot who makes the excuses. It isn't funny, Vernon. And it really has to stop.'

'Be fair. I'm getting better. Once upon a time, I would have gone off without telling anyone. I definitely wouldn't have asked you to go in my place.'

A pair of businessmen entered the pub, laughing raucously. She watched one of them loitering deliberately, determined to come last in the race for the bar so that his friend would be forced to buy the first round. There are criminals everywhere. 'Promise me something,' she said, turning back to Laverne.

'What?'

'Promise me you won't go on that course. Send someone else.'

'All right,' he said. 'If it's that important to you.'

She glanced at his beer glass. It was now completely empty, but neither Laverne's mouth nor the interior of the glass bore the faintest trace of tell-tale foam. Savage stared at Laverne incredulously.

'How do you *do* that?' she said.

# SEVEN

North Abbey lies three miles out of Ilkley, on the edge of the moors. It was once the home of Cistercian monks, until Henry VIII razed the abbey to the ground and, in its place, built a country mansion that he never saw. In the seventeenth century the house fell into the hands of the North family, who had made their fortune in wool. The present owner, Hugo Prince, claimed direct descent from Thomas North, who had fought alongside Richard the Lionheart. Prince was known to be a rich American who dabbled in new age practices. He had no criminal record.

This much Vernon Laverne knew, as he motored up the winding drive to the Abbey. And it had taken WPC Robinson a dozen phone calls and a trip to the public library to furnish him with the above information.

Then he had decided, rightly or wrongly, to discover the rest for himself. Dialling the number on the invitation, Laverne spoke to a courteous American woman called Yolande Henerberry, who had instructed him to attend on Saturday, at ten o'clock sharp, and to bring his invitation and his 'gift' along with him. Laverne wasn't sure what kind of gift the woman had in mind, or indeed what gifts, if any, he possessed, beyond his ability to wiggle his ears and his tendency to always look for the best in people, while fully expecting the worst. But he had pretended to understand what the woman was talking about, not wishing her to mistake him for a man without mystical tendencies.

The house crouched (or rather hid) in nine hundred acres of desolate, overgrown parkland, its Tudor origins masked by a crumbling and blackened façade of grand Georgian symmetry, with high dark windows and fanciful columns. Laverne didn't care for the place. And as he eased the Rover through the main gates into the central courtyard, he couldn't help wondering whether he'd acted foolishly in coming here.

Savage would be furious with him when she found out. Dawn was *already* furious with him. That night, he ought to have been accompanying her to a charity dinner-dance in aid of the hospice where she worked as a volunteer. But all his instincts told him that he would do more good, and ultimately avert more suffering, by joining the promised 'Quest for the High Self'.

There were already several cars parked in the courtyard. Laverne locked the Rover, and extracted a compact overnight bag from the boot. Lastly, he set the car alarm, lest anyone should be tempted to go in search of the 'High Self' in his beloved 1971 P5 coupé. A cheap-looking board with a white cardboard arrow affixed to it proclaimed 'Life Healing Weekend: This Way'. The arrow pointed towards an oval doorway underneath a Grecian arch. The door led into a dark, low-ceilinged passage, lined with indifferent antique oil paintings. On the wall facing the entrance was another arrow, pointing right. With his head expediently lowered, Laverne walked down the corridor, inhaling the smell of aged wood and beeswax polish. He also became aware of that characteristic dusty airlessness that old houses acquire, as if the dead of centuries are pressing in on the living; half curious, half resentful.

Laverne turned left into a wider passage, lit with fake oil lamps. He heard voices and walked towards the sound, emerging into an airy stone-flagged entrance hall.

There were over a dozen people present, men and women of all ages, some with bags like his own, others bearing rucksacks or small suitcases. They were gathered in diffident little groups at the foot of a wide, impressive oak staircase. There was a first-day-of-term awkwardness in the air, which

Laverne, impostor that he was, felt more keenly than most. A small, elegant woman with neatly styled grey hair and expensive clothes nodded to him in greeting as he approached.

'You are here for the course?' She had a light German accent.

'That's right,' said Laverne. 'Where's Yolande?'

Taking Laverne's sleeve, she pointed to a small, dark woman with high cheekbones and an elfin haircut. 'Over there.'

At that moment, Yolande's eyes met Laverne's. He approached her. She smiled and said, 'Are you Vernon Arnold?'

Laverne nodded. She shook his hand vigorously. 'Great to see you. And have we got a treat in store. Hugo's back from Paris and he's taking two of the sessions himself.'

'Is that good?' said Laverne.

She laughed, assuming that he was joking. With a black marker pen, she ticked his name off on an A4 pad. 'Great to see you, Vernon.' She nodded to a tall Polynesian who was standing beside her. 'This is Miko. He's going to show you all to your rooms.' Miko had sharp, watchful eyes in a flat, heavy-jowled face. He looked like a particularly world-weary bouncer. Cautiously, Miko nodded at Laverne. Laverne nodded back.

Laverne's room was on the first floor, on the south side of the house. It was sparsely and tastelessly furnished. Nothing matched. It was as if all the rejected items from other bedrooms had been moved into his room. A hideous mahogany cradle, big enough to house an exceptionally fat baby, rested by the door. It was probably a priceless antique, but Laverne would have happily thrown it out with the garbage.

There was a small stone balcony outside the window, but his view was marred by a lofty, overgrown elm. A concrete terrace lay directly below, then a network of ornamental gardens sloped upward towards a forest of pines. There, partially obscured by the trees, stood a whitish building with classical pillars. Somewhere, a peacock shrieked indignantly,

111

reminding Laverne of every vacuous award-winning film set on a country estate that his wife had ever forced him to sit through.

An oval baroque mirror hung opposite the plain double-bed. Laverne rested on the edge of the mattress, facing the mirror, and eyed himself critically. He had arrived, as advised, in casual clothes; a thick Arran sweater and brown corduroy trousers. He was posing as an insurance salesman, and there was no reason why an insurance salesman shouldn't have mystical leanings, or wear corduroy trousers. But Laverne felt that his eyes, with their steady, unexcitable gaze, gave him away.

He unpacked and joined the rest of the party for tea and biscuits in a dining room which overlooked a wide expanse of lawn and, in the distance, a melancholy lake. Yolande encouraged everyone to sit in a prearranged ring of chairs. Then she passed around a large floppy felt hat.

'Now, I'd like everyone to present their gifts. For, as Hugo says, we only get back that which we are first prepared to give.'

Laverne had no idea what was going on. Then he noticed that his companions were dipping into their purses and wallets. 'What one gives depends, of course, on one's individual conscience. Only you know what you can truly afford. But we do recommend a minimum of five hundred pounds. But whatever you give, please make sure it's cash. Cash only, please.'

This news appeared to come as no surprise to Laverne's fellow life healers, who were enthusiastically parting with fat rolls of bank-notes. But Laverne had only brought about eighty pounds away with him. When the hat passed into his lap, he sheepishly withdrew three five-pound notes from his pocket and dropped them in, taking care to bury them under the growing mound of twenties and fifties.

When this unsavoury rite had been completed, Yolande handed the hat to Miko, who marched out of the room with it. Then she addressed the gathering. 'Thank you, everyone. Now we've done with the business, let's start on the fun. One or two of you have been here before, but we also have quite a few new faces. So let's introduce ourselves, so everyone knows who everyone is. Yeah?'

Unluckily, Laverne was picked to start the ball rolling. With a dry mouth and a miserable face, he introduced himself as Vernon Arnold, a resident of York and an employee of the Liverpool Victoria insurance company, who was interested in life healing and 'wanted to find out more about it'.

Yolande seemed a little put out by the brevity of this declaration. 'OK, Vernon. But who invited you?'

For a moment, Laverne was nonplussed. Then he said, 'Sheelagh. Sheelagh Daye invited me.'

'Hey,' said Yolande. 'Sheelagh invited Mandy and Sue, too.' A couple of cheerful young women with rather extreme hairstyles nodded and beamed at Laverne enthusiastically. 'Of course, we're all very sad about Sheelagh's accident. But no one who knows anything about that lady can doubt she'll pull through, 'cause Sheelagh is a born fighter. So thanks, Vernon. This is Vernon, everybody . . .'

The other guests introduced themselves. There was a red-bearded man called Mike, who described himself as a 'workshop co-ordinator'. The strident German whom Laverne had already spoken to was called Lilo. She had been told about life healing by a friend, and wanted to try it for herself. The unlikeliest guests were a quiet, pleasant-faced couple called Ian and Estelle Marsland who seemed far too normal to be involved in something like this. Laverne couldn't work out what they were doing there. Then there were Charles and Angus, two amiable gay men in their forties who laughed a lot. 'We came along to the August weekend, and frankly we haven't stopped laughing since,' explained Angus.

They all repaired to a huge conservatory on the south side of the house. It was warm, bright and dry and the floor was

113

covered with rubber matting. Yolande directed everyone to take off their shoes and sit in a circle.

'Some of you will have already heard what I'm about to say a thousand times over, but as life healing relies on the power of repetition, I make no apologies for that. These low spirits are stubborn sons-of-bitches. Right? They need telling, and then some.'

Laverne looked round at his fellow guests, who were all nodding and smiling. To him, however, the American woman seemed to be talking complete gibberish.

'In this morning's session, we're going to make friends with the low self. Just to recap, we each of us have three spirits. A low spirit, a middle spirit, and a high spirit. They're all joined together to form a single spirit, but at the same time they're separate. The middle spirit is the person talking to you now, the guy in the pilot seat.

'The high self is the better part of us. It's the high self that is closest to God, and can work miracles. This is a being that can change our lives, it can change the future. Wow, think what our lives will be like when we're all like Hugo, and in constant daily contact with our high selves.'

This declaration was rewarded with a round of applause. Reluctantly, Laverne joined in.

'But there's a snag. Yeah. What's the snag? Anyone? Angus?'

Angus, a small man with a broken nose, cropped reddish hair and twinkling eyes, said, 'Only the low self can communicate with the high self.'

'Exactly right,' affirmed Yolande. 'If the middle self – the person we know as "I" – wants something, it can't ask the high self directly. Only the low self can communicate directly with the high self. The low self has to tell the high self what the middle self wants. What "I" want, basically. And that low self is one stubborn mother. It's lazy and, frankly, none too smart.

'It clings to complexes that are hard to shake off. If you

catch a bad cold and tell the low self to ask the high self to cure you of that cold, the low self will just think, "Hey. What's the point? Why should I bother? Everyone knows there is no cure for the common cold." So he'll refuse to pass the message on. The low self needs constant commands before it'll take new information on board. But there *is* a short-cut. We can *make friends* with the low self, make it work for us, get it on our side so it'll do anything to please us. So lie down, everyone. Make yourselves comfortable.'

Yolande got to her feet and stood in the centre of the ring of reclining adults.

'OK. So close your eyes, and in your mind call to your low selves. That applies to everyone. Come on. You're calling to a very precious part of you, so do it with love. Remember that the low self is very emotional. It responds to affection. Make it feel wanted.'

Laverne, with his eyes closed, reflected that this was how it must feel to be a long-stay patient in a mental hospital.

'Hey, Vernon,' barked Yolande suddenly. 'Why so gloomy? Smile! The low self is your friend!'

While the group broke for lunch, Laverne, rather the worse for wear, strolled out into the pine forest. He was chewing a turkey sandwich which he'd brought from home. The day was cloudless, but perpetual twilight reigned under the trees, the branches intertwining to form a perfumed canopy in which birds and squirrels nested. The forest floor was soft beneath his feet, a carpet of earth and rotting pine needles.

Laverne now believed that he had made a serious error of judgement. If only he had listened to Savage. He did not belong here. He knew nothing of the hidden potential of the human psyche, and cared less. How, then, was he to judge whether he was among sincere pilgrims or dangerous charlatans? To Laverne, all psychotherapists seemed like charlatans. The new age had not only passed him by; he had deliberately crossed the road to avoid it.

115

And he was honest enough to recognize that his innate prejudice against people like Yolande Henerberry (even her name provoked him) hardly formed the basis for a fair, objective investigation. In fact, regardless of her bizarre beliefs, she struck him as being wholly sincere.

So it was settled, then. He would return to his room, collect his belongings, and quietly slip out to the car, leaving his fellow guests to greet the New Year with Hugo and Yolande. Dear God! What a prospect.

As he doubled back on himself, he saw the girl walking towards him through the trees. She looked pale and fetchingly forsaken, like a model from one of those Pre-Raphaelite paintings that he both revered and despised. She had torn off a strip of bark and was absent-mindedly grinding it between her fingers. Laverne came to a standstill, mesmerized and alarmed, knowing this woman could not possibly be here.

He was gazing at the beggar girl with plaited and beaded hair that he had met in Stonegate on Christmas Eve. He knew her instantly, whereas she, slowly walking past him, took a few moments to place her mysterious benefactor.

'Hey,' she suddenly said. 'I *know* you.'

She loped over to him, grinning expansively. She was touchingly beautiful and once again her mere proximity was enough to make Laverne feel coarse, old and unattractive. She pointed a finger at his face.

'York,' she said. 'Yeah, yeah; I'm right, aren't I?'

'You're right,' he conceded shyly. 'Christmas Eve, wasn't it?'

'Yeah. Hey! I don't believe it . . . This is just amazing!' Exuberantly, she whacked him in the chest. 'You're the one who gave me twenty quid!'

Poker-faced, he held out his hand. 'No, I only lent it to you. Come on. Hand it over . . .'

For a moment, she looked horrified. Then she realized he was joking. 'You . . .' She laughed. 'You made my Christmas,

116

you did. Me and a mate got pissed out of our skulls, thanks to you.'

'Oh. Sorry.'

'No, it was great! You completely freaked me. Twenty pounds. I'd only been there for about five minutes. I mean, talk about luck!'

She was tall, possibly about five feet ten. Laverne saw that his original impression of her appearance had been erroneous. Her facial resemblance to Anjali Dutt was minimal. She was dark like the murdered girl and shared a similar height and build. But all that the two women really had in common was the aura surrounding them; a feeling of haunting vulnerability that aroused Laverne's protective instincts.

Nodding downwards, he said, 'I see you remembered to get dressed this time.'

She followed his gaze, not understanding. Then a short laugh as what he meant sank in. 'Oh, you mean the boots. Yeah. I don't usually walk about with no shoes on. I've just noticed that when you're begging, people are more generous if you're barefoot.'

Disapproval must have flickered across his face, for she added, 'But, come on, what else can I do? You can't get the dole if you haven't got an address. They'd let people like me starve. I mean it. Literally starve . . .'

Hating himself, he said, 'You could always try working.'

Defensively, she replied, 'I can't handle that kind of press-ure. It does my head in. That's why I had to pack in medical school. The workload gave me a nervous breakdown.'

'You gave up medical school? That's a shame.'

'Why? Why is it?' she said, suspecting him of further moralizing.

He smiled innocently. 'I just think it'd be nice to have a doctor who looked like you.'

They exchanged introductions. She told him her name was Alison Reffel. Laverne repeated the same lie he'd been telling all day. 'But I promise not to sell you insurance, if you promise to call me Vernon.'

There was an awkward silence as they emerged from the forest. Laverne was convinced that the girl's presence here was no coincidence. There could now be no question of leaving. He had to stay and see this thing out.

They came upon a small, railed garden, to the left of the doleful mausoleum. Alison leaned over the gate. 'Have you seen this?' she marvelled. 'Dogs. Can you believe that? A cemetery just for dogs.'

Laverne peered over the high railings, then saw the tips of tiny gravestones emerging from the thick, rancid under-growth. He saw a few names: DOBBY and BOGGLE and elsewhere the words LOYAL UNTO DEATH.

'What a world,' she sighed. 'I'll bet those dogs got a better funeral than our grandparents. Mastiffs, they were called. Bloody massive great things.'

She led him up the steps of the mausoleum; a crumbling mini-Parthenon, green with moss, tangled ivy and decades of neglect. 'This is where they buried the human members of the family.'

'I think I'd rather be with the dogs,' said Laverne.

A Latin inscription carved into the heavy lintel above the oaken doors read: FACILIS DESCENSUS AVERNO.

'See that?' said Alison. 'Know what that means?'

'Mind your head?' guessed Laverne.

'Nope. It means "Easy Is the Path That Leads Down To Hell".'

'Funny sort of message to hang over your dear departed.'

'Isn't it just?'

She pressed the toe of her boot against one of the double doors. It creaked open. Inside, the building was damp and neglected. There was an aroma of ancient urine. The floor was strewn with dead leaves.

'Jesus!' exclaimed Alison. 'Talk about bad vibes . . .'

Laverne said, 'Hot and cold running water in every coffin.'

118

It was a poor joke, but Alison laughed anyway. They walked out into the cold, crisp afternoon.

'So how did you meet, then? You and Prince?'

'He found me on the streets.' She nudged him in the ribs. 'Just like you did, big boy.'

'A friend of yours, is he?'

'A friend and a lover. He lets me stay here from time to time.'

'Generous of him,' said Laverne.

Catching the sneer in his voice, she said, 'No. It *is* generous. Hugo's special.'

'Just not special enough to let you live here permanently, eh?'

This touched a nerve. 'No. I could probably stay here more often, if I wanted to. But it's a question of freedom, er . . .' She struggled to remember his name.

'Vernon.'

'Yeah, sorry. It's a question of freedom, Vernon. If you depend on other people, you can never be truly free . . .'

His brow creased in consternation. 'But isn't begging depending on other people?' She didn't reply. 'Besides, we all depend on each other for something. Don't we?'

'Yeah, well. You're a different generation. The whole concept of personal freedom is probably a bit hard for you to understand.'

Laverne felt like arguing, but manfully decided to let the matter drop. Walking in a clockwise direction, they rounded the woods until they were gazing across the lake at the western façade of the house. Alison threw a pebble into the reedy, stagnant water. Laverne, ever the policeman, thought it just the sort of pool to sink a corpse in.

'Kind of drear, wouldn't you say?' suggested Alison.

'Come again?'

'Drear. Isn't that the sort of word a nineteenth-century writer would have used to describe a view like this? Someone like Poe. "Dark and drear." Don't you think?'

119

'I wouldn't know, Alison,' said Laverne. 'I'm not very well read.'

'No,' she mocked. 'I'll bet you read the *Reader's Digest*.'

'Rubbish,' said Laverne. 'I read a very good car magazine called *Popular Classics*.' He glanced at his watch. 'Nearly time for the afternoon session. Better be getting back.'

Amazement crossed Alison's face. 'What? You mean to say you're one of the paying guests?'

'I am indeed,' he confessed. 'I want to know what this life healing game is all about.'

'Whatever for? You're completely the wrong sort of person.'

'So you've told me,' he ruefully reminded her. '"People of my generation don't understand anything." Wasn't that what you said?'

Unexpectedly, she leaned forward and kissed him warmly on the cheek. Laverne was visibly embarrassed. 'Hello. What was that for?'

'I don't know,' she said. 'I just felt like it.'

She linked his arm, and together they walked back to the house.

# EIGHT

Alison and Laverne parted company at the south gate. She promised to catch him later. He hurried to the conservatory, where Yolande and the group were respectfully gathered around a thin, pallid man with a shock of carefully back-combed fair hair. He watched Laverne's entrance with eyes that were both alert and amused.

'Ah, Vernon,' said Yolande, rushing forward. 'You're a little late. Hugo's here . . .'

She led Laverne into the centre of the group and introduced him to the blond man. 'Hugo: this is Vernon Arnold. Sheelagh invited him. Vernon, say hello to Hugo.'

Accepting the outstretched hand, Laverne said, 'Hello to Hugo.' Prince's palm was strong, dry and cold, and it maintained its grip for what, to Laverne, seemed an almost indecent length of time.

At around six feet, Prince was marginally shorter than the Superintendent, but he had a way of tilting his head to one side that made it seem as if he was looking down on Laverne from a great height. The pupils of his large, upward slanting eyes were a shockingly pale shade of blue-grey, and seemed to stare slightly past Laverne's left ear, into the infinite distance. Prince's face creased into a charming smile. 'You're the insurance salesman?'

'That's me all right,' said Laverne unimaginatively.

Prince was possibly in his early forties, slim, lean-jawed and elegant. He wore a dark, immaculate three-piece suit. A golden watch-chain dangled from his waistcoat. He would have been ideally cast as a well-mannered gunfighter in a Western.

Abruptly, Prince released Laverne's hand, effectively dismissing him. Yolande clapped her hands to gain the group's attention. 'OK, everyone. This afternoon, we're in for a treat. Hugo is going to talk to us about mana. But first, there's something not too great I have to discuss with you. This morning, we passed around the hat and you all handed in your gifts. Well, we've counted up and we've got a problem, in that the collection is way below the estimated figure. I don't know what happened, here. Either all of you donated slightly less than the recommended amount, or maybe just one person misunderstood and gave too little. All I know is that the figure we had in mind was meant to be at least five hundred per head, minimum. Someone must have donated way below that.'

The group members assumed innocent expressions and scanned each other's faces, searching for incriminating twitches. Laverne felt a warm glow of secret pride.

Prince continued. He had a light, almost boyish voice. The accent was the familiar languid sneer of a rich, educated American. 'It isn't that I need the money . . .' He laughed, and the women in the group laughed with him. 'I'm OK for money.' More laughter. 'All that troubles me is that someone here is short-changing themselves. If one of you has given too little, then you're bound to suffer a self-induced punishment, and that's terribly sad. Your low self is bound to know you've been less than generous, and develop a guilt complex because of it. Now, as we're here to eradicate our complexes, and hopefully heal our lives, I think you'll all agree that whoever's responsible is behaving in a crazy way. Really.'

Everyone except Laverne nodded, or murmured in agreement. Yolande and Prince walked amongst the group, studying each member. When they came to Laverne, he couldn't help noticing that their eyes lingered on him.

Finally, Prince waved his arms in the air, as if banishing the unpleasantness from his presence. He turned his back on the company and said, 'All right. I now know who the guilty party is.' This statement prompted a collective gasp. 'I also know that the reason the person concerned didn't pay was because they felt that their weekend here wasn't worth the money. Incredible, but true. But let's forget about it for now. We haven't got to live with that person. No, sir. They've got to live with themselves. The rest of us are going to have fun. Coats on, everyone. Coats on. We're going outside. I'm going to show you the power of mana.'

With Prince and Yolande leading the way, the party crossed the west lawn and circled the lake. Laverne saw blue smoke rising from the trees as they approached the woods. The sweet sound of distant bells in full peal drifted down on the still air.

They stopped at a small thatched lodge, hidden in a copse of decaying oaks. The cottage was adjoined by a series of outhouses and potting sheds. A sprightly old man (whom Prince introduced as Mr Meakin) was throwing logs on to a blazing bonfire.

'A nice blaze you've got going there, Robert,' observed Prince. The elderly gentleman looked suitably gratified, and nodded, continuing to fuel the fire. 'Bob? If you could just leave us for a moment?' Prince asked.

Still nodding and smiling, the ancient retainer vanished into one of the outhouses.

Prince removed his overcoat and jacket, then passed them to Yolande. Laverne wondered what was about to happen. 'Mana is an Hawaiian word, meaning "vital force". Mana can protect as well as nourish us. What you are about to see is not god-like, or superhuman, but a demonstration of a very *human* ability.'

Prince approached the flames, and sank to his knees. Laverne had to restrain himself from rushing forth and hauling the American clear. Without averting his face from the heat, Prince aggressively thrust his forearm into the centre of the fire.

This feat was accompanied by a massive intake of breath from the onlookers. Angus fainted, and Yolande had to attend to him. Prince showed no signs of suffering, although black smoke seemed to be rising from his incandescent arm. One of the men exclaimed, 'Jesus Christ!'

'Yes,' said Prince, without looking round. 'The comparison is justified. I am protected by exactly the same energy that Jesus of Nazareth used to work his miracles. Throughout the ages, mana has been called many things. Christians know it as the holy spirit. The very breath of God.'

Prince withdrew his arm and showed it to the group. It was unblemished, as was the sleeve encompassing it. He invited Laverne to feel the skin of his hand. It was perfectly cool to the touch. Prince's face had been inches away from the flames, but it had also escaped harm. His eyebrows and hair had not even been singed.

Laverne grinned. 'That's some trick, Hugo.'

Yolande admonished him. 'No, Vernon. It's not a trick. That's a terrible thing to say . . .'

Prince shook his head at her, not wanting or needing her support. 'Vernon: if I told you that you also could place your arm in that fire, and not be harmed, what would you say?'

For a few seconds, there was no sound but the crackle of burning logs.

Laverne said, 'I'd say "Sorry, but I'm not insured against fire damage."'

'Oh, but you are.' Prince reached forth and grabbed Laverne's wrist. For a man of slight build, he was disconcertingly strong. 'Let me show you.'

Laverne experienced a stab of fear. But his instincts told him that this was not a moment for weakness.

'Do you trust me?' demanded Prince.

Absurdly, Laverne said, 'Yes . . . but don't I need to take my coat off?'

Prince shook his head. 'Don't worry. I won't let you burn.'

He allowed Prince to guide him towards the bonfire. When they were about a foot away, Laverne realized that he could no longer feel the heat. As they crouched down, Prince released his grip on Laverne's wrist and instead placed his own right hand in Laverne's left. Then he looked Laverne in the eyes.

'How much faith do you have, my friend?'

Laverne had none. But before he could reply, Prince leaned forward and plunged their joined arms into the very heart of the fire. Laverne clenched his teeth, expecting absolute agony. But he felt no pain, no sensation at all, beyond a faint, delicious tingling. Laverne exhaled in sharp relief, and then, watching the flames embracing their extended limbs, erupted into nervous laughter.

He felt Prince's hand squeeze his. In congratulation? Or in warning? Laverne could not say. Trembling, he withdrew his arm and saw that Prince had played a trick on him. Although his flesh had not burned, his clothing had been reduced to black ash. The arm of his overcoat, his sweater and the underlying shirt sleeve had been forged together to form one smoking rag. Laverne raised his hand and inspected the damage in amazement. The charred remnants fell away, leaving his entire right arm, as far as the shoulder, exposed to the chill afternoon air. Prince threw back his head and laughed, and the rest of the group joined in. Laverne, who had lost a good shirt, sweater and overcoat, failed to see the joke.

Grinning jubilantly, Prince leaned forward and whispered in Laverne's ear.

'That's for being a cheapskate.'

Vernon Laverne was sobered and depressed by his experience in the woods. He had expected Hugo Prince to be a common swindler. This had not proved to be the case. If Prince was a mountebank, he was a formidable one; an illusionist of the highest order. His trick with the bonfire had made Laverne look a fool. No. Worse than that. An amateur.

At six p.m. the group met for dinner in the banquet hall, a dark, polished and panelled rectangle overlooked by an authentic Elizabethan gallery. Prince, Yolande and Alison were not present. The diners were waited on by Prince's domestic staff, most of whom seemed to be of Polynesian or Asian extraction. Portraits of Prince's ancestors lined the walls. Their fat, soft faces sneered down at the guests with the universal complacency of the pampered gentry. None of them appeared to bear the faintest family resemblance to the present Lord of North Abbey, which for Prince was very good news indeed.

The mood at the table was noisy and sportive. Laverne was forced to fend off numerous bad jokes about 'being 'armless' and 'having surprises up his sleeve'. The only guest to show real sympathy for Laverne was Ian Marsland, who seemed bemused that Prince, a man he plainly admired, had behaved in such a way.

The main course was a game pie comprising various inhabitants of Prince's estate. It was spicy and delicious, but Laverne's appetite had been blunted by the events of the day.

And when Lilo started amorously rubbing her foot up against his leg under the table, he judiciously decided to skip dessert. Complaining of fatigue, he retired to his room and lay on the bed, grumpily flicking through the pages of *Popular Classics*.

After twenty minutes or so, a knock sounded on the door. Laverne feared that it might be the thick-skinned Lilo. In a calculatedly infirm voice, he asked who was there.

'It's Alison. Are you all right?'

He opened the door, and she walked in, trailing a cloud of patchouli oil. 'Yes, of course I'm all right,' he said. 'What is it?'

She touched his brow. 'Are you sure? You sounded funny.'

'I was feigning serious illness, if you must know.'

Boldly, she walked to the bed, turned over his magazine and smirked at the cover 'You weren't joking, then? About your choice of bedtime reading . . .'

She was wearing a baggy, rather unflattering grey sweater with tattered old jeans. Yet she still looked adorable, and Laverne felt, in his staid, old-fashioned way, that she shouldn't really be in his room, particularly as it was after ten p.m.

'Well, young lady, what can I do for you?'

She giggled. 'God, you're a bit on the formal side, aren't you? What a grouch. Can't I come in and say hello if I want to?'

He looked crushed by this remark. 'Oh, yes. Sorry. 'Course you can.'

'Anyway, I told Hugo about you. About you giving me that money at Christmas . . . He was rather impressed. He wants to know if you'll come along to his private drawing room and have a drink with him.'

'What? Me on my own?'

'No. Me as well. And Yolande'll be there.'

'Is Yolande his wife, then?'

'No.' An ironical half-smile. 'But she'd probably like to be.'

He considered her proposal. 'Well, I don't know, really. Your friend Hugo annoyed the hell out of me today. I don't know whether you're aware of it, but he ruined my best coat, pulling one of his silly stunts.'

Beaming playfully, she walked over to his wardrobe and opened it, then whisked out Laverne's Abercrombie overcoat, which was neatly draped around a hanger. 'Do you mean this coat?'

His mouth dropped open. The missing right sleeve had been completely restored. The garment looked as good as new. Laverne tugged at it sceptically, suspecting some further prank. Leaving the coat in his arms, Alison reached into the

127

wardrobe again, producing his ruined shirt and sweater. They, too, were in perfect condition.

Laverne swore mildly and shook his head. 'Well, that's unbelievable. It really is.'

'Yeah . . . He thought you'd be pleased. He sent me up with them while you were at dinner. He wanted to surprise you.'

'Then he's succeeded. Again. But . . . how? Are they different clothes, or what?'

She shrugged and grinned. 'Dunno, mister. It must be magic. Come on, Hugo's waiting . . .'

Prince lived in the north wing, among dusty, cobwebbed closets and locked rooms that never saw the sun. Laverne thought that this probably accounted for the man's pallor. Alison led him down rickety timbered passageways, past little dark flights of stairs that seemed to lead nowhere. Long narrow mullioned windows looked out towards the park and the drab, windy moor.

Emerging into a wide, long gallery that traversed the breadth of the house, Alison knocked once on a solid oak door. Then they entered.

Prince was standing by the hearth, warming himself by a generous fire. Yolande was sitting crosslegged in a leather armchair. A vast and rather gorgeous tapestry, depicting a simple motif of fish, waves, and clouds, dominated the wall behind her head. Dispassionately, she watched them walk across the room before returning her attention to the book on her lap.

'Hello, hello,' enthused Prince, patting Laverne's arm. 'I was hoping you'd be wearing that new suit of clothes I made for you.'

'How did you do that?' said Laverne.

Prince smiled indulgently. 'Ask me another time. When you know me a little better . . .'

Laverne noticed the intensity of Prince's stare, which he suspected had been deliberately cultivated. He thought it was the sign of a professional confidence trickster; the look in the eye that distracts attention from the hand in the pocket.

Light-heartedly, Prince said, 'Thanks again for the donation, by the way. I'll be able to retire on the fifteen pounds you gave me.'

Laverne smiled grimly. 'How did you know it was me?'

'Because you're the only person here who thinks I'm a fraud.'

Laverne struggled to justify himself. Prince hushed him. 'Please. I couldn't care less. Forget about it. Your donation was a calculated insult. We both know that. But Alison tells me that you gave her money at Christmas, when she was in dire need. That's enough to convince me that you're worth having in my house. Now. I have an excellent fifty-year-old brandy. Will you take some with me?'

Laverne accepted his offer, then perched himself on a rather lumpy horsehair sofa. Alison dragged a large cushion into the centre of the room and sank heavily on to it. Then she reached up her jumper, fumbled in her shirt pocket, and removed a small tin of tobacco, a packet of cigarette papers, a cheap lighter and a small lump wrapped in silver foil. Laverne had an unpleasant feeling that she was about to break the law.

Prince, meanwhile, had walked over to a well-stocked drinks cabinet in a corner of the room. With his back to Laverne, he tipped alcohol into two glasses, taking great care to make both measures equal. Returning, he passed one of these glasses to Laverne, who was gazing in disbelief at a large oil painting above the fireplace. It was a hideously incompetent depiction of a rabbit-laden poacher being torn down by two enormous, slavering mastiffs.

Prince followed Laverne's eyes. 'A family heirloom. What do you think?'

'Tasteless in the extreme,' confessed Laverne.

'Fair comment. But, you know, this painting illustrates a major law of nature. It reminds us that the weak will always bring disaster upon themselves if they trespass into the domain of the strong. That's a lesson worth remembering, my friend.'

Laverne offered no response.

Without looking up from her cigarette papers, Alison said, 'Sieg heil.' Affectionately, Prince mimed a kick at her rump with the toe of his boot.

Raising his glass to Laverne, he said, 'Anyway, here's to you, Mr Arnold. May you find what you're looking for.'

They drank to this.

'Come on,' said Prince. 'You haven't seen the chapel.'

'Have you got your own chapel?'

'I do.'

Laverne was baffled by this Americanism. 'I didn't ask to marry you. I asked if you'd got a chapel.'

Prince laughed. 'This guy's funny. I like him.'

They went next door, to a beautiful stone-walled chamber with a huge, oval stained-glass window. There was a row of candles burning before the altar. On a plinth behind them stood a bronze carving of a knight, a sword in his left hand, a cross of gold in his right. The knight's unvizored face was calm and benevolent, but his eyes were blindfolded.

'See this fellow? He represents my ancestor, Thomas North, who fought in the Holy Land eight centuries ago. I never knew him, yet I often miss him and wish he was with me. Does that sound foolish to you?'

'No. Not really. What's the blindfold in aid of?'

'It's a symbol of a soul in exile. Sir Thomas was feared while he lived, and feared after his death. It's quite a story. The good people of York thought he was in league with the devil. When he died, they put chains on his corpse and buried him with his head between his legs, in a field outside the city. That was the kind of impression he made on people.

'Later, one of his descendants paid a substantial amount in bribes to have his bones moved to the crypt at York Minster. That's where he is to this day. He's been there so long that

130

his grave isn't even marked. He's just buried beneath some goddamned paving stone. It irritates me that those who have been dead for a long time are regarded as less and less important as time goes on, until in the end even their memory is buried.'

Laverne sipped his brandy, feeling it catch fire in his belly. 'That's the way the world is, I'm afraid.'

'I'm currently fighting a legal battle to have his bones disinterred and brought here, where they belong. I want to bring him home, Vernon. I believe the dead should be with their families.'

There was a scuffling sound behind them. Alison skipped down the aisle of the chapel. She was carrying a lighted joint and humming to herself. The heady smell of hash filled the air.

Prince wrinkled up his nose. 'Alison; haven't I asked you not to smoke that stuff in here?'

She took a deep blast on the joint and offered it to Laverne. He politely declined. 'Has he shown you this?' she said, waving at the oval window. 'This blows me away.'

'She's actually rather intelligent,' said Prince, 'but you wouldn't know it to listen to her.'

She snatched a candelabra and held it up to the glass. 'It's too dark to make out the colours in this light, but have you seen what's going on? Come and look . . .'

Laverne looked. Each of the panels depicted a separate demon, and each demon boasted its own unique and grotesque physical characteristics. In all, there were thirty-one assorted fiends. Together they danced around the window's heart, where the damned writhed eternally in a sea of flame.

'Are they your ancestors, too?' asked Laverne.

'That window came from the original abbey on this site,' said Prince. His tone was noncommittal. 'Fifteenth-century. Priceless.'

'And it faces the north,' added Alison ingenuously, the dope making her garrulous. 'The evil quarter. Creepy, or what? In

131

the old days, people believed that when evil spirits came into your house, they always approached from the north. Did you know that?'

The Superintendent looked at Prince. Prince was watching him closely.

'No,' said Laverne. 'I didn't know that.'

# NINE

At four in the morning, two men met in a service lift at York Infirmary. They were each wheeling heavy trolleys.

'Post-mortems?' joked Jack, pressing the button for the basement.

'That'll do nicely,' replied the other.

Then they laughed. This was one of many standing jokes between them; pleasantries that eased them through the boredom of their shift. Both men were porters; Jack a year away from retirement, Marcus in his twenties, already seeking more lucrative employment. He kept his job-hunting no secret from the older man, who had once gone to the trouble of training him. In fact, Jack actively encouraged Marcus to better himself. 'This is a mug's game,' he was fond of saying. 'You wanna get out, mate, while you're still young.'

Almost as an afterthought, Marcus reached into the inner pocket of his spacious overall, took out a video cassette and slipped it to his companion. 'Here you go, pop.'

The older man accepted the tape with enthusiasm. Its box bore a glossy, lurid cover and the legend *Black Bum Bandits*. 'I hope this is better than the last one you borrowed me,' said Jack.

'*Lent* you,' corrected Marcus. 'Not "borrowed". "Lent." Where's your diction?'

'In me hand, when I watch films like this . . .'

The two men roared with ribald laughter. Jack pocketed the tape and the lift juddered to a halt. One by one, they stepped out into the corridor, wheeling the lifeless bodies of Derek Tyreman and Sheelagh Daye before them.

*

Laverne slowly opened his eyes, confused by the unfamiliarity of his bed and the musty, alien smell of the room. Then he remembered where he was, and immediately felt depressed.

He had been dreaming about soldiers defending a lonely coastline, firing at an enemy over the waves, and the sound of their guns had followed him into the waking world. He could still hear the ominous muffled booming of exploding shells. And there was a light in the room, a subtle milky glow seeping in through a chink in the curtains. His overcoat hung on the wardrobe door, and its folds were touched with silver.

He left his bed and peered through the curtains. His first impression was that there was a ball of white fire nestling in the upper branches of the elm tree outside the window. Then he realized that it was the moon, so full and bright that the tree and the lawn and the sombre woods had turned blue with its brilliance.

Then he heard the booming sound again, monotonous and grating. Annoyed, he unlocked the french window and walked out on to the balcony. Through the elm's whispering branches, he could see the pale mass of the family mausoleum. This was where the noise seemed to be coming from.

There was a moment of peace. Then another series of resounding crashes, gradually growing fainter until they ceased altogether. As Laverne looked more closely, he imagined he could discern a procession of pale lights moving around the base of the building. At last they, too, faded away.

He switched on the bedside lamp and picked up his wristwatch, swearing when he saw the time; seventeen minutes past four. He rummaged in his overnight bag until he found a pencil torch and a small crooked length of wire. Then he slipped on some socks and shoes and bundled his coat over his pyjamas. He slipped the wire into a pocket and, guided by the modest beam of the torch, stepped out into the pitch-black corridor.

There was a service staircase at the end of the passage. This led him down to the kitchens and the servants' common rooms on the ground floor. His torch illuminated huge, intimidating basins and pans arranged on sturdy tables. There was a faintly disgusting odour in the air that reminded him of school dinners.

The kitchens were obviously infested with rats. A nervous scuttling sounded behind him as he knelt to insert his wire rod in the lock of the glazed tradesmen's entrance. (Housebreaking was a skill he'd picked up at police training college.)

The lock surrendered without a struggle, and the door opened on to a small kitchen yard, discreetly hidden from polite eyes by a high privet hedge. Then he rounded the building and after glancing cautiously about him, strode past the sleeping flower beds.

His way was lit by the chasing moon, and a light but icy breeze chilled his pyjama-clad legs as he crossed the park. There was a pitiful child-like squeal from the pines. The noise made Laverne shudder and he guessed that some small creature had fallen foul of a predator.

The grubby off-white marble of the mausoleum shone like bone in the moonlight. As he drew near to its doors, he stopped and listened. He could only hear the wind, whistling softly in his ears. Aiming the thin beam of his torch straight ahead, he mounted the steps of the building and, as Alison had done earlier that day, coaxed the doors open with one foot.

It is unlikely that Laverne would ever have admitted to such a prosaic thought, but when he slid the torchlight over the contents of that tomb, he seriously wondered whether he was dreaming. Three of the deep stone coffins had been uprooted from the floor, and laid on end. Their lids were still secure and they were arranged neatly, in a row. Laverne judged that it would have taken a hefty crane to lift one of the sarcophagi, let alone three.

Around the walls of the chamber were three grave-shaped depressions where the coffins had lain. Laverne directed his torch at each of these hollows, and saw damp, freshly uncovered earth. He mused on the awesome force that had made this act of displacement possible, and then remembered a boy impaled on railings, and a young woman hurled like a rocket at the walls of her room. And his disquiet turned to fear.

He had no idea what had recently occurred under that roof, and at that precise moment had no wish to know. With as much haste as his dignity would permit, he vacated the charnel house.

The moon was at his back, casting his shadow before him as he hurried towards the house. But when the moon slipped behind a bank of cloud, and its radiance was momentarily dowsed, Laverne glanced around and thought he could see another shadow skimming over the ground at his heels. He was not a particularly imaginative man, but could not shake the conviction that something had followed him out of the mausoleum and was now rushing to catch up with him. He increased his speed, but the disagreeable sensation would not go away. By now, he was sufficiently disturbed to break into a run. When he reached the kitchens, he was sweating and shaking, and had to summon all his self-control to re-lock the door. While tampering with the lock, he fully expected to hear footsteps on the gravel outside and see a blurred face pressed against the glass in the door frame. But nothing happened. He was safe. No longer caring whether he was heard or not, he rushed back to the safety of his room.

In the morning, Yolande presided over another workshop and Laverne, once again, made no effort whatsoever to commune with his 'high self'. When the session was over, he went in search of Alison. She was in the music room, playing a one-fingered boogie on a seventeenth-century harpsichord and polluting the atmosphere with yet another illegal cigarette.

As she was the only person at North Abbey that he felt comfortable with, he invited her out to lunch. She accepted,

136

on condition that he paid. They drove into Ilkley, to enjoy a pint and a toasted cheese sandwich in a homely pub.

After they'd eaten, he watched her take a long draught of ale, then wipe the foam off her mouth with her sleeve. 'You know, that's something I've never got used to – the sight of a woman drinking out of a pint pot.'

She poured scorn on him. He took it like a man.

They trekked up on to the moors, and Alison talked about her childhood in Devon, and how she loved her parents.

'You're not really homeless, then, are you? If you get on with your parents, you could live with them.'

'I said I loved them. I didn't say I got on with them.'

The ground was hard and frosty underfoot. Laverne could feel the icy cold rising through the soles of his shoes. Wisps of mist were starting to drift down from the heights. Attempting to appear casual, he said, 'By the way what's a "Death Prayer"?'

She stopped and looked at him quizzically. 'It's an ancient Hawaiian curse. Why?'

He tried to conceal his excitement. 'You've heard of it, then?'

Warily, she said, 'Sure. What makes you ask?'

'Oh, I've just met someone who's dying from it.'

She stared at him strangely, but said nothing.

He glanced up and saw three distant figures silently coming towards them through the mist. Laverne guessed that they were hikers, who had chosen to leave the moor before the weather got any worse. Following their sensible example, he and Alison turned and walked back to the car.

By dusk, the mist had turned to freezing fog. The park of North Abbey was completely engulfed, so that the house seemed to be riding on a slow, billowing cloud.

That evening, Hugo Prince held a New Year celebration for his guests, friends and business associates. A large marquee had been attached to the conservatory, and a string quartet serenaded the glittering visitors with selections from Bach, Haydn and Vivaldi.

Laverne washed and changed, and at seven-thirty went down to join the party. He estimated that there were about three hundred people there: rich, self-conscious mystics from all over the world. He had never seen so many beards, pony-tails and amulets in one place before. There was an abundance of food on offer, but nothing that Laverne could readily identify. He ate as little as possible and drank no alcohol. All his instincts told him that tonight he would have to stay sober and alert.

Yolande, looking vampish in a low-cut black velvet gown, found him hovering by the sweets trolley. 'Vernon, what happened to you this afternoon?'

'Ah, sorry about that. I got lost in the fog.'

'You missed one hell of a workshop.'

'Oh, damn! I didn't, did I?'

She gave him a lethal smile. 'You're fighting us, aren't you?'

'Pardon me?'

'You heard, buster. You're fighting us. Don't deny it. But we'll heal your life, with or without your help. Just you wait and see. Now ... someone was asking for you earlier. Who was it? Oh, yeah, Lilo.' She waved to a group standing by the door. 'Li-lo!'

While her back was turned, Laverne nimbly slipped away. Then he elbowed and excused his way through the jabbering throng, looking for Alison. He found her in the marquee, sat at the feet of the musicians.

She surveyed his serviceable, inexpensive sports jacket and toasted him with a tumbler full of wine.

'Hey. Here's to us ... The worst-dressed couple here.'

She was already slightly drunk. Laverne thought he could hear bitterness in her voice. She was still dressed in the baggy jumper and jeans she'd been wearing the day before. In a comically pompous voice, he said, 'What we lack in sartorial elegance, we make up for with good looks and intelligence.'

This made her smile.

The music stopped, and the musicians trooped into the conservatory. Laverne and Alison followed them. Something was about to happen. Hugo Prince was standing in the centre of the floor, holding a slim microphone, and his many admirers had formed a circle around him. Prince wore a black frock-coat that was presumably meant to appear Byronic, but in Laverne's opinion merely made him look like a camp ringmaster at a circus. But Laverne's opinion had no relevance here. For most of the onlookers, Prince possessed a fascination that was daring, startling and intensely sexual.

Then he spoke. 'Good evening, ladies and gentlemen. I presume you know who I am.' The guests cheered with a fervour that Laverne found disturbing. Prince paused to bow, and nod at various familiar faces. 'There aren't so many of us this year, mainly because of the appalling weather. But that shouldn't stop the rest of us from having a good time.'

A chorus of feeble cheers.

'Every year, I throw down the old "mana challenge", offering a sizeable cash prize to anyone who can beat me at my own game. And every year, surprise, surprise, I get to keep my money.

'This year, I've raised the stakes, in the hope that one of you valiants out there will just stay on their feet for once. That's all I'm asking. Just stay vertical. Ten thousand English pounds to anyone who can stand up to me. How about it? Who thinks they can take me?'

Laverne turned to Alison. 'What's he doing?'

'Showing off.'

Prince outstretched an arm in welcome. 'First of all, a demonstration. Miko? Let's hear it for Miko, ladies and gentlemen . . .'

Miko appeared at his employer's side, unhappy and ridiculous in an ill-fitting tuxedo. When the applause had died down, the towering Polynesian faced Prince, evidently steeling himself for some kind of assault. He squared his shoulders

139

and thrust out his deep chest. Prince held up his right hand, with the little finger extended. 'Ladies and gentlemen, I present to you, one pinkie.'

Laughter. Then, Prince took a step towards Miko. The big man adopted a low fighting stance, his eyes on the hand that was slowly reaching for him. With infinite delicacy, Prince stretched out his arm until his little finger touched Miko's chest. This dainty action had a dramatic effect. Instantly, the Polynesian keeled over, as if he'd been punched by a prize-fighter. The people standing behind Miko caught him as he fell, then staggered themselves under his immense weight. With difficulty, they laid him on the floor. He was completely unconscious.

A collective sigh of awe. No one applauded. Smiling genially, Prince said, 'Anyone else care to try?'

Miko groaned as he came round. Apart from this, there was no sound. 'No one?' asked Prince. 'Not even our friend the policeman?' A few perplexed murmurs passed through the crowd. 'Oh, yes. Didn't I tell you? We have our very own house detective. He's pretending to be an insurance salesman, and he'd actually make a very good insurance salesman. But, in fact, he's Detective Superintendent Vernon Laverne of the CID. Yes, I'm talking about you, Vernon. Where are you?'

Laverne began to blush and perspire. Alison, her face blank with disbelief, took a step away from him.

'Ah! There he is! There's our friend the detective. Hi, Vernon. Vernon's investigating a murder, folks. And because we life healers are such sick cranks, he thought he'd better check up on us.'

Laverne began to inch towards the door. 'Hey, don't go. I want you to take up the challenge. What's the matter, Superintendent? Afraid of my little finger?'

Laverne halted, turned, slowly pushed his way through to the centre of the room. Mockingly, Prince pointed the microphone at him. 'Would you care to say a few words?'

Some of the guests laughed. Laverne glared at Prince. 'No?

OK. Well, maybe you can tell me where you got that jacket. That's a real humdinger.'

This time the laughter was more general. Laverne sensed a subtle shift in atmosphere, and realized that the smiling faces that surrounded him were starting to enjoy his humiliation. Laughing, Prince raised his little finger and floated it towards the red-faced policeman. Laverne looked into Prince's eyes and saw a fleeting gleam of cold hatred. At that moment he knew, beyond doubt, that Hugo Prince was a murderer.

For a few tantalizing seconds, Prince held his finger a mere centimetre away from Laverne's chest. Then he struck.

What followed astonished everyone, including Laverne. At the moment of contact, the American's feet literally left the ground and he flew backwards, bowling over several spectators as he fell. Yolande rushed to his aid, making various emotional outbursts. Prince threshed on the floor, at first spluttering for breath, then giggling manically at his own misfortune. Laverne turned to face the guests. In awed silence, they made way for him. With his head held high, he marched out of the conservatory.

He went up to his room and washed his hands and face. Then, calmly and methodically, he packed his bag and went downstairs. Yolande intercepted him in the entrance hall. Laverne expected a stream of abuse from her, but instead she addressed him with quiet humility.

'Hugo wants to talk to you. Is that all right?'

He nodded, his curiosity aroused. Together, and in silence, they travelled to the north wing. She accompanied him to the door of the chapel, smiled and walked away. Laverne entered. The stone walls were golden with the light of many candles. Prince was waiting for him by the altar, under the beautiful arched window in which the damned would always burn.

Prince seemed to have erased all memory of his recent embarrassment. He had recovered his familiar icy poise and touched Laverne's sleeve in greeting. There were two glasses of red wine on the altar. Wordlessly, he passed one of the

141

glasses to Laverne, who saw that the pupils of Prince's strange, upward-slanting eyes were hugely dilated. Had Laverne not known better, he might have suspected his host was in love with him.

'Such a sad world, don't you think, Superintendent? So sad, that one might be led to believe that it had been created by a devil. A devil that grieves for the very souls he destroys.'

Laverne placed his bag on the floor and stared into Prince's eyes, wondering why they failed to reflect the light. 'Spare me the claptrap, Prince. You can talk as much as you like. You're very fond of talking. All the best con-men are.'

'You've hardly been a model of honesty yourself, Laverne. An insurance salesman. I ask you . . .'

'At least I don't charge money for the lies I tell.'

'Oh, please. There's no need to go through the motions. No one can hear you now. Only me, and I can keep a secret. I'm a Kahuna. A high priest of Huna. And I know a Master when I meet one. So relax. Please. And tell me.' Prince leaned forward, and in a half-whisper said, 'Where did you learn the art?'

Laverne sniffed at his glass. 'What art?'

'Come now. No one has ever resisted my party trick before. You were so charged with mana that it felt as if I'd been hit by a truck. I suppose I deserved it. It was very funny of you.' Prince laughed unconvincingly. 'A witty thing to do.' His eyes sharpened. 'Who taught you magic?'

Laverne sighed. 'Nobody's taught me anything. I don't believe in magic, Huna or otherwise.'

After a long silence, Prince bared his teeth in a sardonic half-smile. 'Yes. Yes, I think I actually believe that. And yet, despite your obvious vulgarity and lack of breeding, you carry yourself like a true adept. I find much to admire in you, Laverne. That's why I'm letting you go.'

'Letting me go?' spluttered Laverne. 'I think you've got that a bit wrong, haven't you? It's me who's letting *you* go . . . for now. But before long, I'll be back with a warrant for your arrest, and the charge'll be murder. Let's see how smug you are then.'

'Murder?' The voice was silky, amused. 'Who am I supposed to have murdered?'

'Two people that I know of. Maybe more.'

'And tell me, I'm curious. What method did I use to despatch these unfortunates?'

'You brainwashed them.'

Prince shrieked with laughter. 'What an antiquated term.'

Laverne reddened. 'You brainwash weak and impressionable people into thinking they're cursed. First, you tell them you're going to kill them with something called the Death Prayer. Then their own sheer bloody terror and gullibility finish the job. I'm going to put you away for a long time, Prince. I think you're using hypnotic suggestion as a murder weapon, and what's more, I intend to prove it.'

Prince smirked. 'Hypnosis? I don't hypnotize people, Laverne. I *pray them dead*.'

'You admit you've killed people, then?'

'Oh, of course. And not just one or two, as you rather quaintly allege, but literally hundreds. To paraphrase that line from *Goodbye, Mr Chips*, I've killed hundreds of people, and all of them worthless.' Prince smirked, proud of his witticism. 'I am served by many spirits. With their assistance, I shall endeavour to rid the world of all racial and spiritual impurity. If you persist with your investigation into my affairs, I will first humiliate and isolate you. Next, I will strike a blow at your innermost heart. Finally, when your life is no longer worth living, I will take it away from you.'

'I think you need psychiatric help.'

'Why? I'm not mad, Laverne. Nor am I breaking the law. I pray people dead. Is there a law against that? What are you planning to charge me with? Uttering ritual curses without a licence?'

Laverne was irritated by this barrage of words.

'I don't care how I do it. I'm going to bring you down.'

143

There was a moment's calm, while Prince subjected Laverne to his peculiar, unwavering gaze. 'I like you. You have certain qualities.'

'One of them is the ability to recognize drivel when I hear it.'

Prince laughed. 'We shouldn't be fighting. Really, we shouldn't. I've no wish to eradicate a man like you from the world. I like you. So be sensible and forget all this law and order nonsense. I'm being nice to you, for God's sake. I usually kill people who oppose me. But I'm giving you the chance to walk out of here unharmed, and live the rest of your life in peace. You can't stop me, so why provoke me by trying? Call off your investigation. You can never win. Accept that, and have a drink with me. Let's drink a toast to peace between us.'

Laverne replaced his glass on the altar. 'I don't drink with criminals.'

Prince laughed again. 'Oh, always so serious . . .'

Laverne adjusted his tie, preparing to leave. 'I'm on to you, Prince.'

Still smiling, Prince said, 'Accept my offer or I'll see you dead, Laverne.'

'Not before I see you locked up.'

'Come now . . . Who will believe you? You have no evidence. No witnesses.'

A woman's voice said, 'He's got one witness.'

Both men turned to see Alison standing in the entrance to the chapel. Prince was momentarily dumbfounded. Then he hastily walked towards her, the palm of his hand outstretched in conciliation. 'Alison. You were listening?'

She was trembling with emotion. 'You swore to me! You promised that you had never, ever used the Death Prayer.'

'I haven't. Truly I ha—'

'Don't lie!' There was a hysterical edge to her voice. 'I've just heard you boasting to him about it.'

'What? You think I was serious? I was just fooling around

144

with him. I wanted to see how much he'd believe. Jesus Christ, I thought *American* cops were stupid, but this fellow deserves some kind of award.'

He grabbed her sleeve, but she snatched her arm free. 'I know you, Hugo. Don't lie to me. I *know* what you've done . . .'

Emotionally, she tried to flee, crashing into the door frame in her haste to escape his presence. Prince snatched at her and she fought him off. As she ran out into the long gallery, she released a strange, muted sob.

Prince walked over to Laverne. His face was now dark with displeasure. 'Out. Go on. Get off my property.'

Laverne picked up his bag. Briskly, he walked to the door. He paused, and turned round. Prince was facing the altar, with his back to Laverne.

'Oh, and before I forget . . . Happy New Year.'

Prince did not respond.

Laverne went out to the car. As he was revving the engine, Alison banged on the window. She was holding a bulky carrier bag. Laverne was pleased to see her. He unlocked the passenger door and she bustled in. 'Where to, madam?'

She moaned and clutched his coat, pressing her face against his arm.

'Hey . . . hey . . .' he said gently. 'What's all this about?'

'We have to get away from here.' Her eyes were red and watery. 'We have to go now.'

She seemed to be drunk with despair. Or perhaps she was simply drunk. After placing her carrier bag on the back seat and checking that her seat belt was secure, he slammed the gear lever into reverse and backed blindly out of the courtyard. Recklessly, he swung the Rover round until its bonnet pointed at the main drive. Then, its headlights scything through the fog, the powerful car surged forward.

'I've been so stupid,' she said. 'I've known about Hugo for ages. It was obvious what kind of a person he was. I saw all the signs and just chose to ignore them. And now he's going to kill us. Oh God, oh God, I know he is . . .'

'Who? Prince? Give over,' scoffed Laverne. 'He's just a big-head.' He opened the glove compartment and took out a silver flask. 'Here, have a swig of this.'

She removed the stopper and took several gulps. He reached out to lower her arm. 'Steady, now. You'll make yourself bad.'

'Bad?' She looked at him strangely.

'It's a northern expression. It means ill. Poorly.'

'Take me somewhere holy. Find me a church.'

'All right. Calm down, now. I won't let anybody hurt you.'

# TEN

The fog thickened, and visibility dwindled to ten yards. For safety's sake, Laverne slowed to a crawl. It took three hours to reach York, with Alison growing more and more convinced that Prince was personally responsible for the bad weather and that she and Laverne were about to be mangled in a preordained road accident. They reached the city shortly before midnight.

Laverne parked his car illegally in a side street and, linking Alison's arm, led her through the swirling murk to the Minster. They approached from the south, and at first sight the cathedral looked to be in darkness. Laverne's spirits plummeted, because it seemed to him that Alison was in a dangerously nervous state. What would he do with her if the church was closed?

But as they rounded the building, flickering golden light glowed in the lofty West Window. Through the glass door panels, people could be seen chatting animatedly.

Then a tall, stooping figure stepped out of the fog. Laverne tensed, expecting trouble. It was a round-faced man in a torn, shabby raincoat. He was about fifty, with weak eyes and a mild southern accent. 'Excuse me, mate. Do you know where there's a hostel or somewhere to kip down for the night?'

'No, sorry,' said Laverne quickly.

'I've tried that place,' he said, pointing vaguely over Laverne's shoulder. 'But they're full. I've just come up from London and I haven't eaten. I'm starving. You couldn't take me for something to eat, could you?'

Laverne delved into his pocket, withdrawing three pound

coins and some small change. He emptied this into the stranger's hand.

'You don't know anywhere I could doss down for the night, do you?' the man persisted. 'I'm cold. Aren't you cold? I couldn't come with you, could I?'

'No,' said Laverne. 'Sorry.'

Alison remained staring at the man as he shambled off into the mist. Laverne gently turned her towards the Minster, giving her shoulder a squeeze as they stepped into the nave.

There were about twenty-five people present, all laughing and talking and drinking mulled wine. Laverne, who resented ceremony, and religious ceremony in particular, was reassured by the obvious informality of the gathering.

Beneath a tall, rather beautiful Christmas tree, splendidly pagan in this austere medieval setting, two people served mince pies and wine to the faithful. Two old-fashioned paraffin heaters gave off the only heat, filling the air with a sweet, nostalgic fragrance and reminding Laverne, with searing pain, of a long-dead father making wooden toys for his sons in his workshop.

Everywhere, candles burned. Laverne had always understood a vigil to be half a dozen freezing, semi-starved individuals holding a candle apiece, but this was altogether a more sumptuous affair. It was a feast of fire, and the faces of the celebrants were bathed in golden light.

As they approached the refreshments table, warmly dressed people parted ranks and smiled politely at the newcomers. Laverne decided, a little unfairly, that he was among a lot of sincere, jolly Christian liberals. As a man, middle-class Christians bored him, but as a police officer, he was rather partial to them, since the only crime they were ever likely to commit was playing their Cliff Richard records too loudly.

A bearded man in a purple vestment, a huge silver cross dangling against his chest, was dishing out mulled wine from a steaming urn. Laverne guessed that he was the event's organizer. The haggard woman by his side was probably his wife.

'Lovely to see you. Lovely to see you,' said the bearded man, apparently meaning it. 'Are you staying with us? I do hope so.'

'Yes. We'd like to,' said Alison. Laverne hoped that she was simply being polite.

'And we'd like you to, too,' quipped the Reverend or whatever he was. 'Mulled wine fifty pence, mince pies twenty pence. All the money to go to famine relief.'

'Two glasses of wine. Four mince pies,' said Laverne. If Alison wasn't hungry, he could easily devour the pies without her help.

'My name's Bob. This is Joan, my good lady wife.'

The haggard woman managed a tired smile. It was probably Bob's overbearing cheerfulness that made her haggard in the first place.

'I'm Alison,' said Alison, shaking hands. 'This is my dad,' she added, to Laverne's surprise.

'Hello, Alison. Hello, Dad,' said Bob, handing them white plastic cups brimming with hot wine, purple and smelling of spice. 'Hang on to the cups, by the way. We're running a bit short of 'em.'

A band, fetchingly attired in medieval dress, began to play old English music with authentic-sounding instruments, and a pleasant-faced blonde woman, overweight, homely, just Laverne's type, began to sing in a pure soprano voice.

'Weep you no more sad fountains,
    What need you flow so fast?'

Alison wandered off to watch the musicians, leaving her 'dad' at Bob's mercy.

'You're probably wondering what this is all about,' said Bob to Laverne, who wasn't. 'Well, three years ago, realizing that war creates most of the suffering in the world, I formed York

149

Anglicans for Peace. YAP for short, and no jokes, please, I've heard 'em all. For example, did you know that war is the biggest single cause of famine? So basically, what we do here is get together, sing, and enjoy ourselves, stopping every hour for five minutes of prayer and contemplation, just praying for a better world.

'You see, Christ isn't just in Christians, he's everywhere, he's in people coming together in joy, in worship, but most importantly, in love. So thanks for coming, and – who knows? – after tonight you might want to join us. Anyway, God bless and we'll have another chat later.'

'I'll look forward to it,' said Laverne, who was not aware that he'd had any kind of 'chat' at all. But Bob, mercifully, had dismissed him and was now serving another customer. Laverne strolled over to stand with Alison. She smiled up at him and linked his arm. The blonde vocalist sang:

'Rest you then, rest, sad eyes!
　　Melt not in weeping,
　　While she lies sleeping
　　Softly! now softly lies sleeping!'

The performance ended to polite applause. The musicians began to play something livelier. Alison and Laverne moved away to lean against a pillar and talk.

'Feeling better now?'

'Yes, Dad.' She started giggling. 'I'm sorry, I'm sorry. I don't know why I said that.'

Laverne held a comic threatening fist under her chin.

'Yes, I do,' she said. 'Because of the way you were with that traveller outside just now. You pretend to be hard but you're not really like that, are you? I can't imagine you hurting anyone.'

'Don't be so sure,' said Laverne, remembering how badly he'd wanted to beat up the Bolton Strangler. Yet, in the end, he'd restrained himself. Perhaps he deserved some credit for that.

'He was one of Prince's people,' she said.

'What? That tramp? Why didn't you say so? I gave him three pounds fifty.'

'No. You don't understand. He was lost, needed looking after. Just the kind of person that Prince would exploit.'

'Like you, you mean?'

'I can look after myself. Whereas I bet that guy outside could barely write his name.'

Laverne took a sip of wine. 'This country's full of homeless people now. I don't know what's gone wrong. It never used to be this bad.'

'They're the disinherited,' she said. 'And it's going to get worse. No hospitals, no dole, no work. This is the new dark age and Hugo means to be its king.'

Laverne humphed. 'He's a pillock.'

'No. He isn't. He's a powerful Black Kahuna.'

'Black Kahuna?'

'Yeah. Kahunas aren't all like Hugo, you know. Traditionally, Kahunas were priests and healers. Holy people.'

She reached into her flying jacket and pulled a travel-weary paperback from the torn lining. 'Like the woman who wrote this book.'

She passed it to him. He looked at the cover. Above a tawdry illustration of a bird in a palm tree were the words *My Life as a Kahuna*. Below this, the author's name: Grandma May.

'It's signed by May herself, see,' said Alison proudly. 'She's a wonderful person. Life healing steals all its ideas from the old Huna religion of Hawaii. If you want to bypass all the crap, and get to the heart of what the Kahunas really believed, read this book.'

'And what if I don't want to read it?'

Alison was visibly aggrieved. It occurred to Laverne that she had just offered to lend him her most valued possession,

151

and he had turned her down. 'No, no,' he said. 'I *do* want to read it. Thanks.' He inserted the paperback into the inside pocket of his overcoat.

'That book was written by a genuine Kahuna. Like I said, Hugo is a Black Kahuna, because he uses Huna magic as a weapon against others. He's no better than a sorcerer, yeah? But even the Black Kahuna is powerless against an opponent with a clear conscience.'

Laverne managed a bitter laugh. 'That rules me out.'

She lowered her wine to study him solemnly. 'I think you're wrong, you know. I think he's already tried to pray you dead, and failed. I see you smiling, treating this like a big joke, but you know, the Death Prayer isn't funny. You've seen what it can do.'

He rammed a mince pie into his mouth, tilted his head in half-agreement.

'Last night, I talked about you with Hugo. I told him that I thought you were quite nice for your age.'

Laverne laughed at this back-handed compliment, spluttering pie crumbs into the air and splashing his hand with wine.

'No,' she reaffirmed, misunderstanding him. 'It's true. For your age, you're not bad at all. Hugo said that perhaps you and I were meant to be together, and that I should listen to what my low self was telling me.'

Laverne started to sneer.

'The low self lives here,' she said, ignoring him and patting her solar plexus. 'In the seat of our emotions. You make me feel funny here, and that's because my low self has taken a liking to you. Probably acting on instructions from my Aumakua or high self.'

'You take the high self and I'll take the low self. I have to be honest with you, Alison, love. This sounds like utter rubbish to me.'

'Of course it does,' she said reasonably. 'That's because your middle self, your reasoning self, the self you present to the world, has developed prejudices and passed them to your

152

low self. The low self is very stubborn, and once it's accepted that something is so, changing its mind isn't easy . . . In fact, it's almost fucking impossible.'

He wrinkled up his nose in distaste. He hated to hear women swear.

The band began to sing without accompaniment. They sang a lament in Gaelic and their mingled voices were magnified by the huge cathedral, their sweetly eerie dirge bouncing back and forth from wall to wall, age to age. Laverne and Alison, seduced by the sound, listened, and Laverne looked sadly into her strange, violet eyes. *It isn't that I don't want to touch you, my love, or that I don't feel the same sad tugging in my guts. It's that I love my wife. I know that hurt always follows desire. And what's more, I'm too fond of sleeping at night, thank God.*

She looked up at him in wonder. 'For a moment, there, I thought you were crying.'

'I never cry,' said Laverne gruffly. 'Haven't cried for years.'

'Where was I?'

The wine was dulling his brain. It took a few seconds to remember. 'You were saying you fancied me. In spite of the fact that I'm past it.'

She elbowed him jokily. 'Oh, stop it. No, when I told Hugo I liked you, he got quite excited. And Hugo doesn't get excited about anything. He said that not to give myself to you would be a betrayal of my soul.'

'Which one?' said Laverne facetiously.

'Like I said,' she continued evenly, 'your prejudice is strong. It makes you deaf to warnings. What I'm trying to tell you is that tonight we learned that Hugo knew you were a policeman when you arrived. But he didn't share that knowledge with me, did he? Instead, seeing that I liked you, he more or less encouraged me to sleep with you.

'I'm supposed to be one of his lovers. He's not a generous person, so why would he do that? Because he wanted to make you guilty, and therefore lower your resistance to the Death

153

Prayer. And how did he know you were immune to the Death Prayer? There's only one possible answer. He must have already tried to kill you, and failed.'

This time, Laverne couldn't bring himself to sneer. He immediately pictured his house on Christmas night, recalling the bruised infant and the groans on the stairs. Although everything he had heard about the Huna religion offended his common sense and upset his digestion, he knew that the girl was right. Prince had indeed tried to kill him.

'So it's guilt, is it? He can only kill me if I have a guilty conscience?'

'That's right.'

'Well, it's hypnotic suggestion, then. He tells people he's going to pray them dead. If they already believe in the Death Prayer, so much the better. And as for the guilt thing ... Well, most of us are guilty about something.'

'God, you can be stupid.' She gave him a pitying look and held out her hand. 'And I need another drink.'

Amused, he gave her a five-pound note and she walked away, leaving him to eat mince pies and drop crumbs down the front of his overcoat.

She returned with two drinks, although he hadn't asked for one. He placed his first cup, still half full, on the cold stone floor by the pillar. 'So why am I such a thicky? That's what you were saying, wasn't it? Policeman Plod, thick sod.'

She shook her head vigorously, and her hair rose and fell, casting the pungent smell of patchouli oil into the chill air.

'No. Not thick. Just naïve. You don't seem to understand what you're up against. Prince isn't some kind of shady stage hypnotist who one day got bored of making people bark like dogs and thought, "Hey, I know; I'll kill people."

'He's a powerful sorcerer and he's murdered many people. Stop deluding yourself. The Death Prayer doesn't work by trickery. It works because Prince controls dead spirits who attach themselves to the chosen victim and sap them of life force.'

154

'What?' said Laverne. 'Like estate agents?'

'Why do you keep joking? It isn't funny. Can't you see that?' she pleaded. 'It isn't funny for the victim, or for the souls who do his bidding.'

'Do you believe he can pray *you* dead?' he asked seriously.

Her eyes darkened. 'Yes. I do.'

'Why? What are you guilty about?'

'I had a baby eighteen months ago. A boy. It wasn't Hugo's son, but he helped me out. At the time, I couldn't cope with a child. I couldn't cope with anything. I'd just had a breakdown. Hugo let me stay at the Abbey and arranged for my baby to be adopted. I'm beginning to have serious regrets about that.'

Laverne asked, 'If he was so generous, why didn't he let you and the kid stay at the Abbey? He's not short of a bob or two.'

She averted her eyes sullenly, knowing this to be unanswerable.

Gently, Laverne said, 'Do you want your son back?'

She shrugged. 'I still probably couldn't cope with him . . . I mean, my life's such a mess. But most nights, I dream about him. Just holding him.'

She related this without self-pity, seeing her plight as commonplace, her misfortunes unexceptional.

After pondering the matter, Laverne said, 'Don't worry. I shouldn't imagine any adoption Prince has arranged is legal. Leave it to me.'

'What can you do?'

'Lots of things. I'm magic, too, you know.'

'You can't take away the guilt, though. I still let my baby down.'

He hushed her. 'No. You didn't. You had no home, no money. No one can blame you for that, Alison. We'll get you sorted, you'll see.'

She took his hand. 'Hey, Dad.'

'But you've got to promise to do something for me.'

'And what's that, Mr Superintendent, sir?'

155

'Help me nail Prince. I may not believe in the Death Prayer but that bloke's a bloody menace. I want to see him locked up.'

As Laverne spoke, he stamped his feet energetically. She watched this impromptu tap dance with puzzlement. 'What's up?'

'Pins and needles,' he explained.

Her face darkened.

'The Death Prayer,' she whispered.

He laughed and said, 'No. Just pins and needles.'

A stout woman in a green duffle-coat interrupted to hand them both hymn books. 'Carols at midnight,' she said. 'Sing out!'

Then the woman grinned yellowly from ear to ear. She wandered off to repeat the same trite little speech, over and over again.

'Look,' said Laverne, 'I'm thinking of heading back. Why don't you come home with me? We've got plenty of room. I could put you up for a few days.'

'What about your wife? Won't she mind?'

'You don't know Dawn. If I tell her you're homeless, she'll put you straight to bed with cocoa and a hot water bottle.'

'But won't she think it's a bit, you know, funny?'

'No. She once brought home a couple of homeless kids herself, you know. They drank all my whisky and took off with the video. Oh yes, we've had confused pensioners, mentally handicapped brush salesmen, stray dogs ... you name it. One more lost cause won't make any difference.'

She looked mildly affronted. 'Oh, sorry, I didn't mean you were a lost cause. You have to excuse me, Alison, I'm a bit clumsy in my speech. A typical policeman, really. Well-meaning but stupid. Now, shall we make a move?'

But Reverend Bob was eagerly regarding his watch, warming up the company in preparation for midnight.

'I make it any second now ... any moment now ...'

Silence. Then the oak figures of the striking clock, four

centuries old, hammered out the hour. Everyone cheered. Laverne observed Alison. For the first time, he saw hope in her eyes.

'Gimme a hug,' she said.

He obeyed, sensing no awkwardness in himself or the girl. She might have been his own daughter, so natural did this embrace feel. Then they were parted by the woman in the green duffle coat, who first kissed Alison, then Laverne.

'Peace on earth starts here tonight!' shouted the irrepressible Bob. Tiresomely, everyone took him at his word, and circulated, exchanging personal hugs and greetings. Alison bounced away to shake hands with a wheelchair-bound man and his wife. Laverne was once again cornered by Bob.

'God be with you,' he said, gripping Laverne's hand in both of his own and pumping it vigorously.

'Not "Bob" be with you! I said "God" be with you!'

A small woman and her teenage daughter approached Laverne. The mother seemed to have won first prize in a sincerity contest. In contrast, her gum-chewing daughter eyed Laverne reproachfully, as if he was personally responsible for this orgy of heartiness. Over her head, he saw Alison being tapped on the shoulder by a little old man he hadn't noticed before.

The stranger was dressed in a long grey clerical robe, and had white, shoulder-length hair. He must have been no more than five feet tall. His thin, wan face radiated kindly intelligence. Alison turned to face him, and at that second, someone walked by, momentarily obscuring Laverne's view.

When he glimpsed Alison again, she was on her knees. The robed stranger was standing back to admire his handiwork, looking on with warm interest as first one, then another onlooker cried out in alarm. In his left hand he held a long, curved knife. A bright fountain of blood appeared to be spurting from the top of Alison's skull.

Dry-mouthed, Laverne ran to her. The blood was not coming from her head, as he'd first assumed, but from a deep wound in her chest. Uncomprehendingly, she was struggling to stem the flow with her fingers, but her stabbed heart was siphoning blood into the air like a geyser. Frightened, Laverne tried to assist her by pressing his hands over hers, but hot blood sprayed into his face and eyes and spattered his clothes.

She collapsed, gasping for breath. He held her head and she gazed up at him in grave wonder. Then she died in his arms.

The Minster bells, in full peal, raged in his ears as they ushered in the year. Bereft, he lurched unsteadily to his feet. As one, the onlookers backed away from him. He had suddenly become the focus of their attention. One of the women was shrieking hysterically. Laverne shook his head as if to clear it. Then he turned to Alison's killer, who was striding away towards the south transept. Swearing silently, Laverne moved to follow him.

The Reverend Bob, who played rugby, shouted something incomprehensible and, attacking from behind, thrust a beefy forearm under Laverne's chin. Quickly, without malice, Laverne elbowed Bob in the gut and, wriggling free, hurled him heavily against a pillar. Winded, Bob sank to the ground, clutching his belly.

Then, his heart sending shockwaves through his frame, Laverne raced after the murderer. His diminutive quarry was now a pale blur, hurrying eastward. As he chased the gaunt, purposeful figure, salt water rolled off his face. The sweat of anguish was pouring out of him.

The tumbling, spiralling bells greatly added to his discomfort; at this proximity, there was no music in their voice; theirs was the mad, jubilant clamour of hell. You were there and couldn't save her. Couldn't save her. Couldn't save her.

Beyond the central tower, the cathedral was in darkness. As he bounded over the crossing, a morbid chill seized him, like the shadow of an iceberg as it blocks out the sun. High in the tower above, St Paul raised his sword. The fifteen Kings of

England that flanked the entrance to the choir inclined their faces towards him as he passed.

Plunging deeper into the gloom, Laverne felt his resolution waver. A babel of whispering voices blew over him like a cloud. His legs, attending to his misgivings, abruptly weakened. His courage seemed to drain away and he came to a standstill. Angry shouts sounded, far behind him.

The diminutive figure ahead, almost luminous in the dark, had also stopped. It was now no more than ten yards away. Laverne saw the robed form turn to the west in a single, graceful motion.

Although Laverne could not see his face, he knew that the little man was now looking directly at him. He shuddered, recollecting the assassin's thin, gracious smile.

Afraid to appear a coward, Laverne barked, 'Police! Don't move!' Then, trembling slightly, he forced himself to advance. When he was within three paces of the figure, he became aware of a vile smell, like rotting vegetables. The old gentleman seemed to nod, once, twice, as if willing Laverne forward. On an impulse, Laverne glanced over his shoulder, and saw his own body, still standing where he had left it, watching his progress in dreadful silence.

Instantly, out of sheer panic, he lunged back into this other Laverne, yet his limbs felt alien and he found himself fighting for breath like a newborn babe. His own choking gasps filled his head. He was shocked by how helpless he sounded. But after a few seconds he managed, blissfully, to breathe and the crisis was averted. He was safe inside himself again.

The old man, who had been coolly regarding this drama, suddenly lost interest and, turning sharply to his left, disappeared into the crypt.

Then, as if to signal the death of hope, the cathedral bells died away. After all, there was nothing to celebrate. Tragedy had visited York Minster. From now on, nothing holy could dwell here. Perhaps nothing holy ever had.

Without purpose or conviction, Detective Superintendent

Laverne walked to the crypt. He already knew what he would find there. The iron gate across its entrance was chained and padlocked. Through its bars, he could vaguely discern narrow sunken steps, and below, the utter blackness that housed the wealthy and the damned. There, under the Domesday carving of hell, slept the murderer of Alison Reffel. Thomas North, Knight of York, a man who had been dead for seven hundred and eighty-eight years.

# Eleven

In a horrified stupor, Laverne staggered back to the girl's body, sat beside her and refused to budge. The York Anglicans for Peace now held a vigil of a different kind. They kept watch over this ashen father who squatted on the floor, covered in his daughter's blood, and they also kept their distance.

The Reverend Bob's wife was jabbering hysterically but her husband, too shocked to comfort her, paced up and down the nave with his hands behind his back, waiting for the police to arrive. His fellow vigilantes stood guard, sickened into silence. Now and then, when one of them dared to whisper, Laverne would stir from his grim trance to paralyse the guilty party with a crazed, condemnatory stare, like a grieving dog keeping watch at its owner's graveside.

At last, a solitary patrol car arrived. Its two uniformed occupants, a man and a woman, were expecting another trivial call. Since ten p.m., when their shift had commenced, they had already dealt with four drunken scuffles and one case of serious name-calling. As they sidled into the cathedral, their plain, honest faces were devoid of interest or enthusiasm. Then they saw Laverne, sitting beside Alison's blood-soaked corpse.

Shaken out of his complacency, the male officer cried, 'Fuck me rigid!'

Hearing this, one of the Christian women tutted in disapproval. The WPC immediately radioed for help. Then, against Bob's advice, she approached Laverne and tried to talk to him. Bob regaled her partner with his personal account of the incident. 'He attacked his own daughter, and you can see the results for yourself. He killed her and ran away. I tried to stop him, at which point he attacked me as well.'

The constable bit his lip and shook his head. This was all too much for him. 'I can't see that, sir. Can't see it at all. That bloke's in the CID.'

Bob looked sceptical. 'He can't be.'

'He is though. He's famous.'

'Well,' predicted Bob darkly, 'he'll be even more famous after this.'

The woman in the wheelchair and her partner approached the exit, and the constable, remembering his responsibilities, was obliged to bar their way. 'Sorry. No one leaves. We'll need to take statements from everyone present.'

Reinforcements arrived. Bob, who seemed to be under the impression that he was in charge, followed the police around, making speeches. 'This is a black day for me. And a black day for York Minster. In fact, a black day for all York churches . . .'

Laverne, who was incapable of making any kind of statement, was led away. They drove him to Fulford Road, and in dreadful awe photographed his gory hands and took scrapings from beneath his fingernails. Then, officers wearing polythene gloves helped him out of his blood-blackened clothes. He sat in a corner of the incident room, diminished and ridiculous in his vest and underpants. Someone sent for Etherington.

It was hoped that he might persuade Laverne to communicate. Etherington, horrified by the situation but flattered by the trust that had been placed in him, questioned his boss repeatedly. But Laverne's only utterance was 'Where've they taken Alison?'

The custody sergeant, a morose pot-bellied bigot called Halford, recorded this statement in a thick black ledger. He then sent his assistant, an equally morose constable, to find some clean clothes for Laverne. The constable returned with a crumpled uniform, but Laverne refused to wear it.

162

'Typical CID,' commented Halford. 'Thinks he's too good to go back into uniform.'

Detective Superintendent Ron Vestey, the highest ranking officer on duty, came down from his office to marvel at the incident room's latest exhibit. He had known Laverne for years and, envying his success, had always prayed that his rival might one day be dishonoured. But now that this day had dawned, Vestey, perversely, was not happy. He vented his displeasure on Halford.

'George, get some clothes on him, you stupid bastard. You can't leave him like that . . .'

Halford explained the situation. Vestey calmed down a little, took the uniform over to Laverne and tried to coax him into it. Laverne resisted strenuously, and Vestey gave in. Deflated, he took Halford and Etherington aside and confessed his bewilderment.

'What's the procedure on this one? Eh? What do we do? Because I'm fucked if I know.' He looked at Halford. 'Any ideas, Georgie?'

Halford shook his head and made foolish steam-train noises with his pouting lips.

'There's no precedent, is there?' offered Etherington.

Vestey frowned. 'No president? What are you talking about?'

'Pre-ce-dent,' repeated Etherington, standing his ground. 'I mean, it hasn't happened before, sort of thing.'

Vestey remarked on Laverne's peculiar state of mind. 'Maybe we should call a doctor? What do you think?'

This suggestion struck them all as inspirational. For foisting Laverne on to a doctor might make them look compassionate, rather than merely incompetent. Until the doctor's arrival, they locked the pride of North Yorkshire in a cell. A young WPC, sent in with a mug of tea for him, burst into tears at the sight of the great detective, shivering in his string vest, and had to be sent home.

The doctor duly arrived, a taciturn, grey-haired Nigerian.

He examined Laverne, and quickly concluded that he was suffering from severe shock. Vestey, looking on, uncharitably commented, 'I don't need a fucking doctor to tell me that.' In retaliation, the physician furiously demanded that Laverne be wrapped in clean, dry blankets. Chastened, Vestey saw that this request was carried out.

In the meantime, Geraint John had been summoned from his bed. He arrived after three, wearing casual clothes and smelling of alcohol, his hair tousled, the collar of a paisley pyjama jacket showing over the neck of his sweater. When he discovered that Laverne was locked in a cell, he railed at Vestey. 'You bloody what? You haven't charged him with anything. We don't even know if there is a charge, yet!'

Red-faced, Vestey defended himself. 'You haven't seen his clothes, sir. Covered in blood. Caked in it. It doesn't look good . . .'

They were standing in the corridor that led to the cells. Geraint, six inches taller than Vestey, paused to hold a thick forefinger under the Superintendent's nose. 'Don't fucking argue, Ronald. I'm telling you he shouldn't be in a cell.'

Vestey half-raised his hands in surrender. 'OK. Point taken.'

The Superintendent unlocked Laverne's cell and departed. John entered. Laverne scarcely seemed aware of his presence. Carefully, John rearranged the blankets around Laverne's shoulders, so that the folds covered his underpants. Then, he sat beside his friend on the hard, thin mattress and for a long time the room was silent.

On Geraint's orders, Laverne was sent home. Dawn, stirred from her bed at four-twenty a.m., was appalled by the sight of him. Etherington, the unlucky bearer of ill tidings, told her there had been an 'incident' in York Minster. When pressed, he added what little he knew: that a girl had been stabbed, and that one witness had implicated Laverne.

Not knowing what to think, feeling sick with worry, she

164

helped Laverne upstairs and urged him to rest. The police left without troubling her further, but she knew they would return. Laverne lay on his bed all day, too electrified by distress to sleep, too sick at heart to rise.

Desperate for more information, Dawn rang Lyn Savage's home number, but all she got was an answering machine. She left a message, asking Lyn to call her as soon as possible. She also phoned Geraint and spoke to Fran, his puzzled wife, learning that Geraint had left the house in the early hours and not contacted her since. She called his direct line at headquarters, only to connect with yet another answering machine.

Unpleasantly, she was obliged to lie to Jennifer. Her daughter's family had been invited to a New Year's Day lunch, but Dawn had to call to put them off. She said that Laverne had contracted flu, and that it wasn't safe to bring Harriet to the house.

By the evening, Laverne had recovered sufficiently to shower and dress. He consumed a meagre supper and, holding his wife tightly by the hand, answered her questions with brief, weary answers, so that little by little she was able to build up a picture of his weekend and its grisly conclusion.

The phone rang. She answered it. It was a man with a suave, deep voice, and a Home Counties accent. Claiming to be a reporter from a respectable national daily, he asked to speak to Laverne. Quaking slightly, Dawn informed the journalist that this was impossible. She glanced over at Laverne, who was sitting on the sofa, a glass in his hand, pretending to listen to a Duke Ellington record. Rapidly, the caller transferred his attention to Dawn. Did she realize that her husband was now the chief suspect in a murder inquiry? Calmly, she replaced the receiver.

She crossed the room to steady the glass in Laverne's hand, which was tilted at a hazardous angle. 'Careful,' she said, in as casual a tone as she could muster. 'You don't want to ruin the carpet.'

Then she left the room and mounted the stairs to their bedroom. Without turning on the light, she walked to the uncurtained window and peered out. It was just as she had thought. They had descended *en masse*, in eerie silence, like birds of prey. Three huge lorries were parked outside the house. A host of photographers, lighting technicians, camera operators and sound recordists were gathering in the drive.

The sight made her heart accelerate. She sank on to the bed, forcing herself to breathe deeply. If she was to be any use to Vernon, she had to stay calm, or at least not grow any less calm. He needed her, and she knew exactly what she had to do. These people were simply not going to go away, but if she co-operated by giving them a brief interview, perhaps she could minimize the damage. It would be like amputating a gangrenous leg; almost insupportably repugnant, but necessary.

She entered the bathroom to rinse her face with lukewarm water. Then she dried herself on a clean, dry hand towel. After brushing her hair and checking that she didn't have food between her teeth, or stains on her sweater, she marched downstairs and unlocked the front door.

Her sudden appearance sent a ripple of consternation through a posse of journalists, who were hovering on the step like indecisive carol singers. When it became apparent that she was willing to talk, their colleagues surged forward to join them, aiming lights and great phallic microphones at her face. Dawn was hardly relaxed, but she agreed to wait until the bumbling BBC crew had set up their camera.

It took less than three minutes. Was the Superintendent available for comment? No. He was too upset by last night's events to talk to anyone. And how did he feel about being accused of murder? So far, Dawn replied, no one had accused him of anything. What was the nature of his involvement with Alison Reffel? Alison, Dawn replied, had been assisting Laverne with a murder inquiry. 'Our main thoughts at this time are with Alison's family. No more questions, please.'

She closed the door, locked and bolted it. A wave of dizziness overcame her. She leaned against the wall until she felt better. Duke Ellington was still jazzing it up behind the closed living-room door. She inhaled deeply, and walked in. As she appeared, Laverne looked up at her sadly, his eyes full of respect. He knew exactly what she'd been up to. She noticed that he'd taken the phone off the hook. He patted the empty half of the sofa, and she sat down beside him.

He took her hand. 'What are we going to do?'

'The same as we always do.'

He managed a tired smile. 'I'd like to send some flowers to Alison's parents.'

She gave his hand a squeeze. 'That's a nice idea. Where do they live?'

'I don't know.'

'We can find out.'

They sat in silence. After a while, Dawn said, 'You don't think you're to blame, do you? For Alison dying, I mean.'

'No,' said Laverne firmly. 'And if I did, I'd be dead myself.'

'I don't know what you mean.'

'Good,' said Laverne. 'Let's keep it that way.'

The press were already regrouping at seven the next morning, when Dawn opened the door to take in the milk. It was still dark outside, but she could see about half a dozen of them lurking by the gate. Headlights flashed through the trees. A slow procession of vans and trailers were rumbling up the lane towards the house. She snatched the milk and closed the door sharply. What did one call a group of journalists? She wondered. A scoop? A defecation?

Laverne had managed a few hours' sleep, and was already, rather unrealistically, talking of going into work to 'clear the air'. But he had no wish to brave the media hounds. The doorbell chimed repeatedly, and was left unanswered. They kept the curtains drawn, unwilling to be captured by the dreaded zoom lens. A photographer found her way into the back garden, while Dawn and Laverne were eating breakfast in the kitchen. Dawn managed to draw the blind just in time.

One second later and a colour portrait of Laverne with egg dripping down his chin would have appeared on the front page of the *Daily Mirror*.

Dawn rang Jennifer, who had been trying to contact them since last night. 'I saw you on *News at Ten*, Mum. I couldn't believe it.'

'How did I look?'

'Very nice. But what's going on? What's Dad supposed to have done?'

'He's done nothing wrong, darling. Your father's just been a bit unlucky.'

This turned out to be something of an understatement.

Lyn Savage arrived at mid-morning. She brought four uniformed officers with her, and posted them at the gate. Laverne wasn't sure whether they were intended to keep the press out, or him in.

Savage sat with Laverne in the dining room. Dawn made them a pot of coffee and left them to it. Initially, the conversation was decidedly stilted. Savage looked almost as pale as Laverne. After a few diversionary remarks about press intrusion, she came to the point.

'You might as well know that they're suspending you from duty.'

'What a surprise. Bring in the smelling salts.'

'Mr John sent me. He wanted you to know straight away, rather than have to wait for the official letter of notification. You'll get the letter anyway, but in the meantime . . .'

'Don't bother turning up for work.'

'You'll be suspended with full pay, of course.'

'Great,' he jeered. 'So I get the lousy money without having to do the lousy job.'

'Oh, Vernon,' she sighed. 'I asked you not to be stupid, didn't I? I told you that an officer of your rank can't go around pretending to be someone else. That sort of stuff is for all those little detective constables who think they're in *Undercover Cop*.'

168

He sipped his coffee and sulked.

'None of this would have happened if you'd only *listened* to me. It's not as if you're stupid. You know how highly I rate you.'

'It doesn't sound like it.'

'Well, you make me so bloody cross. What's happened isn't just bad for you. It's bad for me, and it's bad for the force.'

'Don't you mean "the service"?'

'Shut up,' she fumed. 'I asked you, didn't I? I said, "Please can we have a good old-fashioned murder inquiry, with the murder team backing up the team leader." You were the team leader, by the way, in case you hadn't realized. And what happens? You go off on one of your little crusades again. Only this time, a witness is murdered while you're three feet away. All you had to do was take my advice. Just once. I would have walked through hellfire for you.'

He had stopped sulking and was now studying her sympathetically. The blood had risen to her cheeks. Her voice was angry, but her eyes showed deep hurt.

'Is that it?' he said.

'No. That isn't *it*. I also want to say that I'm sorry. Sorry you're in trouble and sorry that I wasn't more honest with you. You were already under investigation, and I should have warned you.'

He shrugged philosophically. 'It wouldn't have made any difference if you had. I already knew.'

'I beg your pardon?'

'People have been asking questions about me for years, Lyn.'

'You mean you knew? Well, that's worse. You knew what they were thinking and yet you *still* carried on breaking the rules?'

Unperturbed, he slurped his coffee, left his chair and drew back the curtain to let in the light. Startled by the sudden movement, a robin dipped and darted away across the frosted lawn, plunging into the hedge at the bottom of the garden. 'So who's taking over from me?'

'Who do you think?'

He looked at her. 'Oh, no. Not Vestey . . .'

'No. Me.'

'Oh. Good,' he said, evidently appeased. 'That's what I would have recommended.'

'You're in no position to recommend anything, really, are you?'

'No need to be like that. I could save you a hell of a lot of time by sharing what I know.'

'Which is what?'

'That Hugo Prince is the man responsible for these murders.'

She was unimpressed. 'You've got evidence to support that, I take it?'

'Well, it depends on your definition of evidence. But I'll bet Derek Tyreman is dead by now, isn't he?'

This surprised her. 'Yes,' she said quietly.

'And Sheelagh Daye?'

'Yes. They both died early on Sunday morning.'

'I'm right, then. Prince killed them both.'

'Ah. And I suppose he killed Alison Reffel too, did he?'

'Certainly did. Or at least arranged to have her killed.' He sat down again, leaned forward to look into her eyes. 'Listen, Lyn. You're going to have to suspend your disbelief. Because what I'm about to tell you is pretty hard to take. Just bear with me . . .'

He began to talk about the Death Prayer, his experience at North Abbey, and how he'd been forced to accept, against his better judgement, that Prince was a genuine black magician served by an army of malevolent spirits. She attended to him in silence, controlling her innate scepticism, taking care not to react to the more preposterous aspects of his story. But as she listened to the man she had followed and respected, the expression in her eyes slowly changed from wounded indignation to pity.

Savage spent the rest of that day wondering what to do next. If, as she suspected, Laverne's mind was unhinged there was a chance that he was indeed guilty of murder. But she also knew that Laverne had only confided in her because he trusted her. She was not convinced, therefore, that anyone else had the right to know the details of their conversation.

That night, she consulted Ian. He was lounging in bed, reading a building journal. His response was infuriatingly dismissive. 'Don't be stupid. Tell everyone. Your friend Laverne's up shit creek without a paddle. You talk about loyalty. Loyalty to what? A fella who's probably lying through his teeth to protect himself from a prison sentence? All right, he may not be a murderer. But the bloke's a nutter. He's got to be. My advice is tell everyone. Tell your mother. Tell the dog.'

She hauled a nightdress over her head. 'Thanks a lot, Ian. Thanks for that calm and balanced judgement.'

'Well . . .' he scowled dismissively, and turned the page of his magazine, feigning deep interest in an article about concrete. 'I've no patience with you sometimes.'

She went downstairs to the living room, and rifled through her handbag. The dog, hoping that something edible was about to manifest, padded over to her and did its best to look deserving. After tipping the bag's contents on to the sofa, she found what she was searching for: a creased calling card. She glanced at a clock on the mantelpiece. It was ten minutes to eleven. Too late? Perhaps. But this couldn't wait.

She grabbed the phone and tapped out the number on the card. There was a slight delay, then the ringing tone. It sounded far away, as if the phone at the end of the line was on the moon. There was a crackling noise, followed by a gruff male voice. 'Yep?'

'Oh, hello. I'd like to speak to Mr John.'

A few seconds passed. 'Who is that, please?'

It occurred to her that she might have dialled the wrong number. 'Savage. DI Savage?'

'Speaking. What can I do for you?'

She felt her confidence shrinking. She had forgotten about the man's cool arrogance. 'Oh. I, er, you told me to ring if I had anything to tell you about Vernon . . .'

A sigh. 'A bit late for that, isn't it?'

Deflated, she said, 'I don't know. You tell me.'

There was a burst of static, as if he was moving the phone across the room. Then he spoke again. 'All right. How are you fixed for tomorrow?'

She was taken aback. 'Excuse me?'

'We can talk tomorrow.'

'Oh. Fine. Well, anytime in the morning would suit me.'

'I was thinking of lunch, actually.'

'Oh. Great. Fine.' The dog was whimpering in the kitchen. 'Lucy: shush!'

'What?'

'Oh, sorry, I was talking to the dog.'

'Oh?' He sounded vaguely suspicious. 'Tomorrow, then. I'll pick you up at one.'

The line went dead. She switched off the phone. Then, without turning on the light, she walked into the kitchen to see what was worrying the dog. Outside, it was raining heavily. The black window panes were awash. Lucy was at the door, clawing. 'What is it, dog?' she soothed. 'Want to go out?'

She walked back to a board beside the fridge where the keys were hung, then glanced over to the kitchen window and saw a white disembodied face looking in at her. Although the image was blurred by rain and condensation, she recognized Laverne instantly. She cried out, and the dog rushed to her side, whining. Savage closed her eyes, then opened them. He was still out there, gazing coldly. Then, slowly, the face shrank back into the darkness, leaving Savage staring at the night and the rain streaming down the window.

# TWELVE

Lyn Savage disliked Chinese food, but Geraint John thought he was doing her a great favour by taking her to lunch at the Silver Dolphin, York's finest Chinese restaurant. So she humoured him by pretending to be honoured.

Privately, she thought the Deputy Chief Constable was looking haggard. He had possibly added four or five pounds to his waistline over Christmas, and his eyes seemed to have lost some of their sparkle. But he still resembled a rich gangster, his polished gold cufflinks gleaming as he jabbed a fork into his dim sum. Whenever he moved, his expensive cologne wafted across the table to her.

The restaurant was cool and spacious. Tropical fish puffed and pouted in a tank behind Geraint's chair. There were only about half a dozen other diners, but Savage and John spoke in low voices, because the subject under discussion was dear to their hearts.

'I shouldn't be buying you lunch,' remarked John, mock-stern. 'I should be giving you a right royal rollocking. What did I ask you, eh? What did I ask you to do?'

'You mean I should have phoned earlier.'

'A week earlier. If I'd known he was thinking of playing silly buggers, I'd have been able to step in and do something about it.'

'I'm not making excuses for myself, but he promised me he'd send someone else to Ilkley. I mean, I can't keep track of him *all* the time.'

Geraint grunted, acknowledging the sense of this.

'The fact is, no one should *have* to keep track of a senior police officer. Vernon isn't a fool. He knows the difference between right and wrong. This had to happen sooner or later. By the way, is your dim sum a bit on the tough side?'

She nodded. 'Rather chewy.'

'Shouldn't be chewy, though. Good dim sum should melt in the mouth.'

He called a waiter over and unceremoniously sent the dumplings back. The waiter returned with a second batch that were no better than the first. Geraint complained again. The manager oozed forth to dispense profuse apologies.

'I don't want an apology, Mr Chan,' said Geraint. 'I want the high standard of cuisine that I've come to expect from your establishment. This lady hasn't been here before. Imagine what kind of impression you're making on her.'

He imparted this speech calmly, confidently, as if he actually couldn't care less whether his dumplings were tough or not. Savage realized that he was flexing his muscles for her benefit. She was not impressed. When the injured manager had returned to his closet, she said, 'Honestly. It's not that important, is it?'

'It is important,' he avowed. 'Haven't you seen the *Egon Ronay* and *Les Routiers* stickers in the window? Earned by good food and good service. No, Lyn. These people get too complacent. They think they can get by on their reputations. Well, they can't. They need their arses kicking now and then. Same as police officers. They need reminding that they can't get by with shoddy practices . . .'

'Which brings us back to Vernon.'

'No, no. What Vernon did wasn't shoddy. It was bloody insane. Insane isn't the same as shoddy.'

'It's funny you should say that.'

'Why? You agree with me, do you?'

She told him about her recent conversation with Laverne, and his contention that Prince was a genuine black magician. As he listened, John kept tutting and shaking his head.

174

'Dear me. Dear, dear, dear. The lad's ill, really, isn't he? He's got to be. He needs help. It's a bloody shame . . .'

They ordered their main course. John chose something called a 'Silver Dolphin Special'. Savage disappointed him by opting for a plate of stir-fried vegetables.

'Are you on a diet or something?'

'I don't eat lunch, generally. Physiologically, human beings only require one square meal a day.'

'Pardon me, DI Savage, but you're talking bollocks.' He laughed, showing beautiful white teeth. Had a less overbearing personality inhabited that immense frame, Savage might have found him attractive.

'No,' he said, fingering his napkin absent-mindedly. 'It's all been rather unfortunate. Of course, some think Vernon might have stabbed the girl, but I've seen the statements taken from the witnesses at the scene. None of 'em saw a thing, apart from Vernon trying to stop the victim bleeding to death. And that's hardly a crime.

'But let's not pretend. Only a miracle could save Vernon now. I'm afraid Mr Neville tight-arse Wood has got what he's always wanted.'

'Neville Wood?'

'That's the chappie. I shouldn't really tell you this, but Wood has had it in for Vernon for years.'

She was flabbergasted. 'But why?'

'Partly jealousy. But that's not the whole reason. 'He's a stickler for order, our Chief Constable. Ever seen his office? Not a speck of dust anywhere, not a file out of place. Fresh flowers every two days, at his request. Honestly, if you went in there, not knowing whose office it was, you'd think a woman worked there.'

She raised an ironical eyebrow.

'The point I'm making is that anyone who likes neatness isn't going to like Vernon. If you like things to be logical, you're hardly going to take kindly to a report that says, "Went to Buxton to interview the missing child's parents. Obtained

175

no useful leads, but on the way home caught the murderer anyway."'

Although she was feeling depressed, this made her smile. 'I think you're exaggerating a little, aren't you?'

'Maybe. A little. But you see my point? Anyone who likes order is going to see Vernon's entire career as a kind of sustained confidence trick. Plus, Wood doesn't like Vernon as a person.'

'Has he admitted that?'

'Has he hell. That sort of fella never admits to anything. He's teetotal, so you can't even get him to be honest when he's pissed. But I can tell. He's never sent Vernon a personal letter of congratulation. Not once. When Vernon caught the Rapist, Wood sent a memo out saying the "case had been brought to a satisfactory conclusion". When, in fact, he should have said: "Three hundred unsolved murders and, fuck me, we finally caught somebody." No. Wood wants Vernon out. And it looks as if his wish is about to be granted.'

Geraint sighed, suddenly impatient. 'Anyway, what is it you wanted to talk to me about?'

'Well, I was going to suggest that you and I got together, made a case for Vernon having some sort of breakdown. I mean, he's obviously in need of medical attention. We could pressure them into being lenient with him.'

'Nah. No point. Even if it worked, he'd only be put out to grass. They'd take him out of the CID and shove him behind a desk somewhere. Frankly, I think that'd kill him.'

After the main course, Geraint asked her if she wanted anything else. She declined. He was obviously in a hurry to get away. He called for the bill, and the waiter respectfully informed them that there would be no charge – 'because of the complaints'.

When they were outside on the pavement, Geraint chuckled gleefully. 'How about that? It was a nice meal, too, apart from the starter. I should complain more often.'

Suddenly heartened, he invited her to walk with him for a

while. They found themselves in the Shambles, with its overhanging timbered houses. A party of nuns were shuffling out of the shrine of Margaret Clitherow, the saint who was crushed to death four centuries ago for hiding a Jesuit priest. 'We had a bit of law and order in those days,' joked Geraint John.

'Oh, don't,' protested Savage.

'Oh, yes. If you were cheeky to a policeman back then, you didn't just get a clip round the ear, you know. You had weights piled on you, bit by bit, until – '

'Shut up.'

He smiled down at her. 'No, but seriously, has it ever struck you what a bloodthirsty place York is? These Yorkshire bastards hate everyone. They always did. Catholics, Jews, Mancunians. They've had it in for us all, at one time or another.'

'What about people from the Channel Isles?'

'Why? Is that where you're from?'

She nodded. 'Jersey.'

'Jersey? There's nothing there, is there? We went there for a day, once. It doesn't seem like a proper place, Jersey.'

'Why do you say that?'

'Well, it doesn't seem to have any proper history. People just settled there and learned to knit. Hence the name: Jersey.'

There was a rumble overhead, followed by a crack of thunder. 'Oh Christ,' groaned Geraint.

The storm broke with sudden violence. Rain sliced down, making them hunch their shoulders and bow their heads. They were in Low Petergate. 'This way,' said Savage, guiding him down the narrow passage that led to the little church of Holy Trinity. They sheltered under its arched doorway, watching the rain fall. After a while, when the torrent showed no sign of abating, Savage glanced at her watch. 'I'd better be getting back.'

'You'll get bloody soaked,' warned Geraint.

'I know. But I've got things to do . . .'

He gently took hold of her arm. 'No, come in and sit down for a few minutes. You haven't told me what's on your mind.'

'There's nothing on my mind.'

'Yes there is. Why won't you talk to me?'

They entered, and sat under the roll of honour, facing the font. Geraint produced a pack of sugarless chewing gum from his overcoat. Wordlessly, he passed a stick to Savage and took one for himself. There was a creak to their left. An old man in a sou'wester peered in, camera in hand, water dripping off his spectacles. He began to unscrew the camera's lens cap.

'Sorry,' said Geraint. 'We're closed.'

The tourist mumbled an apology and stumbled out. Savage was disgusted. 'That was an awful thing to do.'

Geraint sniggered. 'Oh, give over . . .'

After a while, he said, 'You *still* haven't told me what's bothering you.'

'Nothing. There's nothing,' she insisted, but the lie brought blood to her cheeks.

'You must think I'm daft, Lyn Savage. Come on. What's the matter?'

She took a deep breath, tasting the damp hymn-book-scented air. 'If I tell you something about Vernon, will you keep it to yourself?'

'That depends. You might be about to tell me he's having an affair with my wife.'

'If only it were that straightforward. No . . . You're the only person I can discuss this with, really. I just don't want it to get back to Neville Wood.'

Geraint released a 'humph' of scorn at the very idea. 'No chance of that. But look, Vernon's a friend of mine. If it's anything awful, I'm not sure I want to know.'

'No. It isn't awful . . . If you must know, I've seen him snooping round my house at night . . .'

Geraint John looked away and let out a measured sigh. 'Like I said, the lad needs help. It's a bloody shame.'

*

Laverne was interviewed by two police psychiatrists, both of whom pronounced him of sound mind, and therefore responsible for his own actions. This was exactly what the Chief Constable wanted to hear. But because Laverne was one of his own officers, Mr Wood called in a team from West Yorkshire Police to investigate the murder of Alison Reffel. They interviewed Laverne at his home, at Fulford Road, and on one occasion, for no obvious reason, obliged him to drive all the way to their headquarters in Wakefield.

But they had no real case.

All they had was the Reverend Bob's statement, which was finally and irrevocably discredited by his wife. After a fortnight had passed, and she had recovered sufficiently from the shock of the killing, she bullied the police into taking a statement from her. Her testimony exonerated Laverne and firmly contradicted everything that her husband had said, for she alone among the peace vigilantes had seen Alison being stabbed through the heart by a little old man.

Her eerie story was corroborated by science. A serologist, examining the distribution of the bloodstains on Laverne's clothes, backed the Superintendent's claim that he had not attacked Alison Reffel, but merely endeavoured to block her fatal wound with his hands. Dr Ernest Swallow, forensic pathologist, estimated that Alison Reffel had died of a single, powerful downward thrust from a sharp knife, which had severed her aorta. Judging by the angle of the wound, and the force with which it had been administered, the pathologist concluded that the attacker had held the murder weapon above his head with both arms fully extended before striking the fatal blow. Taking the victim's height into consideration, this meant that the murderer himself could have been no more than five feet two inches tall.

The investigating officers filed an interim report in which they stated, rather stuffily, that Laverne had been eliminated from their inquiries due to a 'paucity of evidence'.

After three weeks, the press hounds disappeared from

179

Laverne's door. The police guard dwindled to one officer, then none. Laverne sat at home, mostly alone. Dawn worked at the hospice four days a week. He had never spent so much time in the house without her before. He passed a great deal of time in silence, gazing out of the window, watching the grey days drift by. Slowly, he began to notice the world around him again; birds in the garden, dark hurtling clouds, the delicate branches of winter trees groping for the light.

He recognized that the continuing investigation into his alleged misconduct was nothing more than a formality. His employers had to be seen to take their time, before reaching the verdict they had reached already. His career was over, and he knew it.

Geraint dropped by one afternoon, told a lot of jokes, reminded Laverne of the fun they'd both had as rookies in Manchester. Neither man alluded to Laverne's predicament, but on his way out, Geraint, rather tactlessly, handed Laverne a worn paperback called *Enjoying Early Retirement*.

Dawn was concerned about him, but not afraid. She knew that he had to deal with pain in his own way. He had always hated fuss and attention. It was the same story whenever he was ill. He was like a sick animal that crawls away and hides itself until it recovers or dies.

She knew that he was too stubborn and strong to wither, or abandon hope entirely. He always had a new plan, some scheme that would get him out of trouble and make life worthwhile again.

His latest plan was that, with or without the police, he would destroy Hugo Prince.

He phoned Savage to ask for her impressions of the master of North Abbey. Had she met him yet? Embarrassed, she told Laverne that she couldn't discuss police matters with him, as he was now, technically, a member of the general public. This news came as a nasty surprise. Like most police officers, he had come to regard the general public as a rather unsavoury bunch.

His clothes and possessions were finally returned to him, having yielded nothing incriminating. Among them was the book that Alison Reffel had begged him to read: *My Life as a Kahuna* by the dubious-sounding Grandma May. Some of its pages were stained with blood. But although he burned his ruined clothes, he kept the book. On a cold afternoon in February, he settled by the fire, hot coffee at his elbow and the paperback on his lap.

There was an entire chapter on the Death Prayer. Laverne tried his best to read it. After a few sentences, he felt himself growing irritable; by the second page he was in the grip of mild nausea. The prose was cheap and cheerful, and the author's dictates so uniformly dogmatic that Laverne was forced to do the only decent thing. He hurled the book across the room.

But later, hoovering the car, he found a carrier bag on the back seat. He had forgotten all about it. The bag contained all the worldly belongings of Alison Reffel. A battered toilet bag; a few T-shirts; some socks, underwear, a box of sanitary towels; a worn kimono that Prince had probably bought for her. He held the garment against his face, inhaling the warm scent of her body again. And he came to a firm decision.

He recalled that Alison had spoken highly of the author of *My Life as a Kahuna*. Appreciating that without help he could never hope to snare Prince, Laverne re-entered the house. He walked over to a mahogany bureau, opened a drawer, and withdrew a pen and writing pad.

Then, with much groaning and crumpling of paper, he composed a letter to Grandma May, c/o The Talisman Press, Bristol.

At five o'clock he walked through swirling leaves to the post box at the end of the lane. As soon as he had dropped the letter through the slot and heard it fall, he felt a hot rush of shame. Slouching back to the cottage, he glumly wondered whether there was not something undignified, even effeminate, about appealing to a strange woman for help.

181

Two days later, he travelled into York and paid a visit to the city library, where he spent a morning among bored students and coughing pensioners, perusing a pile of stout historical reference books. In R. Doad's estimable *Ancient Guilds of England*, he found what he was looking for:

> In 1188, there occurred one of the most shameful episodes in York's history, when Rabbi David of Coney Street was stabbed to death in Marketshire (latterly known as Pavement), one of the city's two principal market places. The crime appears to have been motiveless; that is to say, no motive has been chronicled and passed down to us.
>
> The Rabbi's assassin was Thomas Northe, wool merchant, later knighted by King Richard I for his involvement in the third crusade. Northe's crime appears to have gone unpunished, apparently because of the unwillingness of the populace to bear witness against him. Arguably, Northe's action triggered an escalating climate of anti-Semitism, culminating in the infamous pogrom of 1190, in which the city's Jewish population was effectively wiped out. On his return from the Holy Land, Northe was to found his own masonic order. See: KNIGHTS OF CHRIST.

Laverne consulted the index, and turned to the appropriate page. This is what he read:

> The Knights of Christ, a lodge founded by Sir Thomas Northe in the last decade of the twelfth century, merits attention in that it brought the leaders of all York's masonic brotherhoods together under one banner, while leaving them free to preside over the business of their respective guilds. The tradition that the sect indulged in

pagan practices, including human sacrifice, is purely apocryphal. There is no record of the authentic Knights of Christ after the year 1348, when the black death ravaged the city, although various factions laying spurious claim to the title continue to surface from time to time.

Laverne returned to an empty house. It was Friday night; Dawn's evening shift at the hospice. She had left a scribbled message on a memo pad by the telephone. 'Ring May. Penzance 371010. PS. DINNER IN OVEN.'

This threw him into confusion. It was miraculous enough, given the inefficiency of the Royal Mail, that the letter had reached Grandma May at all, but the promptness of her response made him actively suspicious. He brewed himself a pot of tea and, mug in hand, seated himself by the phone. Then he practised lifting and replacing the receiver a few times before finding the resolve to make the call. The phone rang several times, then a woman answered, repeating the number he'd dialled. The voice was calm, elderly and, to Laverne's ears, quite accentless.

'May?' he said. 'Laverne, here.'

'Well, hello, Mr Laverne.' Warmth entered her voice. 'I was hoping it might be you.'

'You rang,' he blundered, 'so I suppose you got my letter.'

She laughed. 'Well, you did say you were a detective.'

He suddenly dried, having no idea what else to say to her. After a long silence, she spoke again. 'So dreadful about Alison. She was a lovely girl. She had such lovely ways. So of course I'd be happy to help you.'

'Oh, thanks. I'm grateful. What do you suggest, then?'

'I suggest you come down to Cornwall and stay with me for a day or two.'

'Cornwall? But that's miles away.'

'Yes. But won't it be worth it?' She sounded disappointed. 'I can't help you over the phone, I'm afraid. Not really.'

He considered this. 'I don't know ... I'll have to ask my wife.'

She brightened. 'Bring your wife, too. Come tomorrow.'

'Where do you live?'

She dictated an address in St Ives, Cornwall. Rather shell-shocked by her friendliness, Laverne wrote it down.

'Hadn't you better think about this?' he persisted. 'I mean – let's be honest – you don't even know me.'

'On the contrary, Mr Laverne. I feel I know you very well.'

There was a soft click as she replaced the receiver.

# Thirteen

At five in the morning, Laverne stowed a small case in the Rover's sizeable boot and set off for Cornwall. Frank Sinatra sang to him as he roared down the motorway in the dark. The album was *Songs For Swinging Lovers*, the only Sinatra album that Laverne could bear to listen to.

He had left Dawn, his own swinging lover, asleep in Huntington. She had been less than enthusiastic about his latest excursion. Although she made no attempt to keep him at home, Laverne thought she had looked at him strangely, just as Lyn Savage had done. It appeared that only the psychiatrists who had recently examined him were convinced of his sanity.

He broke his journey only once, stopping for brunch at a motorway service station outside Exeter, where he consumed a plate of chips and a slightly hostile steak and kidney pie. This was swilled down with a warm brown liquid that was sold as ground coffee, but seemed to contain more ground than coffee. After this triple insult to the palate, he visited the washroom to wash his hands, smooth back his hair and urinate, but not necessarily in that order. Then out into the drab late morning to refuel, consult *The AA Book of the Road*, and resume his journey.

The big, handsome automobile sailed effortlessly through the traffic. Laverne tried to enjoy the drive, but was dogged by a sense of irretrievable loss. He had last made this trip with his parents and his sister on a family holiday in the late fifties.

Death had taken them all, just as it had taken his son and Alison Reffel. The world was indifferent to their loss, just as one day it would be indifferent to his. Life was better suited to people like Hugo Prince, who could trample over the living and the dead without remorse. Imagine the strength in that; never to doubt or fall prey to pity or sentiment.

Laverne's bluff, uncivil manner managed to convince most observers that he was exactly what he appeared to be: a hard-headed Yorkshire bastard. But inside, Laverne was still that serious, overly sensitive boy playing on the shore, feeling inexplicably sorry for his parents as he watched them paddling in the sea. He scowled with self-reproach and beeped his horn at a perfectly innocent motor-cyclist. Vernon Laverne: the lady detective. Was it any wonder that Prince had run rings round him?

He reached St Ives by the early afternoon. The Rover seemed as wide and ungainly as a bus in the narrow, unaccommodating streets. Overhead, low clouds threatened rain and turned the water in the harbour black. Gaily painted boats rocked frenziedly on their moorings, as if in anticipation of some imminent disaster. Laverne followed the curve of the harbour to the end of Quay Street, then turned right on to Smeaton's Pier. With some reluctance, he parked his car under the sea wall at the mouth of the pier, among briny puddles and cobbles shiny with fish scales. Then he went in search of Grandma May.

She lived in a stout, whitewashed fisherman's cottage on three levels. The front entrance faced back down Quay Street, and anyone poised behind the net curtains in the sitting room would have had ample warning of Laverne's approach. He peered up at the veiled windows, detecting no movement behind them. Then he mounted a flight of stone steps that led to the front door. There was no doorbell, so he announced his presence with a stout brass knocker. No answer. He knocked again, but nothing stirred within. Despite her mystic powers of precognition, Grandma May had failed to predict his time of arrival. Feeling tired and grubby after his long journey, Laverne walked into the town.

The cobbles of Fore Street glistened wetly, Most of the shops were boarded up, and a mood of out-of-season gloom prevailed. He noticed a faded, sun-yellowed sign in a shop window: PLEASE DO NOT FEED THE SEAGULLS, AS THEY ARE BECOMING VERY AGGRESSIVE.

He entered a dark, empty café to order tea and a hot pasty from a downtrodden man in a baggy fisherman's sweater. Then he sat by the window, watching the passers-by; the locals, brisk and unattentive, and the visiting families plodding past in their cagoules and woolly hats. He bit into his pasty. It tasted of nothing but old age. He groped in his overcoat, and yanked out Grandma May's book, thinking to give it one last chance. But the chapter titles alone were enough to discourage him: 'Changing the Unwanted Future' and 'How to Work Miracles'. He closed the book and rammed it back into his pocket crossly.

He had to face it: the occult repelled him. Anything to do with magic and spirits made him sick and smacked of ignorance and self-deception. So why was he here? He sighed, knowing the answer. Because he had nowhere else to turn.

Laverne downed as much of the tea as he could stomach and stepped out into the windy street. He returned to the cottage and this time his knock was rewarded by the thud of feet on stairs. A handsome elderly woman opened the door. She had fine, bright, fearless eyes.

'Hello. Is May at home?'

With a smile and a nod, she admitted him to a pleasant, homely sitting room, full of cheap furniture that looked as if it dated back to the 1930s. A tall grandfather clock stood beside the entrance, as if on sentry duty. 'Is May at home?' he asked again.

'I'm May.' She grinned, offering her hand.

Suspicion must have shown on his face, for she added, 'Yes, I know. I'm not Hawaiian, or even half-Hawaiian. Blame my publisher for that. He thought I'd sell more books if I pretended I didn't come from Yorkshire.'

He smirked. 'Yorkshire?'

'Leeds, to be exact.'

'Know it well.'

'A right dump.'

'It could have been worse. You could have been born in Barnsley . . .'

'I *was* born in Barnsley.'

His face dropped. She looked indignant for a moment, and then burst out laughing.

He fetched his case from the car, and she showed him to his bedroom on the top floor. There was a single bed that was about two feet too short for him. May had disguised the chipped and tired seaside furniture with lace shawls and lengths of bright fabric. The room smelled faintly of sand and moth balls.

Outside his door was a second sitting room, with an awesome view across the bay to Godrevy Point. There was no sea wall to separate the cottage from the Atlantic – the cottage *was* the sea wall.

May threw open the windows, filling the room with the shriek of seabirds and the roar of the ocean. Cold fish-tainted air blasted Laverne's face as he watched the gulls hover and wheel above the turquoise waves. May studied his profile, liking the look of his worn, kindly face.

'Wind's playing up,' she remarked. 'High tide tonight.'

That evening, Laverne took May out to dinner. He had hoped to sample the local lobster, but she was a vegetarian, so they ended up in a small candle-lit bistro, dining on something called mushroom stroganoff. Apart from the waiter, the cook, and a solitary mumbling old man with a flat cap and a thick moustache, they were the only people in the restaurant.

'You're a big lad,' May pointed out amiably.

'I won't be for much longer if I carry on eating muck like this.'

She beamed, reminding him of a North American Indian

with her tanned, wrinkled face and her neatly bound and plaited white hair. 'Oh, stop your moaning. I'll cook you a proper Sunday lunch tomorrow.'

They were silent for a while. He toyed with his food unenthusiastically. Suddenly, May surprised him by saying, 'Yes. I'll mention it to him.'

Laverne wondered who she was talking to. She looked into his eyes. 'The god says you should eat more fresh vegetables.'

He tried not to mock, but his mouth sneered of its own accord. 'The god? What god?'

'The high self. The god. My god. Haven't you read my book?' She paused to cock her head on one side, attending to her inaudible, invisible companion. Then she cackled delightedly. 'Oh. It's like that, is it? The god says you think my book's rubbish.'

'Er . . .' He began to reply, then stopped himself. He was nettled by her play-acting. The woman hardly needed to be psychic to know that her book would appal him. One only had to look at his dour face, his sensible brown trousers and his fawn herring-bone jacket to see that he had never danced around a stone circle in his life.

She eyed him calmly. 'So you think I'm a fraud, do you?'

He returned her gaze steadily. 'You behave like one.'

She rolled her eyes light-heartedly. 'Oh, God. I can see you come from Yorkshire . . . All right. I'll tell you what I already know, shall I? You carry a great sorrow . . . Yes, you've known great sadness . . .'

This infuriated him. 'Oh, who the hell hasn't?'

She carried on as if he hadn't spoken. 'This is the picture I see. This is what the god is showing me. Stairs. A flight of wooden stairs. A little lad, a toddler, stands at the top of 'em. He misses his footing, the poor lamb. Down he falls, hitting every stair on the way.' Laverne felt an icy chill rising from the nape of his neck to the crown of his head. 'When he's at the bottom, he lies still, on his back. Just lies there. He isn't crying . . . he's too shocked for that. Then I see a lady, a dark lady, running down the hall to him. She's got a nice face. She's the little lad's mum.

'She bends over him. "Are you all right, love?" she says. "Does it hurt?"

'He doesn't answer, but his bottom lip is starting to tremble. She reaches out, gets ready to pick him up. She slips one hand under his knees, the other under his arms. I see a man coming down the stairs. A big man with a moustache. He can see what's about to happen. He yells, "No! No!"'

Laverne had turned grey. Slowly, he placed his knife and fork down on his plate. When he spoke, his voice contained a terrible weariness. 'All right. You've made your point.'

There was no need for her to continue. He knew this story all too well. How often had he sweated and anguished over that moment? For his warning had come too late. Dawn lifted Tom, and as she did so his head rolled back and dark blood spilled from his open mouth. The fall had broken his neck. Had Dawn left him lying there, and phoned for an ambulance, their son would still be alive today. Laverne did not blame his wife, but she had never forgiven herself.

'I'm sorry, Vernon,' said May. He could tell that she meant it. She reached over the table and placed her hand on his.

Afterwards, it was too cold and blustery to walk. They returned to May's kitchen to sip brandy by a real coal fire. She had been right about the high tide. The kitchen window had to be shuttered to keep out the boom and swash of the sea. To relax him, she talked about herself for a while. She had been married twice, and twice divorced. She had two children in their thirties, with families of their own. Framed photographs of unremarkable grandchildren were proudly displayed throughout the cottage.

In her youth, she had been a dancer. Looking at her strong-boned face, Laverne imagined that she had once been very beautiful. Then she showed him a photograph of herself, as a twenty-two-year-old chorus girl, and he saw that he was mistaken. She had always looked more or less the same, give or take a few wrinkles.

'When I gave up dancing, I became a medium,' she reminisced.

'Now you're an extra-large,' quipped Laverne.

'No, listen. I was a successful medium. People came from all over the world to contact their loved ones through me. But I quickly cottoned on to the fact that the messages those loved ones sent were either trivial or plain useless. Have you never noticed that? The kind of spirits that appear at seances might say, "I've got a message for Fred. Does he remember a green hat?" But they never say anything useful, do they? Or even intelligent. That's because the only spirits that appear at seances are low spirits, who love a joke at the expense of the living. They do. They enjoy buggering about. So I packed in mediumship, and went in search of a better class of ghost.'

She sipped her brandy and threw a fresh log on the fire. 'In the sixties, I went off to America, on a lecture tour organized by the American Spiritualist Society.'

'That spells ASS,' commented Laverne.

She laughed drily. 'You noticed. Anyway, it was then that I met my second husband, God rest him. A Hawaiian called Johnny Kim. It was Johnny who introduced me to Huna. And I knew I'd finally found what I was looking for. I've been a Kahuna ever since. Johnny was a very good teacher, by the way. One of his pupils has become quite famous since. A fella by the name of Hugo Prince.'

'Small world.'

'Not really. Johnny had a reputation and Prince was a rich man who sought him out. Prince learned what he could – although Johnny made him pay through the nose for it – and then Prince used what he'd picked up to start all this life healing nonsense.'

'Is it nonsense?'

'Of course it damn well is! Huna isn't about personal gain. It's about helping others. The ancient Kahunas were first and

191

foremost priests and healers. Prince has taken something worthwhile and made it trivial. Trivial.'

'And the Death Prayer?'

She looked him in the eyes. 'What about it?'

'Did your husband teach Prince the Death Prayer?'

'No! No way. Johnny followed the high self.'

'And you?'

Her nostrils flared. 'You've got a damn cheek asking me that. I've spent my life trying to help people . . .'

'All right,' said Laverne mildly. 'I only asked.'

She cupped her hands around the bowl of her glass, gently rotating the amber ring of brandy.

'You've got to bear in mind,' clarified Laverne, 'that to an ordinary person like myself, this is all a bit confusing. If I sound ignorant about your beliefs, it's because I am. All I'm sure of is that Hugo Prince is a murderer.'

She nodded. 'You're not wrong there. He's trying to murder you.'

The shutters rattled, as a huge wave crashed against the cottage wall. A cold draught broke into the room. The flames of the fire scraped and bowed. Laverne tried to make light of May's remark. 'Well, maybe not this minute . . .'

'Oh, yes. Now. There are three lost souls standing behind you, even as we speak. They follow you everywhere, you see. They'd like to curl up to you and kill you, because that's what they've been ordered to do. But they can't get close to you, you see, because your vital force is too strong. There's a great shield of light around you, keeping them off. No, I shouldn't imagine our friend Prince reckoned on that.'

'No,' said Laverne, his skin crawling. '"Never be without your shield of light." That's my motto.'

She chuckled appreciatively. 'You see? You're strong. That's a great bonus. But it's not your strength that protects you from the Death Prayer, my love. It's your clear conscience.'

'So I've been told.'

192

She knocked back her brandy. 'It's late. Better get some sleep. Tomorrow's a busy day. I'll get rid of those spirits for you in the morning. Just don't do anything you'll feel guilty about in the night . . .'

He awoke suddenly in the early hours, with the uncomfortable sense that there was someone at the foot of his bed. He raised his head from the pillow, and saw that the room was empty. The sea was now so loud that the waves seemed to have invaded his head and be breaking on the walls of his skull.

His throat was parched. He knew that he had overdone the brandy, and could feel neat alcohol buzzing in his veins. Knowing, from bitter experience, that the only antidote to this condition was pure water, and plenty of it, he roused himself and stumbled through the dark into the next room.

The uncurtained windows were humming ominously before the force of the sea wind. In the night beyond, the lighthouse on Godrevy Island winked calmly and methodically, its meagre beam no match for the overpowering blackness of the sky and the blind, relentless tide.

Shivering in the cold, Laverne crept down to the central floor and, tiptoeing past May's room, entered the bathroom to urinate. Then he descended to the kitchen, where the embers of last night's fire still glowed and smouldered in the grate. He turned on the light, and with his eyes screwed up, poured mineral water into a glass and gulped it down. Outside, a door or a loose shutter was banging monotonously. So this was what it was like to live by the sea in winter. Laverne found it all rather unsettling.

He turned off the light and trudged back to his room. But as he kicked off his slippers and drew back the sheets, he was surprised to see that he was already lying in bed, sleeping peacefully.

After breakfast, May and Laverne climbed the stairs to the second sitting room. May had brewed a second pot of coffee, and Laverne carried it up on a tray. After the rough night, the outer window panes were veiled with a fine mist of sand and sea-salt, giving May and Laverne a rather blurred view of the surrounding bay.

Laverne told her about the deaths of the unknown boy, and Anjali Dutt, his visit to North Abbey and the murder of Alison Reffel. She listened with surprising composure, taking care not to interrupt him. When he recounted his research into Thomas North and the Knights of Christ, she began to nod sagely.

'And now I'm suspended from duty, pending a full-scale inquiry into my past activities. I think it's safe to say that my career in the police is over.'

'Well . . .' She leaned forward to refill his coffee cup. 'You *are* in a bad way, love. Prince has blocked all your paths, you see. He knows what he's doing, that one. And you shouldn't underestimate him.

'I'll tell you why. We all have a high self, a guardian angel. The Hawaiians call this spirit the "aumakua". This angel might be a dead grandparent, or a complete stranger, but it's always someone who loves us and only wants the very best for us. That old man you saw in York Minster . . .'

'Thomas North.'

'That's right. Well, it's coming to me – and the god says I'm right – that the old gentleman is Prince's high self, or guardian angel. Only, in his case, angel isn't quite the right word. Old Thomas is completely evil. He's a demon. A guardian demon, if you like.'

'No,' said Laverne. 'I don't like.'

She narrowed her eyes, warming to her theme. 'So we're up against someone who derives power from suffering. That's what demons do, by the way. They thrive on cruelty and destruction. Prince won't stop, because he's set on becoming stronger. The more people he kills, the stronger he gets.'

She paused, listening. 'Wait. The god says you haven't told

me something important. Something else that happened in the cathedral. What was it?'

He racked his brains. 'I don't know.'

'Yes, you do.' She beamed. 'You've got a gift, you little devil. Why didn't you say so before? Eh? What are you capable of?'

He smiled back at her. 'Bugger all.'

'No. No. That's not true, is it? Tell me again. Tell me what you did when you saw the old man.'

'I've told you, I chased him.'

'What else?'

'I couldn't get near him. He got away . . .'

'Yes. But what else happened? What aren't you telling me?'

He examined the knuckles of his left hand, feeling vulnerable and awkward in the full glare of her attention.

'Vernon: *tell me*.'

He took a deep breath and looked her in the eyes. He had to drag the words out of himself.

'I left my body,' he said.

It had first happened during his son's funeral service. Confused and disorientated by grief, he had suddenly found himself walking down the aisle of Huntington Church, away from the mourners. The other Laverne, stolid and immaculate in his dark suit, remained in the front row, his arm around his sobbing wife. But he himself, this spirit or whatever he was, could bear the pain no longer. So he had walked home across the fields, passed through his own front door as if it were no more than a column of vapour. Then he had gone directly to Tom's room, to stare at the empty bed.

After a short time, he remembered Dawn, left alone in the church. Instantly, he was back at her side, gazing at a small pine coffin from behind his own living, chalk-white face.

In the weeks that followed, he took leave of himself often, sometimes without his knowledge. Twice, Dawn saw him standing beside their bed when he'd actually been downstairs, dozing in an armchair. His double always looked reassuringly solid; and had the same *presence* as the real Laverne, so Dawn was not unduly troubled by these occasional manifestations. In fact, she took comfort from them. For, she reasoned, if Vernon could exist outside his body, then so could her son.

Laverne, however, found the phenomenom disturbing, particularly when he was awake and fully aware of what was happening. At these times, he was able to see himself as others saw him. And the flesh-and-blood shell that he had vacated continued to function in his absence; walking, driving, holding sensible conversations, while he stood apart from it, a passive spectator. None of this made sense to him. He could not understand why the self he had left behind, robbed of its own essence, did not slump like an empty sack.

What disturbed him most was the world outside his body. For although it seemed to be the world he knew, comprising the same buildings, trees and people, his liberated spirit was aware of much that his corporeal self failed to detect. He saw, or rather sensed, that we are surrounded by invisible beings, not all of whom wish us well.

For over a decade Laverne made no further use of his flair for astral projection. With his large feet planted firmly on the ground, he rose in the ranks. He was a competent detective; not exceptional, but honest and thorough. In the mid-eighties, as Detective Chief Inspector Laverne, he was chosen to head the hunt for a brutal maniac who was terrorizing the race-courses of Yorkshire. The killer had a habit of stabbing middle-aged women and leaving their bodies in other people's cars.

When Laverne joined the inquiry, the man the press called the Racecourse Rapist had already claimed the lives of three women. During the next eighteen months he was to murder three more. Laverne interviewed a suspect called Rodney Carter, a pools winner who had been seen in the company of the last victim two days before her death, but Carter had an alibi for the day of her murder. Laverne thought the man was guilty, but had no evidence to hold him. Carter was released.

Under massive pressure to produce a result, Laverne decided to place Carter under supernatural surveillance. He left his body, and began to follow the suspect at every opportunity, finally capturing Carter in the process of torturing one of his many female admirers. Laverne promptly returned to his body and arrested Carter in time to save the woman's life. Carter was searched, and a shiny new screwdriver was found in the inside pocket of his blazer. This proved conclusive – three of the rapist's victims had died by having a screwdriver driven through their eye sockets.

Two years later, Laverne left his body again in an effort to capture the Bolton Strangler, but this time got nowhere. Then, when all seemed hopeless, Laverne was given the kind of tip-off that detectives dream of, and then only in their nightmares.

Driving past Norbury Church on that stormy night in October 1987, Vernon Laverne witnessed a sight that shattered his nerves. Lyn Savage, sitting at his side, saw nothing and would spend the rest of her life wondering what had led the Superintendent to stop outside that church.

Only his wife knew his secret, and now he was about to share it with another. This is Laverne's vision, as described to Grandma May.

By the roadside, in front of the churchyard gate, Laverne had seen seven small figures. A huddle of children, patiently awaiting his arrival, their clothes and hair unstirred by the rampaging wind. Although their faces were indistinct, Laverne recognized them instantly. Graham Allen. Mark Hendry. Lindsay Pike. Heather Knowles. Paul Richardson. Susan Hamer. Annette Ketley.

All the children killed by the Bolton Strangler.

'You couldn't go to them,' said May quietly. 'So they came to you.'

Laverne nodded. Outside the misty window, a gull cried, its voice an ugly complaint.

'That's right,' he said after a while, sipping his coffee and finding that it had gone cold. 'That was enough for me. I didn't want to see anything else like that.'

'Why? They were only children, weren't they?' He had no answer to this. 'So that was why you stopped leaving your body?'

'That's right. Apart from that time in the Minster, I haven't left my body for years. Not as far as I know, anyway.'

'What about last night?'

He smiled. 'How did you know that?'

She laughed. 'I know lots of things.' Without malice, she added, 'I also know how afraid you are. Afraid of your own spirit.'

This offended his manly pride. 'Damn right I'm afraid. All I ever wanted to be was an ordinary policeman.'

'And that's why, when you were chasing the Animal, you didn't leave your body once?'

'Correct.'

'And what happened?'

Laverne eyed her resentfully, almost choking on his reply. 'I didn't catch him.'

# Fourteen

She lived in the heart of Swaledale, on a once-thriving farm that the recession had reduced to a smallholding. In the four years since her husband's death, Kate Hibbett had been forced to sell off two-thirds of her land to neighbouring farmers. She had a son, Tim, who came home from university to help at the weekends, and a farm-hand who worked part-time, but she bore the brunt of the pressure herself.

And it showed. Sitting in her kitchen, gingerly sipping tea from the none-too-clean mug that she had given him, Merton thought she was looking old. She was in her mid-forties; darkly handsome, only slightly heavy about the hips. But the bags that had first appeared under her eyes after her husband's death had now become permanent features of her long, intelligent face.

'The problem with Chuck isn't health, Kate,' said Merton gently. 'I'm afraid it's age.'

Mrs Hibbett nodded hastily, to cover up her disappointment. Chuck was a Friesian, her best milker. Merton had been called out because the cow's yield had dropped drastically, in the hope, no doubt, that he could offer a more helpful diagnosis than the advance of time, for which there is no cure.

'It's up to you what you do about it, but I know a man who'd give you a fair price for her.'

She nodded.

To soften the blow, Merton said, 'As for the fee, pay me when you can.'

She gave him a tired smile. 'It'll have to be eggs again.'

'Eggs'll be fine.' It was Merton's antiquated policy to accept payment-in-kind from clients of modest means. There had been a lot of real hardship in the Dales since the mid-eighties. Merton's willingness to barter may not have pleased his accountant, but it kept his fridge well stocked with fresh dairy produce.

He got up to leave, almost tripping over a wooden crate, piled high with old empty bottles. The same crate, containing the same bottles, had been a feature of the woman's kitchen for as long as he remembered.

His eyes fell upon a double-barrelled shotgun protruding from a bucket in the corner. Both gun and bucket were thickly coated with dust.

'Tim not here?' he enquired.

'Not this weekend. He's gone canoeing.'

'Canoeing, eh?' Merton could think of nothing to say about this. Water sports bored him. 'But Matthew's back tomorrow?'

'No. He's put his back out. I'm all on my own next week. Unless you're volunteering?'

She laughed to show that this was a joke. He said goodbye to her at the door and waded through the muddy yard to the waiting Land-Rover.

The Merry Maidens are nineteen upright stones. They stand in a circle, in an unassuming field, on the edge of a winding country road that links Penzance with Land's End. The Maidens pre-date Christ by approximately two and a half thousand years, but to be in their company is to lose interest in time itself.

Laverne was impressed by the monoliths, and the sense of gentle promise that seemed to emanate from them. The same quiet goodwill seemed to waft across the surrounding fields towards him, washing over him in sweet, subtle waves.

May beamed up at him. 'Can you feel it?' she said.

'Yes.' He smiled back at her. 'Whatever it is, I feel it.'

'Just to remind you, that not all spirits are capable of

200

murder. We're in good company, here. We're being watched. But only by those who wish us enlightenment.'

'Whatever that means,' said Laverne, accidentally lapsing into his habitual cynicism.

A Bedford van trundled by, travelling west. Its engine harummed and laboured as it reached the incline in the road. Laverne watched the van until it had passed out of sight. In this landscape, even the sight of an unroadworthy vehicle climbing a hill seemed faintly magical.

Abruptly, May said, 'You've got a special talent, Vernon. You *must* use it.'

She had been nagging him all the way from St Ives. 'Some talent,' he retorted sourly.

'Yes! Yes! A God-given talent! We are all made up of three spirits: a low, a middle and a high spirit. But when *your* spirit travels, it travels as three-in-one. Your *whole self* is present. Don't you see how special that is? Most of us only achieve that state when we die.'

Laverne shrugged. 'What about the spirits that Prince has got working for him? They've died, haven't they?'

'They've died, all right, but they aren't whole spirits. They're low spirits, snared by magic. You've heard of poltergeists? That's another name for low spirits. They're noisy, stupid, and when they're controlled by a man like Prince, they're downright nasty.'

Laverne rested his hand on one of the Maidens. It was a cold morning, but the green, fragrant stone was warm to the touch. He looked at May for a long time. 'All right,' he said eventually. 'But where the hell does he get these low spirits from?'

'He takes them from those he kills ... Or people on the brink of death.'

'How?'

'The low self is highly suggestible. It can't reason very well, so it can easily be bribed, flattered and, in time, completely dominated. A bit like a pet dog. Once it's in your power, you

201

can make it do more or less anything. And like a dog, it loves to show off.'

Laverne listened in silence. There had certainly been more than a touch of exhibitionism to the recent murders. As they walked back to the road, May tapped his arm.

'And another thing, Prince is arrogant. That's a weakness, even for a black magician. He imagines he's above the law. That leads me to think the law is the best way to trap him.'

'You're forgetting one thing, May. I don't represent the law any more. The police are about to give me the boot.'

'Don't let them!' she snapped. 'Remind them how good you are.'

Laverne laughed bitterly. 'How?'

He helped May over the stile in the hedge. When she was on the ground, she kept hold of his hand and stared into his eyes. 'That's what I'm about to tell you, if you'll just listen. Tomorrow night, that man's going to kill again.'

'What man?'

'The man you couldn't catch . . . the Animal.'

Laverne began to mouth an objection, but the expression on her face silenced him.

'I've seen the future, Vernon. I know the name of his victim. I've seen the future and she dies tomorrow night.'

Laverne was exasperated.

'Even if you're right, what the hell can I do about it? If it's in the future, it's already happened.'

She folded his hand in both of hers and squeezed. 'Vernon, love. Don't you understand? You're no ordinary man. You're a Kahuna. A shaman. A holy man. You have the power to *change* the future.'

It was just after midnight and Geraint John was on his third double malt. He was at home, curled up in his favourite armchair, watching a video of *Where Eagles Dare*. He had last seen it at the pictures, years ago, and was surprised how banal

202

it now seemed. Had he matured? Or simply grown too world-weary to be entertained?

His wife was already asleep. He was listening to the film on headphones so as not to blast her out of bed with the sound of machine-gun fire. He was watching Clint Eastwood gun down a load of gullible Nazis when he glanced up and saw Laverne standing beside his chair. His entire body jolted in surprise. He snatched off the headphones.

'Fuck me! Where did you spring from?'

Laverne raised an apologetic hand. 'Sorry, sorry. I did knock, but no one answered.'

'What the fuck's so important that you have to come round at this time. Eh?'

'I need to talk to you, Geraint.'

John wavered. Then, seeing the warmth in Laverne's face, he relented. 'All right. Sit yourself down. But you can't just walk into folks' houses like that, Vernon. It's not nice.'

Laverne nodded in friendly agreement and seated himself on a dainty sofa. John shook his head in a half-admonitory, half-drunken fashion. 'Not nice at all,' he repeated.

'I know. Sorry. But this couldn't wait. I need your help, Geraint. The Animal is going to kill again. I know the victim's name. I know her name and she dies tomorrow night.'

John looked to Heaven for support. 'Vernon, Vernon—'

'You've got to believe me. I know the victim's name.'

'Oh, stop it. Please. If you could only hear yourself . . .'

The Deputy Chief Constable was beginning to get worried. There was a look of calm sincerity on Laverne's face that he had never seen before. To Geraint John, it looked like the unflappable benevolence of a religious zealot. Or the thin fixed smile of a maniac.

'I'm right about this, Geraint. Just as I was right about the Rapist and the Strangler. You've always wondered how I caught them. That's what I'm here to tell you . . .'

Geraint took a sip of his malt – it suddenly tasted foul. He placed the glass down on the coffee table. What did one do with madmen? Hit them? Offer them tea or coffee? No. Keep them talking.

'Go on, then. Tell me.'

'I can leave my body. I know it sounds daft, but my soul can leave my body.'

This struck John as so preposterous that he instantly forgot his plan to humour Laverne. 'Vernon: I'm not listening to this. No. I'm not listening. Go home and have a nice long sleep.'

'Her name's Katherine Hibbett. She lives in Swaledale.'

'Of course she does. Now go home and take a couple of aspirin. Take a whole fucking bottle ... No. I don't mean that ...'

Laverne arose, and slowly moved towards the door. Geraint also ascended, walking a little way behind Laverne to shepherd him out. After a few paces, Laverne turned, smiled, and left the room. But he didn't leave by the door. He walked right through the wall. Or, to be precise, Laverne *collapsed* into the wall, becoming one with it.

Geraint John staggered back, his scalp crawling, his breath coming in short, anxious gasps. 'Fuck! Fuck!'

He heard a voice. His wife had awoken and was calling him from the landing. 'Geraint? Who's there?'

He walked out into the hall, half-expecting to see Laverne standing there, pointing a phantasmal finger at him like Marley's ghost. The hall was empty. 'Only the telly, love,' he shouted. 'I've turned it off, now. Go back to sleep ...'

He re-entered the living room, picked up the telephone and dialled Laverne's number. Almost immediately, the phone was answered and he heard a familiar voice say, 'Yes?'

John exhaled noisily. This seemed to clinch it. Laverne lived miles away. There was no way he could have got home in such a short space of time. 'Vernon. Oh, thank fuck for that ...'

The voice on the end of the line said, 'You didn't imagine

204

it, Geraint. You wanted to know my secret, and now you do. I can leave my body.'

Geraint shook his head, forgetting that Laverne couldn't see him. 'Oh, no. No.'

'Her name's Katherine Hibbett. Help me to find her.'

Prince laid his hand on Yolande's brow and waited.

They were in the chapel at North Abbey. She was seated, and he was standing over her. Her eyes were closed and she was breathing deeply. Prince watched her, coldly, his mouth twisted in a half-sneer. She was more than his ally and consort. She was his medium, and her psychic gifts had already served him well. It had been Yolande who had warned him that Laverne was not at North Abbey to sell insurance. She had supplied him with his name, rank and true purpose.

Laverne was on Prince's mind. The policeman may have been dishonoured, but he was still alive. And Prince could not forget New Year's Eve, or the blinding flash of light as the mana equivalent of one thousand volts had sent him sprawling. No. The man was dangerous.

As he watched, Yolande entered a trance. Her breathing became deep and regular. Then she began to tremble.

'Yes? What do you see?'

'I see him.'

'The policeman?'

'Yes.'

'What's he doing? Does he still hunt me?'

There was a silence. Yolande's head lolled from side to side as if she'd just downed a bottle of Scotch. Impatiently, Prince repeated his question.

'No,' she said eventually. 'He hunts another.'

'What other? My ancestor? Does he hunt Thomas?'

'No. Another.'

'Who? I need a name. Give me a name.'

A pause. She said, 'I cannot see. He hides himself too well.'

*

It had started during the breakdown of his marriage. Just to see what it felt like, he had picked up a young male hitch-hiker in Wensleydale, drugged him and removed his innards while he was still alive. Then he had buried the body in the garden of an old lady he did odd jobs for. That had been eight years ago. No one had ever reported the youth missing, or surmised that the Animal (a strangely apposite name for a veterinary surgeon) had claimed ten victims, not nine.

Merton compared himself, with some amusement, to the serial killers he had read about in books, and seen portrayed in gory, exploitative films. An American behavioural scientist had even appeared on television to offer a 'psychological profile' of the Animal. Merton had watched the programme and been mildly surprised to learn that he had been sexually abused as a child, suffered from a speech impediment and found it difficult to make friends.

In fact, James Merton was widely liked, loved even, both in Swaledale and his native Doncaster. People trusted him. It was true that he had few close friends; but he was hardly the brooding, maladjusted loner of serial killer mythology. Nothing in his past could account for his barbarous crimes. His parents had been no more inadequate and insensitive than anybody else's parents.

After the death of Mrs Standring, he was interviewed by the policeman who was leading the inquiry, a man called Laverne. Merton had liked him, and suspected that the feeling was mutual.

During their chat, Merton told Laverne that he'd taken Betty Standring a food parcel on the night of her death, as he did every week. He had always given her food, rather than money, because when she had cash she tended to fritter it away on booze. At this point, Merton had wept so convincingly that Laverne had offered him his own handkerchief and promptly left, never to return, instructing a WPC to take his statement.

In truth, Merton had never felt pity for any of his victims.

Even as he held their severed and dripping organs before their screaming faces, the sheer awfulness of what he was doing had always failed to move him.

Yet Merton did not believe that he was a monster. Rather, he saw himself as an exceptionally well-rounded individual. He did not despise humanity. Nor did he despise himself. Merton loved, grieved, laughed, worried and struggled in the normal human way. It just so happened that, from time to time, he liked to take people apart, slowly and with unbelievable cruelty, making sure that they felt everything.

But he was kind to children and animals.

# FIFTEEN

As Geraint John's black Daimler inched down the narrow, twisting track to Roseberry Farm, the light was fading and the snow that had been steadily falling from mid-afternoon was beginning to stick. John turned to Laverne and gave him a slightly apologetic smile.

'The last one on the list, flower. If this one's no good, we've had it. For today, at any rate. I don't fancy being stranded in a winter-fucking-wonderland.'

Laverne bit his lip, watching the sweep of the windscreen wipers. There were fresh tracks in the road ahead. Tyres with a heavy tread had only recently passed this way.

'Don't you think we should forget it?' urged the Deputy Chief Constable. 'There's always tomorrow.'

'Not for this woman there isn't,' said Laverne. 'Not if we don't find her.'

All day they had searched the farms and villages of Swaledale. Nowhere, not in one of its modest grey-brown sandstone houses, had they found a woman by the name of Katherine Hibbett. An Amelia Hibbert, aged ninety-three, and a family of rather fat Hibbards from Reeth, but no Katherine.

Geraint took a small square flask from his thick overcoat and removed the stopper with his teeth. Then, one hand on the wheel, he took a mouthful of rum.

'You shouldn't drink and drive,' said Laverne.

John half-laughed. 'What are you planning to do? Breathalyse me?'

He offered the flask to Laverne, who hesitated, and then took a modest swig. The rum vouchsafed him a moment of well-being; an instant surge of alcoholic enlightenment, worthless, forgotten as soon as it is experienced.

They reached the end of the track and turned left into a bleak farmyard. The farmhouse itself looked squat, desolate, and unoccupied. The tyre tracks they had been following circled the building in a wide arc, taking the vehicle that made them out of sight. The Daimler came to a halt.

Geraint stopped the engine. For a while, absolute silence reigned. Then, two bedraggled Alsatians emerged from a dingy barn and raced towards the car, barking and fretting.

'Mad dogs. That's all we need,' grumbled John. 'Where did you get this woman's name from, anyway? A Christmas cracker?'

'How many more times, Geraint? I got the name from someone I trust.'

'What? Someone you met when you left your body, was it?'

'No.'

'Oh, I see. They left their body to come and chat to you, did they?' John tutted in disapproval. 'I've never heard anything like it . . .'

'I take it you don't believe what you saw last night?'

Geraint gave a half-shrug that turned into a shudder.

A little sadistically, Laverne said, 'Maybe you'd care for another demonstration?'

Geraint John sat up sharply in his seat and waved his gloved hand at Laverne, as if warding off evil spirits. 'No, no. You're all right. I believe you.' But he could not resist adding, 'Fuck knows why.'

They left the car and locked it. The Alsatians ceased to bark and began to claw and paw at their legs, whimpering mournfully. Geraint John, afraid of getting dog hairs on his new tweed trousers, pushed them away. 'Off! Get off! You bloody things.'

The front entrance faced them; a green door with flaking paint, nestling beneath a crude arch. Above the arch, a date was stamped into the stone: 1875. The small, ungenerous windows were dark and seemed to shout, 'No one home.' But from the chimney above, a trail of dirty brown smoke spiralled up to meet the descending snowflakes.

'Go on, then.' With a hint of belligerence, John nodded towards the green door, implying that although he was willing to act as Laverne's chauffeur, he was buggered if he was going to debase himself by enquiring after a woman who probably didn't exist anyway.

Raising a gloved fist, Laverne prepared to knock. Then he paused. He'd heard something. A glance at Geraint's face confirmed that he, too, was aware of the sound; a high-pitched, harrowing wail that rose and fell, outraging the beauty of that quiet winter landscape.

'It's a cat,' said Geraint, uncertainly. 'Isn't it?'

They listened. After a lull, the noise resumed, this time tailing off into emotional shouts of abuse. It was a woman's voice. 'Leave me alone, you bastard! No! No!'

The dogs bared their teeth, their hackles rising.

'We'll split up,' hissed Laverne. 'You go round the back . . .'

The DCC vacillated for a moment. He hadn't seen active service for years, and suddenly felt a nostalgic longing for the warm, snug office where he spent most of his working life. Laverne, reading John's face, said, 'You and me together, eh? Just like the old days . . .'

John looked unconvinced. But he gave Laverne a brave smile, and vanished round the side of the building, pursued by the dogs. Without ceremony, Laverne approached one of the lower windows and punched a hole through the pane.

Hearing the umistakable sound of breaking glass, Merton stopped what he was doing and listened.

'What was that?'

Afraid of being hurt again, Kate Hibbett said nothing, merely shook her head. They were in the kitchen. Merton was wearing one of the heavy cotton aprons that he used for surgery. Mrs Hibbett, stripped to her underwear, was bound to the kitchen table by an elaborate system of cords and ropes, her arms and legs trussed tightly together and fully out-stretched. Her face was tear-stained and bloody. In order to subdue her, violence had been necessary. Her mouth was gashed and swollen. There were fresh symmetrical slash wounds on either side of her face – her punishment for resisting, a mere overture before the real entertainment began.

In his bones, he had felt that the time was right. Murder is not a random event; it adheres to its own calendar. There are, there have to be, preordained moments when the world thinks only of itself, closing its eyes and ears so that people like Merton can go about their business uninterrupted. This was such a moment: he had been certain of it. Here was a woman living alone, without a telephone, on a day when police were advising motorists to stay at home. Merton had driven here in the belief that he would not be seen, that no one else would venture up here in such weather for fear of being stranded, and that after his departure, the steadily falling snow would cover his tracks.

But now, hearing the window shatter, he experienced the first hot stirrings of panic.

'You're lying.' Harshly, he squeezed the woman's face in one hand and held the long serrated blade of his shark knife over her eyes. 'Who is it?'

'I don't know ... It could only be a burglar ... I don't know.' She was acting humble, but he thought he could discern hope in her eyes, and the sight infuriated him. He plunged the knife into the table beside her head, where it quivered momentarily before coming to rest. Then he walked across to the rocking chair where the woman's rifle lay.

On closer inspection, this had turned out to be a quality weapon; a Browning trap gun, a twelve-bore. There were only two rounds of ammunition, but he had loaded the gun anyway, as a precaution. Now he snatched it up, flicked off the safety catch and walked over to the kitchen door. He paused, listened, but could hear nothing but his own breathing and the dogs barking in the yard.

He edged out into a small, grubby hallway. Bulging boxes of old books and magazines were stacked high against the damp walls. The house had not been properly cleaned for years. There was only one door leading off from the hall, and it was wide open. Merton thought this door had been closed when he'd arrived, but couldn't be certain. He took a deep breath and nimbly stepped into a large front room.

And found no one.

Peering through the gloom, he saw more junk-filled cardboard boxes and, on the shabby sofa, huge jars crammed with coins, badges and buttons. On a low coffee table at his feet lay three packets of biscuits, all opened, and a half-eaten bar of Cadbury's Fruit and Nut. Anyone who lived like this, thought Merton, deserved to die.

An Arctic breeze sliced through the room, ruffling his hair. He walked over to the broken window, his feet grinding glass into the carpet. Someone else was in the house. There was no doubt about it. He returned to the doorway and listened. From overhead, he thought he detected the barest whisper of movement. Eager not to advertise his progress by tripping over the heaps of rubbish, he crept to the foot of the stairs and started to climb.

The daylight was fading, but the glare of the snow poured through the narrow window at the top of the stairs, filling the house with a spectral glow. Merton had almost reached the landing when something, a subtle shift in the light, caused him to look up. As he raised his head, a large brown object sailed over the banister rail on the landing and smashed into his face, knocking him off balance. It was a heavy cardboard box which split open as it hit him, scattering cookery books down the stairs.

At the moment of impact, the gun went off. A shot thundered through the cottage, blasting a hole in the wall at the top of the stairs. A mound of plaster broke loose and clattered to the floor. Smoke and the smell of cordite filled the air. Before the sound of the shot had died away, Laverne himself leapt over the banister, knocking Merton backwards and bouncing down the stairs on top of him as if the murderer was a human sled.

The two men fell heavily into the hall, where they rolled, struggling for possession of the firearm, an awkward, ungainly mass of flailing limbs. There was a crash from the kitchen. Geraint John ran into the hall and, standing over the grunting, tangled bodies, administered several hefty kicks to Merton's ribs with his size twelves.

'Out of the way!' shouted Laverne. 'He's armed!'

The DCC ignored this advice and recklessly tried to wrench the firearm from Merton's fingers. With another deafening roar, the trap gun released its second round. Geraint John made no sound apart from a muffled 'Uh!' as blood and raw meat sprayed out of his midriff. Then he fell sideways and crashed to the ground.

Laverne relinquished his hold on Merton and ran to Geraint's aid. The big man's face had turned white, and he was clutching his guts with both hands. His expensive suede driving gloves were soaked in gore.

Helplessly, he stared into Laverne's eyes, trying to speak. 'The . . . fucking . . . bastard . . .'

Laverne felt a rush of cold air on his neck. Merton had left by the front door. At that precise moment, Laverne didn't care. His only immediate concern was rushing Geraint and the woman to a hospital.

Merton didn't get far. As he reached the Land-Rover, he saw Mrs Hibbett's Alsatians hurtling over the snowy yard towards him. He fumbled for his car keys and, in his haste, dropped them. Softly, without a sound, the keys landed in the snow, where they were to remain for another twelve hours, until the police, their path cleared by a snow plough, pulled into the farmyard. There they discovered, lying beside his Land-Rover, the frozen, half-eaten body of James Merton, the Animal.

# Sixteen

Laverne's return to work was a quiet affair. Not, however, as quiet as he would have liked. On his first morning, the press were waiting for him in the police car park. Dolefully, he grimaced for the cameras. Walking out of the elevator on to the top floor, he was relieved to find the corridor empty. But as he neared the door to his office, a pretty young detective leaned out of a doorway to give him a shrill wolf-whistle. Laverne wouldn't have minded, but the officer concerned was male.

Savage was alone in his office, waiting for him. As he entered, she rose to her full height, which brought her eyes about level with his chest. She smiled at him and her face literally shone with happiness. Embarrassed, not wanting a fuss, Laverne said, 'Hello, Lyn,' and proceeded to hang up his coat.

Then he turned back to Savage, who was still smiling. Not being able to help herself, she walked into his arms and held on to him. He returned the embrace, feeling the warmth and softness of her body and remembering, a little uncomfortably, that she was a good-looking woman as well as a first-class police officer.

They were still hugging each other when the partition door creaked open and Mills poked his face into the office. Laverne glanced at him, and winked. Mills smirked, his face turning red. 'I was going to suggest we started the meeting, but I can, er, see you're not quite ready.'

Savage waved him away. The door closed. There was a burst of ribald laughter on the other side of the partition.

Laverne thought he heard Mills say, 'They're having a shag in there.'

He and Savage disentangled themselves. Laverne saw her wipe one of her eyes with the back of her hand, but pretended not to notice.

'Well, Lyn,' he said. 'I'm a few months late, but I'm making a New Year resolution. From now on, I promise to listen to everything you say.'

She gave him a playful punch in the belly. 'You'd better, buster. You'd damn well better.'

She smoothed down her jacket and Laverne, feeling like a small child about to take centre stage at the school concert, adjusted his tie. Savage saw what he was doing, tutted and, slapping his hands away, readjusted the knot. 'It was all right to begin with. Now you've made it all crooked . . .'

When she was satisfied with his appearance, she took him by the arm. 'Are you ready?'

He tried to think of something amusing to say; something wittier than 'Ready as I'll ever be.' But nothing came to mind, so he simply smiled and nodded. Savage opened the door to the murder room, and he followed her inside.

Immediately, Laverne realized he'd been tricked. As he entered the room, there was a loud popping sound, and Lawless proceeded to christen Laverne and Savage with champagne from a foaming gold-labelled bottle. The team, all present and correct, began to cheer and Lawless ran to a table covered in a white linen cloth, where he poured the champagne into glasses. WPC Robinson, opening a sister bottle with rather more care than Lawless had displayed, came to his assistance. In the centre of the table was a large rectangular cake. Written across its white surface, in blue letters, was the word LEADER.

After twenty minutes of restrained merrymaking, Geraint John appeared, leaning on a stick. He looked pallid and gaunt. He had only recently been allowed home, after spending six weeks in hospital. Merton's bullet had blown away a third of

215

his stomach and on its way out, for good measure, had dislodged one of his spinal vertebrae. It now seemed likely that he would always walk with a limp. Or, as he himself put it, 'a fucking limp'.

The DCC had not yet returned to work. This was a special visit, in Laverne's honour. At the sight of Geraint John, Laverne went very red in the face and the two men clasped hands like old comrades-in-arms.

'This bugger saved my life,' Geraint informed Savage.

'It was this bugger that put your life in danger in the first place,' Laverne reminded him.

It had been a close call. Laverne had carried the wounded DCC out to the car, leaving a trail of blood in the snow, and gone back for the shocked Katherine Hibbett. Then he had driven them both away, unwittingly leaving James Merton to bleed to death behind the farmhouse.

After riding through a blizzard at insane speed, they had arrived at casualty in Richmond, only to be told by hospital staff that supplies of Geraint John's blood type, O, were running low. By chance, Laverne was in the same blood group, so he acted as a donor. When he'd recovered consciousness, Geraint John maintained that 'O' stood for 'outstanding'. The two men had always been friends and allies. Now they were blood brothers.

'I suppose you've heard the rumours?' said John.

'What rumours?'

'Merton's brother is talking about suing us.'

Laverne and Savage roared with laughter. Geraint laughed also, until pain made him grasp his belly. 'No,' he continued, 'I'm serious. He wants to do us for criminal negligence. He thinks we deliberately left his brother to die.'

Laverne smiled grimly. 'We would have done, if we'd known he was there.'

Later in the day, Laverne set up his trusty projector in the office and Lyn Savage talked him through a fresh set of slides.

216

An x-ray of a femur appeared on the screen. The bone had broken into hundreds of intricate fragments.

'Is this still Anjali Dutt?'

'No,' said Savage. 'We're on Derek Tyreman now.'

He had been slouching in his chair, but this news made him lean forward. 'What? That's Tyreman?'

She flashed to the next slide, which showed the bone in relation to the pelvis. The femur had been massively dislocated. 'We weren't expecting this, because he died quietly, in his sleep. The fractures and dislocations just appeared. But they had nothing to do with the cause of death . . .'

'Which was heart failure,' said Laverne, grimly.

She nodded, and turned on the light. 'Apoplexy, causing a massive pulmonary embolism, according to the death certificate.'

'Clap-trap,' scoffed Laverne. 'What about Sheelagh Daye?'

'Some even bigger words that mean more or less the same thing. Her heart stopped beating.'

'It happens to the best of us, Inspector.'

Savage and Laverne studied each other in silence.

Laverne said, 'When I told you that Hugo Prince was killing people with a curse called the Death Prayer, you had visions of me being wheeled about in a bath-chair with a blanket over my knees. Admit it.'

'I admit it.'

'And what do you think now?'

'Vernon: I honestly don't know what to think.'

'Come on, you must have formed some opinion. You've met Prince, haven't you?'

'Yes.'

'What did you make of him?'

'He was very charming, took great pains to enquire after your well-being. He said he was very sorry about Alison Reffel's death and hoped it wasn't true that you'd murdered her.' Laverne made a low sound in his throat that was almost a growl. 'If you're asking me what we can prove, I have to say "nothing". But if you want to know what I actually *think*, it's that he's as guilty as hell. But what do we do about it?'

Laverne waited for her to continue. Savage sighed and fidgeted, finding the conversation difficult. 'If Prince is really cursing people to death – and I stress the word *if* – well, it isn't a police matter. Sorcery is outside our jurisdiction. The Witchcraft Act was repealed in 1735.'

'1736,' stated Laverne, quietly.

That night, while Dawn was out visiting a neighbour, Laverne left his body. With the lights turned low, he lay on his back in front of the living-room fire, a cushion under his head. He began to breathe deeply and regularly and with his eyes open tried to imagine himself floating up towards the ceiling. A minute passed, and then everything began to glow with a subtle golden light. He felt his physical self growing numb, and a strange euphoria possessed him as his soul began to rise. Then he was drifting, lighter than air, and seen through the eyes of the spirit, the room around him, including the rather haggard-looking body he had just vacated, seemed to quiver with a vivid, vibrant energy.

Then, faster than the speed of thought, he was in St Ives, on the steps of May's cottage. Silently, he passed into the house, walking straight through the front door. He could easily have walked through the wall, but he felt it was more polite to use the door.

The cottage lights were on, but May seemed to be out. He wandered from room to room, appearing and disappearing, until he heard a voice calling from the bathroom. 'Vernon? I'm in here . . .'

The bathroom door was open. The room itself was dark, but light poured in from the landing. Gingerly, he entered and found May lying in a bubble bath. Embarrassed, he apologized and turned to leave. She called him back.

'Don't be daft. I don't mind.'

'You don't seem surprised to see me.'

'The god told me you were on your way. You got my letter, I take it?'

'Yep, I did. And thanks. You said some nice things.'

'I meant every word. I'm proud of you. And your spirit's looking good, too. Very solid.' She extended a foam-covered arm and prodded his leg. 'Feels solid, too. Very good. I'm impressed. That's a real skill you've got there. Some people look like ghosts when they leave their bodies. But I can't tell you from the real you.'

He beamed. 'Which one *is* the real me?'

'Both. And neither. We exist on many levels.'

He sighed. Whether he was in his body or out of it, her capacity for mystical gobbledegook continued to annoy him. 'I came to see if you had any more suggestions. After all, I've done pretty well out of you so far. But I'm still no closer to building a case against Prince. We know he's behind it all, but the actual murders are committed by ghosts. Ghosts tend to be a bit elusive when you try to bring them in for questioning . . .'

She held up a hand to silence him. 'Shhh . . . the god's talking to me. He keeps saying, "Baby, baby." Somehow, I get the feeling that he isn't singing a pop song.' She sat up in the bath, examining him with her fine, piercing eyes. 'He says, "Ask him about the baby." Does the word "baby" mean anything to you?'

There was no need for Laverne to answer. The look on his face told her all she needed to know.

Three nights later, Laverne and his wife attended a dinner in aid of the Police Benevolent Fund. The function was held in York, at the Merchant Adventurers' Hall on Fossgate. There was, of course, no connection between the building's history of masonry and the considerable police presence there that night.

Laverne, stiff and uncomfortable in a dinner jacket, was the guest of honour. He and Dawn sat at the top table. On his

219

left were Geraint John and his wife, Fran. To Laverne's right sat the President of the Police Federation. Then the President's husband. Next, Lyn and Ian Savage. Laverne noticed that Ian was having difficulty smiling but, not being a jealous man himself, had no idea why.

Geraint John was not really well enough to be there, but pride had forced him to make the effort. And not just pride in himself. Vernon Laverne had stopped another killer, and only he, out of all the officers present, knew how and why. This secret knowledge made him feel even more superior than usual.

Now and then, the big man winced and his spouse insisted on fussing over him, thereby drawing unwanted attention to his infirmity. He merely toyed with his main course (Beef Wellington). He had no appetite. Since the operation, his insides felt as if they belonged to someone else. But at least, after the dessert was out of the way, the DCC received a standing ovation and was given the opportunity to say what he had been yearning to say all night: 'Ladies and gentlemen, detectives amongst you will already have noticed the suspicious-looking character on my right . . .'

Laverne arose, more flushed with shame than pride. The diners, despite the dead weight in their bellies, also stood and applauded for three full minutes, bringing tears to Dawn's eyes, and a sceptical glint to Laverne's. He had not forgotten that a few months ago many of the people cheering him now had written him off.

When the applause had subsided, he looked down at the crumpled sheet of foolscap where the main points of his 'speech' were listed, and read: 1) DRUNK, GOOD TO BE.

'Thank you, everybody,' he began. 'It's good to be here. Let's be honest; if you're as drunk as we are, it's good to be anywhere . . .'

This unremarkable pleasantry was rewarded with a roar of laughter, proving that the company was indeed as drunk as he'd alleged. As he spoke, he became aware of a mild floating sensation and the faces around him were bathed in golden light. And then, unseen by any of the diners, with his own voice ringing in his ears, Laverne's spirit floated out of his body, out of the Great Hall, and up into the night sky above the city of York.

# Seventeen

Hugo Prince was in the library at North Abbey, spending a quiet evening with a bottle of good Cognac and his cherished books. He collected Grimoires and Occult First Editions, and the manuscript now resting on his lap was priceless: *The Book of the Sacred Magic of Abra-Melin the Mage*, recently stolen from the Bibliothèque de l'Arsenal in Paris by the spirits in his charge. That, Prince reflected, was the odd thing about low spirits: when directed by a Master, or merely someone they liked, they were capable of truly astonishing feats. Left to their own devices, they wasted their time throwing pebbles and making tedious rapping noises.

Abra-Melin had taught that the prerequisite of successful magic was getting acquainted with one's Holy Guardian Angel. It fascinated Prince; the way that the concept of the high self was to be found in all cultures. Prince's French was not good, and to make matters worse, Abra-Melin's teachings had been rendered in Old French. But the master of North Abbey was patient, and diligent, and with some difficulty was slowly managing to decipher the ancient text. He was in the process of reading and re-reading the section on bringing the dead back to life, when a knock sounded on the door.

Without looking up, Prince said, 'Come in.'

But the door remained closed. Silence. Then another knock.

'Who is that?'

No reply. Was one of his spirits playing tricks on him? No. They wouldn't dare. With a sigh of mild irritation, he left his chair and crossed the wine-red carpet. He wrenched open the

222

door, and saw Laverne standing in the passage. For a few seconds the two men silently regarded each other.

'Laverne,' breathed Prince finally, 'you really are one hell of a gatecrasher.'

Calmly, Laverne picked Prince up by the left lapel and, after a moment's consideration, drew back his arm and slammed his right fist into the American's mouth. Prince crashed to the floor and slid several feet across the carpet, bashing his head on the leg of a Queen Anne bureau.

Laverne strolled over to him. Prince lay on the floor, rubbing his jaw and laughing gently to himself.

Laverne said, 'That's for Alison Reffel.'

Before Prince had time to recover, Laverne dragged him to his feet, punched him in the solar plexus and finished with a beautifully judged upper cut to the chin. Prince reeled backwards into a bookcase, and as he fell a signed copy of Fortune's *Psychic Self-Defence* bounced off his head.

'And that's for everyone else,' added Laverne, relishing the moment.

Prince was hurt. But he kept laughing, as if Laverne's best efforts to subdue him were truly risible. 'You're weak, Laverne. You're weak, and do you want to know why? Because you can't kill. Hitting me is the worst thing you can think of, isn't it, you poor fool?'

Before Laverne could resume his attack, he heard the sound of running feet out in the passage. The door flew open and Miko appeared. The huge Polynesian dithered on the threshold for a few seconds, trying to apprehend the situation. Spitting blood, Prince turned to the manservant furiously.

'Do something!'

Goaded into action, Miko roared, bounded and sprang into the air like a wrestler. Laverne stepped to one side and thrashed out with his left arm, aiding the manservant's flight. Miko fell heavily to earth and lay there, winded. Unhurriedly, Laverne walked to the door, where he met the startled Yolande, draped in a bath-robe. He wished her a good evening and vanished into thin air.

Laverne didn't realize it at the time, but he had made a grave mistake. By visiting Prince in the spirit, he had shown his hand, or rather his soul, to the enemy. And whereas Prince had many tricks up his sleeve, Laverne had only one.

Something of this knowledge glittered in the American's eyes early the next morning, as he met Laverne, Savage and Lawless in the entrance hall of North Abbey. The police officers were deflated by the manner of their welcome. They had been hoping to surprise Prince, but the sardonic smirk on his bruised face told them that the master of North Abbey had been expecting them.

'What happened to you?' enquired Lawless, with his customary diplomacy.

'Ask Mr Laverne, here,' Prince replied. 'The Superintendent seems to have been getting rather confused lately. You better remind him that the police are supposed to beat up suspects *after* taking them into custody, not before. Isn't that right, Miko?'

The Polynesian, who was standing at Prince's side, nodded slowly, fixing Laverne with a resentful stare that was faintly tinged with respect.

Lawless and Savage exchanged puzzled glances. Were they missing something? Laverne reached into his inside jacket pocket, pulled out his wallet and extracted a crumpled photocopy.

'Now, what've you got there?' sneered Prince. 'Could that possibly be a list of all the murderers you've caught this week? No ... too short. Wait, I've got it. It's a warrant for my arrest.'

'Nearly right,' replied Laverne. 'It's a warrant for the arrest of Ms Yolande Henerberry.'

The smile disappeared from Prince's face.

*

After days of discussion, Laverne and Savage had both concluded that interviewing Prince would be a waste of time.
They felt that he was far too slippery and urbane to tell them
anything useful. So instead, they chose to talk to Yolande,
working on the assumption that as Prince's constant companion, she would surely have shared in his crimes, without
necessarily sharing his ingenuity or strength of character.

They were wrong about the strength of character. For most
of the day she sat in the interview room at Fulford Road,
staring coldly at Savage and Laverne, fielding their questions
with half-truths and sneers. She felt no need to have a solicitor
present. She believed that the police had neither the brains
nor the evidence to incriminate her.

She exhibited unease only once, towards the end of the
interview, when Laverne said, 'Alison Reffel told me she had
a baby that Mr Prince arranged to have adopted.'

The merest breath of tension passed through Yolande's face
and body; not so much an emotion as an emotion suppressed.
But the response was sufficiently marked to be noted by
Laverne and Savage and chronicled by the video camera that
was filming the interview.

'That rings a bell, I see,' commented Laverne.

'No, it does not,' she disclaimed tersely.

Savage said, 'And yet, on your own admission, you've been
Mr Prince's constant companion for at least five years.'

'One thing you should know about Alison, she tended to
romanticize. She invented things. She used to like saying she
was homeless. She was never once homeless. She had her own
flat in York and an open invitation to come and stay with us
whenever she pleased. I wouldn't call her a liar. Not exactly.
It was more that she didn't have a firm hold on reality. This
stuff about a child sounds to me like another one of her
stories. I certainly never heard anything about a child.'

Savage and Laverne studied the dark woman for a while.
Then Savage peered down at her notes. 'Well, Yolande, that
strikes me as a little odd. Because the birth of a baby boy, to

225

one Alison Mary Reffel, was recorded the year before last at York Royal Infirmary. Born October eighth. Weight seven pounds eleven ounces.'

Yolande Henerberry sat in silence, watching the police officers while they watched her, and her eyes grew hard and dark. Laverne glanced at the clock on the wall. 'That's enough for now. We'll continue this chat in the morning, shall we? After you've spent the night in a nice cosy cell?'

Laverne lay awake next to Dawn, wondering what Prince would do next. It was 1.35 in the morning. The Superintendent had gone to bed at eleven, and risen after an hour of restlessness to take half a sleeping pill. But the drug had done nothing to soothe him. He knew that with Yolande in custody, Prince was sure to attempt some kind of counter-move. But what? Laverne had to find out.

So he roused himself for the second time that night, but on this occasion left his body behind. Wind roared in his ears as he soared through the dark night to Ilkley, and arrived in the Long Gallery at North Abbey. He had no wish to be seen, so did not materialize. Unseen, he would stalk the Abbey to spy on Prince, just as he had once spied on the Racecourse Rapist.

Footsteps approached. A male servant, bearing a tray, turned into the gallery and walked towards Laverne. The smell of fresh coffee drifted before him. For a second the man seemed to look directly at the Superintendent. But as the man drew nearer, Laverne saw that his gaze was bored and unfocused. He turned away and knocked once on the door to Prince's study. Then he entered. Laverne followed, to find the study empty. The servant placed the tray on a table and left.

Laverne walked through the wall and emerged into the family chapel. There was someone kneeling at the altar, with his back to him, head bowed. From the fair hair and lean, narrow shoulders, Laverne identified the figure as Hugo Prince, praying on his knees before a single, guttering candle.

Noiselessly, Laverne advanced until he was level with the American. Prince remained kneeling, his eyes tightly closed – he showed no awareness of Laverne's presence. In a voice that was almost a whisper, he was intoning a short phrase over and over again.

Intrigued, Laverne leaned closer to listen. And what he heard was this: 'You fool. You fool . . .'

At once, Prince's hand shot out and clasped Laverne by the throat. The American opened his eyes, leapt up and pressed his face into Laverne's, slowly throttling him. Laverne was dumbfounded. He was invisible. How could Prince possibly see him?

The answer, of course, was that this was not Hugo Prince at all, but a spirit posted there as a sentinel. For as Laverne stared, Prince's features faded and became the malignant blue-black death-mask of Derek Tyreman. The ghost hissed at Laverne, and its breath stank of putrefaction and death. With a gasp of disgust, the policeman broke free. As he did so, more spectres passed through the stone walls into the chapel and surrounded him. There were about a dozen of them. Some of them had faces; some had no features at all. Prince had persuaded them that they were dead, and so, even as spirits, they continued to decompose, knowing that this was how dead people behaved.

They were repulsive, frightening and pitiful. Laverne couldn't take his eyes off them. As one, the spirits took a step towards him. Laverne came to his senses and shot through the ceiling of the chapel like a dart of fire. Almost simultaneously, the spirits followed.

There were hundreds more waiting for him outside, hovering in the dark sky, high above North Abbey. At the sight of Laverne, they began to shriek like hideous birds of prey. Then they bore down on him with terrifying speed. Laverne was dimly aware of tearing through utter blackness with a screeching multitude at his heels. A few seconds later, he

227

landed back in his body and sat up in bed, pouring with sweat, his chest heaving.

He could no longer see the pursuers, but knew that they were in the room. The air was icy. Then a sudden barrage of crashes and booms sounded around him. Dawn awoke sharply, instinctively clasping him by the arm. Laverne switched on the bedside lamp, in time to see the dressing-table mirror erupt like a fountain, filling the room with powdered glass. A deep crack appeared in the ceiling, raining plaster down on to the bed. The bedroom door tore off its hinges and staggered into the room like a child taking its first steps, before toppling to the floor. A ball of blue fire, brighter than a magnesium flare, zig-zagged across the bedroom walls, shot out on to the landing and instantly died away.

Then stillness.

Dawn groaned. 'Not again. For God's sake, Vernon. What have you been up to?'

'Nothing,' he said, guiltily.

'Rubbish. You must have been doing something ... That was something to do with you. I know it was.'

Unable to refute the charge, he said, 'I'll make a pot of tea, shall I?'

She sighed and drew back the covers. 'No, I'll make the tea. You can start clearing up.'

She tried to get out of bed and slumped, comically, to the floor. Laverne laughed, and leaned across to help her up.

'You daft beggar,' he said, taking her arm.

She laughed also, and then stopped. Fearfully, she looked up at him. 'Vernon: I can't feel my legs.'

Laverne wasted no time. He dressed, packed some of Dawn's things into a bag, and drove her to York Royal Infirmary, where she was admitted to Casualty. For two hours she lay on a trolley, out in the corridor, because the department was understaffed and there was no bed for her. Laverne waited at her side, holding her hand and directing rude remarks at any

228

nurse or physician unlucky enough to pass within earshot.

On arrival, he had demanded to see Dr Gregg, only to be told that she didn't come on duty for another five hours. Eventually, a tired, mild-mannered young man examined Dawn, and reached the unspectacular conclusion that she was paralysed from the waist down.

While they waited, a bed became available in ward C12, where Tyreman had died. Laverne knew that when a bed 'became available' at four-thirty in the morning, it could mean only one thing.

When she was in bed, Dawn squeezed Laverne's hand and asked him not to be so rude to the staff. Everything, she assured him, would be all right. 'I'm in good hands,' she said. Laverne nodded, while privately having every reason to doubt this.

Later, sitting in the living room of the cottage, he thanked God that he had never mentioned the Death Prayer to Dawn. If she had to die, let it be painlessly, without fear; not with the knowledge that a pack of phantoms were slowly sucking the life out of her. A fearful chill descended on him as he tried to imagine life without her. At New Year, Prince had threatened to strike a blow at his innermost heart.

And now that blow was about to be delivered.

The American had been right. Laverne wasn't a killer. He was a small-time policeman, hampered by antiquated notions of fairness and decency. He was a relic from a bygone age, while Prince, with his chilly indifference to all that was human and humane, was very much a child of his time.

Laverne was losing the fight. And as far as he knew, there was only one person alive who could help him.

Grandma May was afraid. In the night, she'd dreamed that Laverne had been murdered, seen him stabbed to death in a dark cathedral. She awoke to an acute sense of misery and sorrow and when she had spoken aloud to the air, asking the god for guidance, the god had not answered.

229

Two hours had passed, and still there had been no reply. This had not happened to her since her initiation as a Huna priestess. The calming, beloved voice that had guided, nourished and nurtured her for twenty-six years had suddenly been silenced.

She was plunged into such a depression that she sat awake in the dark, perched on the window seat of the upper sitting room. She stared out to sea but saw neither the jewelled lights of the fishing boats passing on the horizon, nor the day breaking like grief above the cold bay. All she saw was the horrific prospect of an existence without the one companion that gave life meaning.

Something drew her back into the present. An insistent, repetitive sound that at first she couldn't quite place. Then she realized that the phone was ringing. She glanced at a small carriage clock on a nearby shelf. It was still early; 6.45 a.m. She could think of no one, apart from Laverne, who would call at such a time. Sighing, she arose and crossed the room. The phone was situated below, in the lower sitting room. Reaching the door, she looked down the steep narrow staircase and saw that she was not alone.

There was an old man standing on the stairs. He was dressed in a long, pale robe and in his left hand he held a thin curved dagger with a dull blade. His gaunt, intelligent face was framed by long white locks of hair. His wide, bloodshot eyes were looking directly at her, and the expression in them was unmistakably evil. But his thin, delicate mouth appeared to be smiling.

May cried out, and began to back away. Simultaneously, the apparition began to ascend the stairs, pointing the knife at her, opening and closing his mouth to utter curses in Ancient English. She rushed to the windows and hurled them open.

There were two early risers standing on the jetty below, and in desperation she called to them. But they remained motionless, looking out to sea, and did not turn their heads.

Overhead, an ominous black cloud rapidly approached the

shore, skimming over the water towards her. As it came closer, she saw that the cloud comprised hundreds of flying figures; dead souls in black and tattered rags. In dreadful silence, the spirits wheeled and spun in the air above her, blotting out the sky.

She turned to face the ghost of Thomas North, who was now almost upon her. He raised his dagger, and, for the last time, May appealed to the god for help. But the god was not listening, and she was dead even before the knife descended.

Far across the country, at his cottage in the north of England, Vernon Laverne accepted defeat and gently returned the phone to its cradle. May was probably away, staying with members of her family. There was no reason to suppose that she spent her life sitting at home, waiting for telephone calls from incompetent detectives.

Wearily, he began to trudge upstairs, hoping to catch an hour's sleep. His face was now as crumpled as his clothes. As he reached his room, the phone rang. He rushed down to answer it, hoping to hear May at the end of the line. Instead, he was greeted by a male voice that took him a few seconds to place.

'How's your wife, Laverne?'

A pause. It was Prince. Laverne's mouth turned dry.

'Who gave you this number?'

Flippantly, Prince replied, 'Oh, I threatened someone at Directory Enquiries with the Death Prayer . . .'

'Leave my wife alone, Prince, or face the consequences.'

'Calm down. That's what I'm calling about. I think we should meet, Laverne.'

'What?'

'You heard me. Let's meet now and settle our differences.'

'No. I'm busy.'

'Ah. The sin of pride.'

'What are you talking about?'

'The size of your ego, Laverne. You aren't busy at all. You

231

just cannot bear to enter into any situation in which you lack total control. But while you sit there, insisting on some petty point of principle, your wife is actually dying.'

Damn the man. He was right. For a long time, Laverne said nothing. Then he sighed. 'All right. Where?'

'I suggest we meet on neutral ground. Somewhere far from prying eyes. Just you and I, Laverne. Alone.'

'Alone, eh?'

Reading Laverne's thoughts, Prince added, 'Apart from the dead, that is. The dead are always with us . . .'

So it was that on the first day of April, Laverne drove out to the ruins of Rievaulx Abbey, in the valley of the Rye, there to talk with Hugo Prince. Laverne arrived five minutes before nine, their designated hour of meeting. It was a fine, cold morning and the sky above the abbey ruins was a searingly beautiful shade of blue.

Prince was waiting for him under the remains of the choir. He was garbed in a long black coat and from a distance his thin, white face looked like a mask intended to frighten children. Laverne, his eyes dark with barely contained fury, came to within a yard of the American and stopped. Prince nodded in greeting.

'You're alone?'

Laverne gave an affirmative grunt.

Prince appraised him for a few moments. Then he walked forward and tapped Laverne lightly on the chest. 'Ah. And I see you brought your body along this time. Good. Good.'

Almost spitting out the words, Laverne said, 'I ought to wring your bloody neck.'

'Do that and your wife will certainly die.'

Laverne stared into Prince's eyes, felt dizzy, had to look away.

'I believe you met my reception committee last night? A policeman with a flair for astral projection. Really, who would have thought it? You've proved to be an interesting opponent.

232

I've underestimated you – I admit it. But I also think that you have seriously underestimated me.'

'What do you want?'

Prince smiled wistfully. 'Ultimately? A world in which white Anglo-Saxon Protestants can live happily together, without fear of contamination from lesser breeds. Did you know that my ancestor, Thomas North, helped rid York of Jews?'

'Yes. I've seen what your precious ancestor can do.'

'He and I are one. The father and the son, without the holy ghost. I hope to carry on Thomas's work, and expand it to eliminate blacks, Catholics and anyone else I take a personal dislike to.'

Prince gave a short humourless laugh that echoed and rang around the stout, crumbling pillars. Laverne failed to see the joke.

'Hugo: have you ever considered seeking psychiatric help?'

Prince grinned, looked Laverne up and down. 'Have you ever considered going to a decent tailor? Here. That reminds me . . .'

Prince dipped his hand into his overcoat pocket, and took out a black leather wallet. He opened the wallet and extracted a slip of paper, which he then passed to Laverne. Laverne unfolded it and stared, uncomprehending. It was a cheque for ten thousand pounds.

'What's this? A bribe?'

'No, no, no. It's your prize for overpowering me on New Year's Eve. Had you forgotten?'

Laverne tried to pass it back. Prince waved it away. "Don't be silly. Put it towards your wife's funeral . . .'

Instinctively, Laverne clenched his fists. 'Don't push me!'

'You want Dawn to live?'

Laverne mouthed a silent obscenity.

Prince smiled. 'I'll take that for a "yes" shall I? And what about your daughter? Your granddaughter? Or that rather attractive policewoman you're so attached to? Because I'll take them all, you know. I'll kill everyone that matters to you.'

Absent-mindedly, Laverne crumpled up Prince's cheque and pushed it into his coat pocket. He said, 'It's got to end somewhere, Hugo. You can't pray everyone dead.' But these words and the voice that uttered them sounded flat, hollow and far away.

'I can pray the world dead,' stated Prince simply. 'However, I am prepared to be reasonable. Eliminate me from your inquiries, release Yolande, and there will be no more strange murders in York. I will continue my work elsewhere, and your wife's life shall be spared. This I can promise. Do you accept my terms?'

Laverne shook his head emphatically.

'Well, look,' said Prince. 'I'll be honest with you. I'm prepared to offer you more. Much more. Because if we fight, it'll probably end in tears for both of us. When dragons fight, blood will be spilled on both sides.'

'What are you talking about?'

'I'm saying that you could be my ally. Think about it, Laverne. A man who can leave his body and a man who forces everybody else to leave theirs.' Prince laughed. 'We could make quite a team, you and I.'

Laverne snorted scornfully. 'I knew this was a waste of time . . .'

Prince's eyes burned into him.

'Magic, Laverne. Real Magic. Have you any idea what I could give to you?'

Weary of this madness, Laverne half-turned, preparing to leave. 'You can give me nothing.'

Then he heard a faint rustling behind him and turned towards the sound. On the site of the high altar was a raised stone ledge, and standing on the ledge was a small boy. He was about three years old, with light brown hair and a chocolate stain around his mouth. He was wearing a blue playsuit and on his face was a familiar crooked smile.

The child called to Laverne.

'Dad-dee!'

Laverne felt weak with excitement.

He forgot about Prince, forgot about everything else that mattered to him. He rushed over to the boy and, scooping him up in his arms, experienced an ecstasy of relief, for the child felt warm and solid, smelled of baby powder and sticky sweets. It was like being reunited with part of his own body. For an instant, Laverne forgot all his pain, because his son was alive and in his arms. Then Tom disappeared, and he was left embracing the air.

Laverne cried out and staggered as if a steel rapier had been thrust between his ribs and twisted. Then he fell, gasping, to his knees. Calmly, Prince walked across to the altar and looked down at him.

'Real magic, Laverne. The past made present. The spirit made flesh. You could have your boy back, whenever you liked. I could bring him back to visit you and Dawn every day. He'd look, feel and behave just like the son you lost. This I will give to you, if you surrender now.'

Trying to shut out temptation, Laverne covered his face. But he could smell Tom on his hands. He let out a roar of anger and distress and his voice trembled as he said, 'It's a trick . . .'

'Trick or not, what does it matter? If he looks, acts, feels like the son you remember, what's the difference?'

Laverne said nothing, screwed his eyes tightly shut.

'Well?' said Prince. 'Do we have a deal?'

There was a long, awful silence. Without looking up, Laverne said, 'Never. I will never, ever bow to you.'

He heard Prince say, 'Then there is really nothing more to be said. You're a brave man, but also, alas, a rather foolish one. Goodbye, Laverne.'

Laverne stared at the earth for a few seconds, unable to shake the image of his son from his mind. Then he lunged to his feet, determined to punish the soft-voiced American for this latest abomination. But Prince had vanished from sight, leaving Laverne alone beneath the empty ragged arches of the ruined abbey.

# Eighteen

He returned to the hospital, where a further shock awaited him. When he arrived at Dawn's ward, her bed was empty. A young girl, a student nurse, was bent over the mattress, busily changing the sheets.

'Where is she?' he demanded.

The girl blinked, unsure how to reply.

'My wife . . . Where is she?'

The girl said, 'I'll get the staff nurse . . .'

His stomach tightening in fear, Laverne followed the girl down the ward to the glass-fronted office where an older nurse, a small woman with bleached hair, looked up from her notes. The student returned to her chores. Quickly, Laverne explained his purpose. The staff nurse prolonged the agony by asking him to sit down. He refused.

'I'm sorry to have to tell you this . . .'

Laverne was aghast. 'What? *What?*'

'I'm afraid Mrs Laverne took a turn for the worse this morning. The Consultant decided that we couldn't take any chances, she was just too poorly . . .'

Laverne could scarcely believe how badly the woman was handling the situation. How did they train these people? 'But how is she?'

'She's on a respirator.'

'So she's alive, then?'

'Well, yes,' said the nurse, in a tone that implied that this point was debatable.

She guided him to Intensive Care, where Dawn lay at the end of a line of eight beds. Laverne pulled up an ugly plastic chair and seated himself beside his wife. The nurse drew a screen around them and left them alone.

Laverne remained there, listening to Dawn's laboured breathing, and the peep-peep-peep of the ECG. This was the woman he loved, an air tube down her throat, her face white and bloodless, her body so still that she might already be dead. He sat there, willing her to return.

Then he felt the pleasant light-headed sensation that always preceded an out-of-the-body experience. He rose above himself and floated to the ceiling, except there was no longer a ceiling, only black and endless space. His wife lay directly below him. There was now no bed or respirator in sight. She was floating on her back, suspended in the dark air, and entwined around her were three grotesque forms. One of the figures embraced her feet, while the other two hugged her sides, one of them resting its head on her chest, the other pressing its dead face against her cheek. This macabre tableau hung in the darkness, suffused by its own pale light. There was no sound. No movement. Nothing.

Laverne watched for a moment, temporarily stunned. Then he remembered that the three creatures around his wife had been sent to kill her. In a desperate panic, he descended to the bed and seized the spirit at Dawn's feet, dragging it off by its hair. It was a middle-aged woman with a badly decomposed face. She spat and clawed at him, furious to be interrupted while feeding. Her spirit was almost weightless, and Laverne found no difficulty in raising it above his head and flinging it far into the dark.

Leadenly, the other two ghosts raised their heads. With a shock of revulsion, Laverne realized that the entity resting on Dawn's chest had a familiar face. It was the boy who had been murdered in the museum gardens. Laverne grabbed him by the hair and heaved him loose. Then the woman's spirit returned and attached itself to his back, where it clung, clawing and screaming.

Her cries alerted the third wraith; a tall thin Caucasian with

238

a strangely black face. Soon all three were grappling with Laverne, coiling their reeking bodies around him, forcing him down. Terror set in as Laverne realized how viciously determined they were. He was being steadily overpowered. Lack of sleep and a mounting sense of hopelessness had robbed him of all his strength. With a final frantic effort, he broke free and dived back to the safety of his body.

As he struggled to compose himself, someone pulled the screen aside. It was Dr Gregg. She looked down at him, smiling faintly. Then he saw her start with surprise as she registered the ghastliness of his appearance. 'You look bloody awful. Are you all right?'

'Just about.' He nodded at his wife. 'She's . . .' He left the sentence unfinished.

Gregg slapped him on the shoulder, rather boisterously. 'I don't know about you, mate, but I'm starving. Let me buy you some lunch.'

'No. I'd better stay here . . .'

'Do as you're told.'


In his present state of exhaustion, Laverne seemed incapable of making the simplest decision. Gregg, playing mother, heaped food upon his plate in a big-hearted, haphazard fashion, hoping to arrive, by chance, at something he found palatable. The hospital canteen was subsidized; the meal wasn't costing her much. And the Superintendent's ashen complexion told her that if he didn't do some serious eating and sleeping soon, he'd end up in Intensive Care himself.

They sat at a central table, surrounded by relaxed, chattering hospital staff. Laverne was reminded, once again, of the gulf between human beings. If Dawn died, none of the people around him would care much. The woman sitting opposite him, for all her good intentions, might be sorry only for a day. Tomorrow, she would have other deaths to fret over, different relatives to console.

239

'She doesn't actually need to be on the respirator,' Gregg was saying. 'Not yet, anyway.'

'Then why do it?'

'So far, she's shown the same symptoms as Derek Tyreman. The post-mortem on Tyreman showed that the root cause of death was paralysis of the central nervous system.'

Laverne frowned. 'Not heart failure?'

'Same difference. If you're completely paralysed, everything fails. But as long as the machine does her breathing for her, we've got time to play with.'

'How much time?'

'I don't know. Until her brain dies, I suppose.'

'Thanks for breaking it to me gently.'

'Sorry. Ignore me. I'm a rude old bag.' She gave him a winning smile and continued to eat.

Laverne forked some baked beans into his mouth, and was shocked by how good they tasted. In his stress, he had forgotten about eating. The food immediately aroused his dormant hunger, and he rapidly cleared his plate. When he'd finished, he looked up and saw that Dr Gregg was watching him pensively.

'Listen ... your wife ... I've seen something like this before.'

'Yes,' he said. 'I know. Derek Tyreman.'

'No. Before Tyreman. Years ago, when I was a junior doctor in the Outback, I treated an Aboriginal girl who claimed she was being haunted by the ghost of her mother-in-law. The girl was suffering from terrible stomach cramps and loss of appetite. She'd cheated on her husband, and believed that his dead mother was punishing her for it. Sounds bloody crazy, doesn't it? But although we couldn't find anything wrong with the patient, she was losing weight at one hell of a rate.

'A colleague of mine, a drunken old bastard who also happened to be the best doctor I've ever worked with, asked the old woman's ghost to leave the girl alone. He couldn't see

240

anything, or hear anything, but he decided to give the patient the benefit of the doubt. So he stayed by her bedside and held a conversation with thin air for half an hour, attempting to make this invisible mother-in-law see reason. After that, the girl made a remarkable recovery. Of course, I was trained as a scientist. I never used to believe in such things . . .'

Laverne sipped his tea, eyed her quizzically. 'Used to?'

Uncomfortably, Dr Gregg explained. 'On the night of Tyreman's death, his body went missing from the morgue.'

Huffily, Laverne said, 'No one told me.'

'Losing bodies isn't the kind of thing hospitals tend to broadcast. We organized a search, and one of the nurses ended up in a right bloody state.'

'Why?'

'Because she saw Tyreman's body outside the maternity wing. It was floating down a corridor, six feet off the ground.'

'And you believe her?'

Dr Gregg blushed slightly. 'I have to believe her. I was with her. I saw it too.'

After lunch, Gregg returned to work and Laverne went out into the corridor to think things over. While appreciating why Dr Gregg had told him about the aboriginal woman, he very much doubted that the three mindless monstrosities attached to his wife were capable of listening to reason. No. Laverne had done all that he could. His best bet was Grandma May. Surely she would know what to do? He closed his eyes, breathed deeply and left his body for the second time that day.

In a matter of seconds, he was in May's cottage. He entered by the kitchen entrance, and slowly mounted the stairs, calling her name. The house felt damp and cold. He found her upstairs, lying in a dark lake of blood that was shaped like Australia. Her head had almost been severed from her body. A fresh cold sea wind poured into the room from the open window. Laverne was saddened and appalled. But as he thought about the woman's simple warmth, and saw what Prince's ancestor had done to her, anger began to course through him like slow, hot poison. And this anger fired him with the energy he needed.

He flew back to his wife's bedside. As before, Dawn's unconscious body lay adrift in darkness. The three spirits had resumed their former positions. Laverne hovered above them. The spirits didn't look up, but Laverne sensed that they knew he was there and resented his presence.

Hesitantly, he began. 'I know that you are extremely clever and gifted. You have the ability to work wonders. You can take away human life. But don't you realize that you're being used? This woman is innocent. She would never intentionally hurt a living thing. I ask you to compare her to the man who sent you to kill her.'

There were no visible signs that the spirits could hear or understand him, but Laverne persevered. 'Can't you see what Prince has done to you? When you died, he separated you from your souls. He cheated you of Heaven. He made you forget who you had been in life. He turned you into slaves.'

Laverne descended, drawing closer to the spirits. 'I love the woman that you're destroying. Love. Do you remember that word? When you were alive, you all had families . . . Some of you had children. People who loved you. For their sake, just think about what you're doing.'

Slowly, the female spirit turned her face to Laverne. He saw pain in her bright eyes. Encouraged, he raised his voice, repeating everything that he had said, assuring them that they were all essentially good and loving, and that Prince had perverted their true natures.

The woman's ghost began to weep and dribble. Her partners, hearing her sobs, slowly lifted their faces and looked at Laverne. He felt the mood in the air shifting slightly, as he repeatedly reminded them that they had once been whole spirits and were now mere shadows of their true selves.

'For the sake of the people who mattered to you when you

242

were alive, I beg you to let this woman live. She's done you no harm. Prince – the man who sent you – he's the one who deserves to die, not her.'

Gradually, one by one, the three spirits abandoned Dawn and floated through space towards him, sobbing softly, their skeletal hands reaching out to him for guidance. As they drew closer, Laverne had to fight to control his nausea. Then a further shock, as from every direction, all the forsaken souls under Prince's command emerged from the heavy darkness.

There was an army of them; a full cemetery's worth. Laverne was completely surrounded. Old, middle-aged and young, some newly rotted, others long dead. Their decline seemed to follow no set pattern; some of the recently deceased, flesh scarcely blue, had already become decrepit, while elsewhere, mere skeletons showed signs of frightening vitality. And all of them were here to listen to Vernon Laverne.

His instincts told him to run, but he stood his ground, trying not to focus on that vast array of floating corpses. 'Listen to me. All of you, please listen.' He pointed to the prone figure lying at his feet. 'This woman doesn't deserve to die. She hasn't hurt you. It's Prince. Prince is the one you want . . .'

There was a deep hush, while the dead watched Laverne, wondering whether to believe him.

As the tall horseman approached, a brace of magpies clattered out of the branches of a withered ash. Two for joy. Prince smiled in satisfaction and gently reined in his mount. She was a grey Danish mare, a six-year-old. He called her Epona, after the Celtic Horse Goddess. By her side trotted Hal, a spaniel who acted as the nervous mare's constant companion, sharing her stable and, when it could get away with it, her food.

Prince's rendezvous at Rievaulx Abbey had left him with a rare feeling of exhilaration. Until now, he had regarded Laverne as a threat. But the sight of that idiot detective

243

running to throw his arms around his son had effectively banished the Kahuna's fears. Had Laverne possessed any insight at all, he would have known that his 'son' was a mere chimera, a life-like impersonation carried out by one of Prince's ghostly disciples. Mimicry was a speciality of the poltergeist.

No. It was just as Prince had thought. Detective Superintendent Laverne was nothing more than an ignorant public servant with one unusual ability. And for all the good it had done him, Laverne's propensity for astral projection might as well have been a talent for playing the mouth organ.

The horse ambled deeper into the woods. He had ridden the mare hard. Steam rose from her flanks. Her warm smell filled his nostrils. He had not felt so strong for a long time. The police stood no chance against him. Yolande would stay silent, knowing what her fate would be if she did not. He would be free to resume his work, with one minor adjustment.

In the past, he had always rewarded the spirits who murdered at his behest by letting them play with the mana that they had absorbed from their victims. This was why Anjali Dutt had been hurled around her flat, and the corpse of Tyreman had taken a night flight around York Royal Infirmary. But in future, his creatures would have to find more discreet methods of disposing of their excess energy. He wanted no more attention from the law.

Prince was approaching the western boundary of his estate. He dipped his head as he rode under the boughs of a copse of ancient oaks. The spaniel was making odd fretting noises in its throat, but he paid the beast no heed.

It was about three in the afternoon, and all day the county had basked in gentle sunshine. The waking earth had responded with sweet odours and fresh green shoots. It felt like the first day of spring. That was why Prince was so surprised when, without warning, the sky turned black and premature night spread over the park.

The spaniel released a strangled yelp and took to its heels.

244

Prince tried to whistle him back, but the dog fled towards the house, barking into the distance. Already pining for her escort, Epona whinnied and twitched, jangling her harness. Prince halted her. Puzzled, he turned to the south-west, looking for the sun. He saw only a black disc, ringed with orange fire. Prince shook his head in denial – a total eclipse, that neither scientist nor mystic had predicted. How could that be?

While he brooded, he realized that the birds in the woods around him had stopped singing. There was an oppressive quiet, disturbed only by the sound of the horse snorting and stamping restlessly where she stood.

Epona tossed her head, showing the whites of her eyes, then in her fear defecated heavily on the woodland floor. Glancing up, Prince saw what was disturbing the animal. The trees were full of spirits, silently looking down at him with fixed expressions of hatred on their faces. They squatted high in the branches like cadaverous apes, motionless, darker than the darkness. There were about a dozen of them, and as he watched, more corpses came winging over the woods towards him.

The horse bucked violently, almost unsaddling its owner. But with a combination of skill and soft words, Prince regained control of her. Undaunted, he surveyed the spirits in the oaks and roared, 'What are you doing, damn you? I didn't send for you! Get out of my sight!'

This outburst only served to enrage his grisly audience. Those perched above him began to screech loudly, their cries gashing and tearing the still air. Infected by their mood, the airborne new arrivals began to fly blindly into the trees and each other, colliding with sickening momentum, until fluttering grave rags and morsels of carrion slowly rained down upon the horse and its rider.

Prince galloped back to the house. He stabled the horse and hurried to the chapel, where he lit a row of candles before the image of Sir Thomas North and knelt down before it.

He had always terrified the spirits. And now they had defied him. What could possibly have gone wrong?

Prince closed his eyes and said, 'Lord of Sorrows, Lord of my Life, Come to me Now.'

A sweet calm descended, like the sudden absence of pain after a bitter illness. Prince smiled, feeling sure that his guardian had heard him and was on his way. While he waited, something made him look up at the great Domesday window through which the sun had never shone. And the smile died on his lips. Because the sun was shining now.

Crimson light poured through the glass, bathing him in its lurid glow. Then the window exploded into a thousand dark fragments, as three flaming shapes burst into the chapel, swooped down and snatched Prince up in their arms. These were the spirits that Prince had sent to kill Dawn Laverne, and now they had come for him. Up they soared, cold elemental fire dancing around their limbs, bearing him out through the gaping oval hole into a darkness from which he would never return. It was like being unborn. As the three spirits carried their prize to their companions in the clouds, the skies above North Abbey resounded to their triumphal cries. But Hugo Prince made no sound.

His maimed and broken body was found the next morning in St Sampson's Square, the part of York that was once known as Thursday Market. Like the deity he adored, Prince had fallen from a great height. Yolande Henerberry, no longer threatened by the power of her Kahuna's curse, made a full confession to Lyn Savage, recounting a catalogue of crimes that gave the DI more than one sleepless night.

The identity of the boy killed in the museum gardens remained a mystery, but Henerberry was able to throw some light on the death of Anjali Dutt. Anjali had been one of Prince's students, until she learned that he used the Death Prayer and had a taste for human sacrifice. Rashly, she attempted to pray the American dead, with fatal consequences for herself and her boyfriend.

Yolande directed the police to the animal graveyard in the grounds of North Abbey, where they unearthed the remains of several small children. Among them, the body of a baby, no more than twelve weeks old, shown by a DNA test to be the missing son of Alison Reffel. For Laverne and Savage, this brought an ugly inquiry to a suitably ugly conclusion.

There was one odd postscript. Dawn Laverne, fully recovered after her ordeal, saw the dead Kahuna's photograph on a TV news programme and insisted that she knew him. Not as Hugo Prince, but as Francis Kent, a rich and kindly American who had made a number of sizeable cash donations to the hospice where she worked. In this guise, Prince had apparently spent long hours visiting the dying, chatting to them with charm and sympathy. To Dawn, this was proof that no one, no matter how black their crimes, can ever be wholly bad. But Vernon Laverne, knowing all that he knew, was unable to share this charitable view.

'Your beverage is served, madam.'

Dawn looked up to see Laverne standing in the doorway, carrying two mugs of hot chocolate on a tin tray.

'Oh, well done,' she mocked, gently. 'It's only taken you twenty-five years.'

At this, his face dropped. 'I'd have been quicker,' he answered, misunderstanding. 'But the milk kept boiling over.'

'What? For twenty-five years?'

Mock-sullen, he cleared a space on the bedside table, set down the tray and passed a mug to her. Then, clasping the remaining mug in both hands, he sat on the bed beside her. She was curled up with a copy of *Good Housekeeping*, a publication that he found almost as interesting as the *Police Gazette*.

'What are you reading about now?' he sneered. 'The latest food mixer, or budget dressing for the menopause?'

Laughing, she rolled up the magazine and swiped him with it. It was the second day of their holiday. He'd taken a week off work, so they could spend some time together. Not just time, but what those awful people who ran business courses called 'quality time'. In the morning he and Dawn were off to Wales for a weekend break with Jennifer and their grand-daughter. Michael Berensford – Praise the Lord – was unable to make the trip due to a hectic filming schedule.

While they sipped their chocolate, Laverne lay on the bed next to his wife, telling her about his grand plans for their future retirement. She responded by falling asleep. Gently, he extricated the mug from her fingers, and replaced it on the tray next to his own. Then, on tiptoe, he carried the tray across the room and turned out the light.

Down in the living room, he made straight for the drinks cabinet, threw open its doors, and with an 'Ahh!' of theatrical delight that was worthy of Michael Berensford, drew out the bottle of Glenmorangie that his murder team had bought him for Christmas. The seal on the bottle was unbroken. The year that had commenced with the murder of Alison Reffel had given him precious little to celebrate.

It was true that he had saved Katherine Hibbett's life, but her face would always bear the scars of Merton's knife and she now suffered from a morbid terror of snow and solitude. And although Laverne had avenged Alison's murder, her child, the child he had promised to trace, was already beyond all help. As always, his victories were tainted with sadness.

Yet he had something to drink to. Laverne settled into his armchair, splashed a generous measure of the malt into his best crystal tumbler and contemplated the fragrant poison with a reverential eye. A toast, then. A toast to no more ghosts, or premonitions, no more journeys out of his body. Let his career end as it had begun. May he literally come down to earth and be dull again; sweetly, blissfully dull.

Before he had time to raise the glass to his lips, he noticed a particularly foul odour. He frowned, wondering where he'd

248

smelled that stench before. Then he remembered. Instantly, his entire body tensed. He put down his glass, moved to the door, and with his guts turning over inside him, slipped out into the hall.

The smell was stronger here. Laverne puffed in distaste and his breath turned to mist. It was the middle of April, yet the house was freezing cold. He shivered, glanced up and saw what he was expecting to see.

The old man was on the stairs, half-climbing, half-floating in a yellow, sulphurous cloud. He had his back to Laverne but as the detective watched, the apparition suddenly stopped. Then it turned its grey head and peered over its shoulder. Seeing Laverne, those inflamed eyes narrowed with recognition. Thomas North slowly spun in the air. In his small, rather refined left hand, he gripped the dagger that had stabbed Alison and May, and Rabbi David of Coney Street, York, in the year 1188.

Before North had time to think, Laverne bounded up the stairs and attacked him. The Knight slashed out blindly with the knife. Laverne leant back, felt the blade cut the air in front of his face. Then, seizing the spirit's left sleeve, Laverne whirled back his arm and hammered his fist into the old man's face.

There must have been more than a touch of mana behind the blow, because the impact sent North rocketing backwards. He hit the wall with a flare of static and disappeared. Laverne inspected his fist with amazement and allowed himself a small snort of amused relief.

Then he felt a sharp, burning pain in his lower back. He turned, saw North standing on the stairs below him, blade upraised, and realized that he had been stabbed. Before Laverne had a chance to retaliate, the old man gave him a deadly smile, thrust the knife up under the policeman's ribs and twisted it. Laverne gasped with astonishment and toppled down the stairs. As he fell, North stepped aside to make way for him.

He landed on his back, at the bottom of the stairs, on the very spot where his son had died. With an agility surprising in one so ancient, the murderer darted down the stairs, kneeled beside the floundering detective and plunged the dagger deep into his heart. Once, twice, three times. Laverne murmured an empty threat and then lay still, sightless eyes staring. He was finished. But just to be certain, the old man pressed the blade over his adversary's throat and slit it wide open.

This was how North had always treated malefactors. He was a twelfth-century knight, for whom killing was an everyday activity. Similarly, the stink that emanated from him was not the smell of putrescence, but a body odour typical of his time. The black lice crawling over his body and through his white hair had been his companions in life and had followed him to the grave. Refusing to acknowledge time, North existed outside it. He was an unliving, undying testament to the power of will.

Carelessly, he wiped his knife on Laverne's arm and straightened himself. Mouthing a black-hearted prayer of thanksgiving, he floated up the stairs to the room where his next victim lay. Arriving on the landing, he sniffed the air and smiled. He could smell woman. Nodding grimly to himself, he opened the door to Laverne's bedroom and peered through the darkness.

There was a gasp from the far wall. A light flashed on. And there she was, sitting up in bed, holding her hands to her face. North gave another of his thin patrician smiles and levitated several inches off the ground. Then he moved diagonally across the room towards the bed.

Unexpectedly, there seemed to be a man lying on the bed beside the woman. As he drew closer, the man raised himself to an upright position, and shouted something. North halted, his white brow creased in consternation. For the figure on the bed was none other than Laverne, the creature that he had only just put to death.

Laverne had dozed off beside his wife, unaware that his spirit was not yet ready for bed. After dreaming that North had found his way into the house, he now awoke to find the nightmare fulfilled. Without a thought for his own safety, he bounded to the floor, putting himself between Dawn and the intruder.

Dawn shouted, 'Vernon! He's got a knife . . .'

As the old man pondered the riddle before him, there was a whisper of movement from the doorway. North swivelled in the air and found himself confronting yet another Laverne, a Laverne that laughed in his face. Infuriated by this conceit, North lunged at the upstart with his dagger, piercing its throat. But as he watched, the fresh wound healed miraculously. At last, North understood. He had been fighting a spirit, not a man.

Then both Lavernes attacked North simultaneously, raining fierce blows upon him, struggling to drag him to earth. But North would not be beaten. He repelled their best onslaughts with a truly demonic strength, and while they grew more and more weary and despondent, he battled on, his knife rending and slitting the air, his eyes ablaze with energy.

Dawn had left the bed and was standing in a corner by the window with her eyes closed. At last, tasting defeat, Laverne returned to his body and threw himself over her, his back pressing her against the wall, his arms outstretched as if crucified. He was breathless, utterly exhausted. His arms were covered with deep lacerations. Blood and sweat dripped off his body on to the carpet. He hardly had the strength to lift his head.

North saw this, and his narrow shoulders shook with silent mirth. Then, still floating on the air, he raised the knife with monstrous deliberation. Laverne let out a bitter sigh. Dawn slipped her hands into his.

He said, 'I'm sorry, love.' By way of reply, she squeezed his hands tightly.

Then Laverne felt a cool breeze on his face. He opened his

251

eyes, and saw that the old man had turned away and was now watching the wall by the bed. Following his gaze, Laverne saw a pale flickering light. Then someone walked through the wall, into the room. Laverne's heart lifted. But his hopes of angelic intervention were swiftly crushed. The new arrival was Hugo Prince.

It was a somewhat degraded Prince, to be sure, for his pale countenance had darkened in death and the sardonic smiling mouth now drooped open, as if amazed by its own demise. But there was no mistaking the Kahuna, or the sheer delight that his presence gave Thomas North.

The old man stepped forward to embrace his son. Then, bobbing his head towards Laverne, North pressed the dagger into Prince's dead hand and patted his arm as if to say, 'Be my guest.'

It was true that if anyone had reason to kill Laverne, it was Prince. But rather than act on the old man's advice, Prince hesitated and turned to Laverne with an odd questioning look in his eyes.

With a thrill of elation, Laverne realized what was being asked of him. This was not Prince, but Prince's low spirit. And because Laverne had been personally responsible for despatching him to the netherworld, Prince now thought of Laverne as his master. North gave his descendant a smile of polite enquiry, not understanding the cause of the delay. But Laverne understood, and looking into Prince's eyes, he nodded his head.

At this signal, Prince spun round and with all his force drove the knife into Thomas North's heart. The old man screamed and threshed his arms, then burst into flames. Prince fastened his hands about his guardian's throat and began to throttle him. Then Prince caught fire also, and the two spirits burned together, dancing through space, spinning away into nothingness.

When Dawn opened her eyes, the room was empty. Laverne helped her to the bathroom, where she was violently sick. Then he gave her two strong sedatives to stop her from shaking, and laid her on the bed. She immediately lost consciousness.

He lay beside her in the dark, fully dressed, makeshift bandages covering his slashed forearms. He kept wondering why the knife that had killed Thomas North should have failed to harm his own spirit. Then he remembered that Prince and North had been different aspects of the same person. And he concluded that while one soul cannot kill another, any soul is free to destroy itself.

Finally, the adrenalin-storm raging inside him abated, and he, too, slept. He stirred a few hours later, to hear the first bird of the day twittering deliriously outside the window. But it was not the birdsong that had disturbed him. Nor was it the stinging soreness of his wounds. Laverne had awoken with the powerful conviction that something else was in the house.

Aching all over, he eased himself off the bed in three painful stages and walked unsteadily to the door. Everything was still. He opened the door and stumbled out on to the landing, rubbing his eyes. Then he stopped and held his breath, seeing that his instinct had been correct.

There were hundreds of them out there, squatting outside the door, crouching on the stairs, pale eyes shining in the early morning gloom. At the sight of him, a host of emaciated hands reached out to pat his legs affectionately. The house was full of dead people.

With difficulty, he made his way downstairs, delicately placing his feet among a throng of bodies. On his way down, he passed a few familiar faces: Derek Tyreman, Sheelagh Daye and, to Laverne's surprise, Albert Bomford, the Bolton Strangler, who had hanged himself in his cell only hours before.

They had come home. Laverne was their Kahuna. They lived only to serve him. All he desired of them at that moment was their departure, but he had no idea how to bring this about. So he found an empty space on the bottom stair, and sat there, wondering what to do next. And all around him, the spirits watched and listened, waiting for Vernon Laverne to come to a decision. None of them cared how long he took. Time only matters to the living. But the dead have all eternity.